WRATH

AVA PARKER

First printing: April 2019
ISBN: 978-0-9862254-8-2

ACKNOWLEDGEMENTS

For my friends and family, and for my readers.
Couldn't do it without you.

PROLOGUE

Dawn, Saturday. Melissa Bauer bounced out of her apartment building in Seattle's University District, did a series of energetic jumping jacks to stave off the October chill, and jogged out to the sidewalk for her morning run. Turning right onto Brooklyn Avenue, she shadow-boxed her way past the Safeway and down the rest of the block until her shoulders and biceps were jelly.

Lot of frustration to vent this morning.

Melissa had spent two hours on the internet last night staring at her sister Becky's Pinterest page, looking at bridesmaids' dresses. Blue, blue, blue. She'd gone cross-eyed. Literally—she couldn't tell one dress from another.

And today she had to meet Becky and her boring bridesmaids to try them all on. Another round of punches. She picked up her pace.

For three months, Melissa had been studying napkins, table settings, reception venues. She'd been involved in serious conversations about 'wedding colors' and 'bridal bling.' She'd been trying starters and mains and fruit fillings and buttercreams.

She'd had no fewer than three Facetimes with Becky's BFF/ maid of honor who wanted to run every detail of the bachelorette party by Melissa, even though Melissa honestly couldn't give a shit.

Becky had probably put her up to it because she felt bad she'd chosen her *sorority* sister over her *real* sister to be the maid of honor.

Punch. Punch. Punch.

She sped up, headed left toward the University of Washington, looped around Drumheller Fountain, came out on the southeast side of campus and headed to Roosevelt Way. Another right past her favorite pancake house and she was on the home stretch.

Two blocks from home, Melissa stopped, stretched her calves and hamstrings, released her neck and shoulders and started walking.

Nice buzz. Maybe she'd get through the day.

Maybe this would be the day Becky found the perfect one-shouldered hi-lo blue satin bridesmaid's dress and ended the madness.

Melissa caught something out of the corner of her eye, did a double-take. Stopped.

A slash of fire-engine red in the bramble. She came closer, leaned over and saw a long black stiletto. Someone had lost her Louboutins in the bushes on Northeast Fiftieth Street. Six-hundred-dollar pair of shoes. Reaching down, Melissa Bauer abruptly froze in place and started to scream.

CHAPTER ONE

Dawn, Saturday. Detective Jerome Kincaid woke up on the wrong side of the bed, answered the phone and stumbled into the bathroom.

"You sound like shit, Jerry," said Judy Carlisle without preamble. "Time to rise and shine, partner, we've got a big day ahead of us."

"We catch a case?" he said gruffly.

This would be Carlisle and Kincaid's seventh homicide case since Missing Persons had been rolled up with the Seattle PD Homicide and Sex Crimes divisions the year before.

"Why else would I be calling at the crack of dawn?" It wasn't exactly the crack of dawn, but close enough.

"Right," Kincaid growled. Retirement party last night and too much whiskey. Both detectives had Ubered home. "What's up?"

Peering into the mirror, Kincaid ran a hand through his mop of red hair and squared his shoulders. He needed a shower, a cup of coffee, maybe a few more hours of sleep. Recapping the Bayer and filling his water glass, he swallowed two aspirin, downed the whole glass and stretched his big frame.

"Dead lady near the university. That's all I know."

"You got a car?"

"I'm going to take Tom's, be at your place in fifteen." Tom, the patient—some might even say long-suffering—husband of Judy Carlisle, father of their two children, successful Microsoft executive, all-around great guy. Kincaid saw a little silver lining—Tom drove a really nice car.

Kincaid showered, put on a suit. Went downstairs and fed Stanley, his happy grey cat. He looked longingly at the Mr. Coffee on his countertop, then looked at the time. Drank two more tall glasses of water and when Carlisle pulled up out front, he felt almost human.

When he opened the door of Tom's S-class, he smelled the black tar that Carlisle drank every morning. "Oh man, Judy, you just made my day."

"Can't take credit," she said, handing her partner a stainless-steel mug of coffee, "Tom had it all packed up and ready to go when I came down this morning." She looked alert, blonde hair tucked under a plaid scarf, eyes shiny and bright, long fingers tapping impatiently on the steering wheel.

Kincaid slid the seat all the way back, stretched his long legs and happily took a drink. "We should always travel in such style." He smoothed the knees of his blue suit, straightened a narrow tie, checked himself in the visor mirror. Sighed with satisfaction. *Not too bad.*

Carlisle said, "There's lip gloss in my purse."

He laughed, smoothed his hair, flipped up the visor. "What do we know?" he asked.

"Precious little," said Carlisle and pointed the car toward the university. "White woman. Blood coming from somewhere, but no one has touched the body yet. She's face down, so we don't have a description." She took a sharp right, sped up. "A jogger found her in the bushes, called nine-one-one. Uniforms have secured the scene and crime scene is on their way. No purse, but she could have an ID in one of her pockets."

A few minutes later they turned onto a street crowded with police cars, lights blinking, sirens off. Neither the Crime Scene

Unit's nor the Coroner's vans had arrived when Carlisle pulled into an empty slot across the street and stepped onto the pavement.

Ducking under the yellow crime scene tape, she and Kincaid followed the patrolman's gesture to a copse of huckleberry bushes. The body was not well-hidden, tucked just far enough into the foliage that no one would trip over her. No surprise she'd been discovered at first light.

Keeping his distance in case the killer had left footprints in the soft dirt around the bushes, Kincaid borrowed a nightstick from a uniform and used it to push aside some of the wispy branches. The woman was lean and well-dressed, lying awkwardly on her stomach. Her pale blond hair was tangled and dirty, matted with leaves and blood.

Kincaid held the branches aside while Carlisle pulled out her cell phone and snapped a dozen pictures. They wouldn't be used as evidence but would help give her and Kincaid a point of reference.

"Nice clothes," said Kincaid. "I don't see a handbag. Maybe a purse-snatching gone wrong?"

"Really, really wrong," Carlisle replied, turned back to the cop. "That her?" she asked, nodding at his patrol car.

"Melissa Bauer. Student at UW. She found the body, and that's about all she knows. I tried to get something out of her, but she just keeps saying her sister's gonna kill her if she's not ready to go at nine." He looked over at the young woman in the backseat of his cruiser. "Bad luck."

Carlisle walked over, pulled open the back door of the patrol car and got in next to Bauer. Kincaid sat in front and they questioned the girl for a few minutes, but it was clear that she really didn't know anything more about the murdered victim, that her trauma was a combo of finding a dead body on her morning jog and dealing with her bridezilla sister.

Carlisle patted the kid on the shoulder. "Every time my sister-in-law gets married, I want to throw myself off a bridge. We'll get an officer to take you home."

As they walked away, Kincaid said, "Does Lauren make you wear taffeta?"

Carlisle sighed. "Every time."

The crime scene van pulled up and the techs began setting up their own perimeter around the body, unloading equipment and snapping photographs. Carlisle and Kincaid knew all of the faces on the forensics unit and they were pleased to see that Kyle Sondheim was leading this team.

Nodding in their direction, Kyle pulled a paper cap over her blond curls and got to work.

———————————

The lady in the bushes had been found in front of an apartment building on a residential block in the University District in northeast Seattle. "Let's talk to the rubberneckers," said Carlisle. "Then we can canvas the buildings." Splitting up, they started asking questions.

Made up mostly of college students, Puerto Ricans and new immigrants, the group of onlookers matched the demographic of the neighborhood. And the canvas didn't take long because no one had seen or heard anything.

Back on the other side of the yellow tape, Carlisle waved Kyle over.

"What do you have so far?" Kyle asked in a sultry voice that made no sense coming from her innocent, milk-fed face and contrasted totally with the hazmat suit, latex gloves and paper booties.

Blinking away the thought that Kyle's voice should really be wearing a different outfit, Kincaid said, "We were hoping you'd tell us."

"Then you're out of luck," she said. "I don't have anything yet. No footprints; looks like the killer swept up the dirt where he walked, maybe with his hand or the sole of his shoe. Not much blood here. I'd guess it's just a dump site, but we'll take soil samples and I'll know for sure back at the lab. We cut the branches immediately around the body and bagged them for trace evidence. Finished the photographs *in situ*. They're just dusting her for prints now. Blah, blah, blah. Mallory should be here soon and then we can move her." To her team she called, "ME's on his way, let's finish it up."

As if on cue, the ME's van pulled up. Decked out in a Tyvek jumpsuit, Dr. Jim Mallory hopped out of the passenger side and walked over carrying a heavy-duty plastic toolbox full of medical instruments.

"We meet again," he said in greeting. Compact but regal, with neatly trimmed salt and pepper hair and a matching beard, Mallory was just shy of Carlisle's five-foot-ten. He had also been at the retirement party the night before, but he'd left early and clearly gotten a good night sleep. "You don't look any the worse for wear," he said to Carlisle. "Though I can't say the same for your partner."

"I'm cultivating the look of a dissolute rogue," said Kincaid with a half-smile. "I hear the ladies love it."

Kyle said, "Did I miss a good party?"

Carlisle said, "The good old boys drank too much Irish whiskey and sang *Danny Boy* fifty times. So, no, you didn't miss a good party."

Mallory grinned, Kincaid shrugged, and they got back to business.

"How far along are you?" Mallory asked Kyle.

"We scanned her prints; I'll run them now, and if she's in the system we'll have an ID shortly." She glanced at the crew. "We're ready for you to move her."

"We're going to knock on some doors," said Carlisle. "Don't find anything good till we get back."

"Hey, get some pictures of the spectators too, will you Kyle?"

said Kincaid. "One of them might be our murderer." This almost never happened, but no stone left unturned.

A cracked brick walkway led from the crime scene to a stucco apartment building. Uniforms were posted at the front and back doors to ask anyone coming or going whether they'd seen or heard anything, but at eight o'clock on a Saturday morning in a building that housed mostly students, there hadn't *been* anyone coming or going.

The front security door had already been propped open and the detectives stepped into the tiny foyer. "You take three and four," said Carlisle, "I'll take one and two."

The noise from the street had woken the place up. The din of gossip and speculation and fear drifted into the hallways.

Carlisle started at the front and made short shrift of her half, taking note when there was no answer, handing out cards and asking questions, but she wasn't getting anywhere. Only one person was able to add anything helpful.

"It was like two or three in the morning," said a woman in her mid-twenties with an obvious hangover and breath so stale Carlisle had to hide a wince. "I parked in back but came around to the front to get my mail. Don't ask me why it seemed important in the middle of the night." She paused, losing her train of thought, came back. "Anyway, I heard a car idling on the street and figured someone was getting dropped off."

When Carlisle asked whether she had seen the make and model of the car, the woman scoffed. "It was on the other side of the hedge and I was drunk. Besides, I don't know a Chevy from a Cadillac, but it must've been kinda loud, because otherwise I wouldn't've heard it." She burped and clutched her stomach.

A few minutes later Carlisle met Kincaid by the mailboxes. "Anything?"

"Nope. No answer at a few of the doors; we can have the

uniforms check back later, but the people I talked to had nuthin' to say."

"I got a woman who puts a loud car idling outside around two or three. No idea what kind of car. Can't narrow down the time. Didn't pay much attention. And she was drunk—probably still is drunk."

"Dubious."

"To say the least."

"Still," said Kincaid, "could be something if the timing lines up with time of death. Or when the body was dumped. We can always press her for more when she sobers up."

Carlisle shrugged. "Let's go talk to Mallory."

"Right on time," said the ME when they emerged from the other side of the hedge. The crowd had been pushed back to prevent cell-phone pics from gawkers when they moved the body, though something always turned up on Twitter.

An empty body bag lay unzipped on top of a blue tarp on the sidewalk. "We'll give her a cursory look here. See what's in her pockets."

While two crime scene techs held twigs and branches out of the way, Kyle Sondheim and Mallory's assistant helped the ME lift and turn the body before laying it on top of the open body bag.

They all stood and took a long look at the woman before them. Her cloudy eyes were blue, her hair an expensive shade of platinum blonde and her clothes were dirty from the ground but very nice. Big one-karat diamond studs shone from her earlobes and a heavy rock sparkled from her ring finger. One side of her head was bloody, but intact. Kyle checked her pockets. "Nothing."

Mallory prodded an arm. "Dead a while, but less than eight hours. And that's probably not what killed her." He pointed to the head wound, checked his watch. "Killed between midnight and two? Don't quote me."

Carlisle snapped a few more pictures with her phone while a

technician placed paper evidence bags over the dead woman's hands and feet. "No way a mugger left that jewelry behind." She turned to Kyle. "Think she was killed here?"

"There's not much blood, depends on what killed her," she said.

Mallory said, "Lividity matches the position of the body. If she wasn't killed here, then she was left here within an hour or two of the murder. Again, don't quote me till I've written my report."

"We have a witness who puts a car idling here around two or three."

Mallory shrugged. "That would work. So would a lot of other scenarios." He turned and began tucking limbs into the rubber bag.

Kyle's phone pinged. She looked at it. "We got a hit on her prints."

"Yeah?" said Carlisle when Kyle didn't go on.

"Aurora Stanhope," she said and turned back to help Mallory.

"Sounds regal," said Carlisle.

"Stanhope," said Kincaid. "Sounds familiar too, but what do I know?" He checked DMV records. "Fifty-seven, five-six, one-twenty-five, blonde and blue. Drives a white Porsche. Not so regal—the hit on her prints came from an arrest record. Reckless driving and resisting. She was booked in the Sheriff's Department."

"*Really?*" Carlisle raised her eyebrows. "Interesting. DUI?"

"Not according to the report," said Kincaid. "Okay, I have a home address on Lake Washington and a business address downtown—she's listed as CEO of a nonprofit called The Economic Development Campaign." He switched over to Google. "Married. Two adult children. Here's a work address for her husband, Robert Stanhope, also right downtown."

"Let's try the home address."

Kincaid nodded, kept reading from the screen. "Listen to this line-up—last month she co-hosted a gala for kids with cancer, before that it was environmental awareness of Puget Sound, before that, Type I diabetes. Aurora Stanhope was a socially aware socialite. Here's something else—after all the social stuff, first two hits on Google are press releases." Reading aloud, he said, "'Aurora Stanhope and her business partner Elizabeth Williams have decided to part ways after disagreements about the direction of their company.'" Raising his eyebrows. "'Stanhope dismisses speculation that Williams was fired from the nonprofit…'"

"When?"

"A while ago, almost two years." A few more clicks took Kincaid to a Facebook page and he began scrolling through it. "Elizabeth Williams. Single mom."

Carlisle was on her own phone. "Pretty. Your age. About."

"Trying to set me up with a murder suspect?"

"Maybe she didn't do it." When Kincaid glowered at her, she shrugged, slipped the phone back into her pocket. "Elizabeth Williams. Add her to our list of suspects, guilty until proven innocent."

"Already done."

CHAPTER TWO

F AMILY NOTIFICATION WAS BAD. ALWAYS. Sometimes, if the
victim had been missing for a while, or lived a dangerous life, it
might be a little less bad. But Aurora Stanhope's husband, as far as
they knew, was in for the full shock and horror version.

They drove to Lake Washington and found the Stanhope's
house in Windermere. A right turn onto the property revealed an
impressive wrought iron gate standing open on a curving driveway.
"This isn't a house," said Kincaid, "it's an estate."

Fifty yards of bigleaf maple and feathery evergreens lined the
drive and parted on a manicured lawn and an enormous French
Provincial mansion. With two and a half stories of pale limestone
and a pitched black slate roof, the home was striking against shades
of green and colorful fall foliage.

"Good thing we're in the Mercedes." said Kincaid as Carlisle
pulled the sedan to a stop in the circular drive. "They might call
the cops if we'd showed up in an unmarked." Getting out of the car,
he did a full three-sixty turn. "How does a lady who lives here"—
his gesture swept the grounds from the main building, passed the
matching carriage house cum garage, and landed on the gardener's
cottage—"a lady who *lived* here, end up dead outside a cheap
apartment building by the university?"

"Let's find out." She looked at her partner. "Stop gawking.
Come on."

Under an impressive portico, Carlisle rang the bell, then

turned to survey the gardens. Two minutes later she was about to ring again when the door opened, revealing a stout, middle-aged Chinese woman wearing a black and white cliché for a uniform. She looked them up and down before asking in an accented voice, "Can I help?"

"I certainly hope so, ma'am," said Kincaid and they both pulled out their badges. "Can we come in?"

"No." She shook her head. "No one's home. Please come back later." The door started to close.

Kincaid put a big hand against the thick door, still brandishing his gold detective's shield. "Actually, we'd like to talk to you, Miss…"

"Mrs. Chang," she said through the crack.

"Can we come in?" said Kincaid, hand still on the door.

She looked at them, then silently stepped aside.

The invitation to enter stopped at a round mahogany table in the center of the circular foyer, a grand two-story stunner with a sweeping staircase leading to the second floor and a white marble-tiled floor. The vaulted ceiling was patinaed copper embossed with Greco-Roman medallions and the whole space was lit on this gray autumnal day by an enormous crystal chandelier. Bucolic oil paintings hung on the wall below the curving staircase, and to the left and right, the room opened respectively to a richly furnished sitting room and a classic gentleman's library.

"What can I do?" asked Chang, interrupting their stares.

Carlisle said, "Mrs. Chang, when was the last time you saw Mrs. Stanhope?"

Almost a foot shorter than Carlisle, Chang stared up at her unblinking for a few beats, without even a glimmer of curiosity. Then, "Last night."

"About what time was that?"

Chang raised a solitary eyebrow and clasped her hands behind her back. Considered. Decided to answer. "She left at eight o'clock last night and did not return. I can tell her you were here."

"Do you live here?" asked Kincaid.

"Yes, Tuesday to Saturday evening I live here. Saturday evening to Tuesday morning I live at home."

"Where's home, Mrs. Chang?" asked Carlisle.

She glared suspiciously. "China Town."

Touché, thought Carlisle. But her address would be easy enough to find with DMV records. She asked, "So you were here all last night and this morning?" The woman nodded. "Could Mrs. Stanhope have come in without you noticing?"

Chang was already shaking her head no, her thick pageboy shaking along with it. "She never come or go without letting me know."

"She always checks in with you?" asked Carlisle.

"No. She always want help, coming and going. Put the car away, bring her tea, find her nightie. Find her keys, get her coat from the closet. Always want help."

"And she didn't want any help after eight o'clock last night?"

Chang looked at Carlisle as if she were daft. "No. Mrs. Stanhope left at eight o'clock and did not return," she repeated.

"Unless she came back and didn't need anything?"

"That has never, ever happened."

"Right. Do you know where she went?"

Another head shake. "No. She never tell me where."

"But she left at eight o'clock? Did she have dinner at home?"

"No."

"So, she could have gone out for dinner?"

"Yes."

"Do you know where she likes to go?"

"No."

Carlisle was tired of the one-word responses. She growled a little. "Did Mrs. Stanhope drive?"

"Yes."

"Okay," said Carlisle, "she took her own car?"

"Yes."

Kincaid stepped forward before his partner got out the rubber hose. "Mrs. Chang, do you know where we can find Mr. or Mrs. Stanhope? It's important that we speak to one of them." He finished with the smile that had melted the hearts of hundreds of witnesses and suspects alike but did not crack Mrs. Chang's stoicism.

"Mr. Stanhope is at his office. Missus, I don't know."

A few more questions got nothing. Back in the car, Kincaid called dispatch and issued a be-on-the-lookout for Mrs. Stanhope's car. "A white Porsche Boxster is kind of edgy for the driveway of a chateau."

"You saw her in a Bentley with a driver?" said Carlisle.

He looked back at the house. "Something like that." Then he added, "Mrs. Chang was concise."

"I was about to wring her neck," said Carlisle. "You know, she never once asked why we were looking for her boss." They both thought about that for a few seconds, found no obvious answer. Finally, she said, "What are the chances she doesn't call Robert Stanhope and tell him the cops are on their way?"

Kincaid settled into the leather seat. "No chance at all."

———————

Stanhope Industries took up half of the twenty-first floor of a thirty-floor office building in downtown Seattle. Another wave of October drizzle had washed over the city, driving the pedestrians off the street, but not the cars. Carlisle parked a few blocks down from the smoked glass edifice and they made their way through the wind and rain.

The heavy doors were locked on a Saturday, but before Kincaid could figure out how to use the intercom a pleasant security guard in his late thirties buzzed the detectives into the deserted lobby. Echoes sounded from their footfalls as they crossed the polished granite floors, and a piano sonata tinkled softly from hidden speakers.

"Afternoon," said the security guard, rising behind a tall mahogany desk, "are you here to see someone?"

"Robert Stanhope," said Carlisle.

He clicked a mouse, scanned a hidden computer screen. "Is he expecting you?"

Kincaid took out his badge. "We need to speak to Mr. Stanhope about a police matter."

The guard looked at the badge, then back at the two detectives. "I'll call up and see if he's available."

"Nope," said Kincaid, in a tone as rigid as a stone wall. "Just tell him we're coming up."

"Right." He made the call and came around the desk, pulling a magnetic fob from a chain on his belt. "This way."

In silence, the three of them rode to the twenty-first floor and the guard turned to the right, where 'Stanhope Industries' was stenciled in gold copperplate across a glass wall with a lobby on the other side of it. The guard pressed a button and a few seconds later a handsome man of average height in a bespoke flannel suit rounded a corner, crossed the reception area and opened the door.

"It's all right, Carl," he said, and the guard went away.

Stanhope introduced himself. Thinning salt and pepper hair accented a deep tan that left fine white laugh lines around his eyes. Probably from a summer spent captaining his yacht, playing tennis, sipping cocktails by the pool, thought Carlisle. The man looked entitled.

"Follow me, Detectives."

At the end of a long hallway, he paused at a door leading to the inner sanctum. "Annie called to tell me you were likely on your way." Then he walked into his giant corner office, heading straight for the chair behind his desk. "I'd offer you coffee, but I don't want to make it," he said, pointing to a discreet bar with half a dozen crystal tumblers and a bottle of scotch, a Subzero mini-fridge tucked in the cabinet. "There's water."

"Nothing, thanks," Carlisle answered for both of them. "Annie Chang?"

He nodded. "She told me you'd stopped by the house."

Carlisle looked around. The room was big and masculine and Stanhope, broad shouldered and imposing, if not very tall, filled it.

"Have a seat," he said, indicating a couple of chairs as he sat heavily in the leather swivel chair behind his desk. "What is it this time?"

"Pardon?" said Kincaid.

Stanhope gestured irritably for them to sit. "Isn't this about my wife?"

They sat. "Sir," said Kincaid, "I'm afraid—"

"Annie told me you were asking about Aurora," he said, frowning. "The children?"

"No, it's not about your children."

"Okay, then it *is* about Aurora. What's the problem? How do I fix it?"

Carlisle leaned forward in her chair, stared at Stanhope until he quieted. "Mr. Stanhope, Detective Kincaid and I are from the homicide division of the police department." She let that sink in. "Your wife was found dead this morning."

Stanhope was silent, blinking rapidly. After a second, he cleared his throat. "What did you say?"

"Your wife was found this morning, sir. Dead," Carlisle repeated. "I'm very sorry."

But Stanhope didn't look very sorry, or very surprised—his face just went blank.

Carlisle and Kincaid exchanged a look. "Mr. Stanhope, do you understand why we're here?"

Silence.

Kincaid got a bottle of water from the mini-fridge.

"Drink," he instructed and Stanhope did.

He said, "Aurora is dead?" Carlisle nodded and he squeezed his eyes shut, managed to reshape his face into the look of a man who understood the gravity of what was happening, then opened them. "She was murdered."

"Yes sir, I'm afraid she was," said Carlisle.

When half a minute passed in silence, Kincaid said, "Mr. Stanhope, do you have any idea who might have wanted to hurt your wife?"

"I don't think so." He fidgeted uncomfortably, "Well, no one who would want to *kill* her. Some people may not wish her well." Suddenly a dopey smile began to spread across his face.

Kincaid waited, raised his eyebrows, and eventually said, "Who?"

Trying to frown, Stanhope said, "That would be a long list, I'm afraid." He waited. The detectives said nothing. "Aurora could be"—he searched for a word—"insensitive, at times." He placed his elbows neatly on either side of a leather desk blotter. Again, he squeezed his eyes tightly shut, resting his head in his hands. He started laughing, choking on his words. "Our children are going to be crushed. I don't know how I'm going to tell them."

Carlisle and Kincaid waited him out. The man was laughing so hard he couldn't speak, tears running from his eyes, snot from his nose. He shook. Hiccupped.

Went quiet.

They let the silence linger, watched Stanhope for signs of guilt or deceit, but the man's expression had gone blank again. Truth be told, hysterical laughter in the face of tragedy was almost as common as uncontrollable tears. Maybe this guy just couldn't believe his wife was dead.

In many ways, cracking up like this was more convincing to the two detectives than weeping. Stanhope appeared to be pulling himself together, directing his energy at maintaining self-control.

Finally, he wiped his eyes with his hands. "Jesus Christ, what's the matter with me?" After a few seconds, he said, "How did it happen? Did she suffer?"

"I wish I could tell you, sir. But we can't be sure of the cause of death until after the autopsy." Carlisle paused, then asked, "Mr. Stanhope, did your wife come home last night?"

Now he got a little shifty. "Well, actually, I don't know. I just flew back from Portland this morning, haven't been home yet."

"Did you speak with her last night?"

"No, I was only gone for the one night." He raked his fingers through his hair. "Look, this is so awful; I have to tell our children." He looked at the phone on his desk, then looked up. "Will I have to identify her?"

"No," said Carlisle. "Not unless you feel you need to. We were able to identify Aurora with her fingerprints, and eventually we'll also show you a photograph. You'll have to sign a few papers, but that's all."

"We would like to talk to your children, too, Mr. Stanhope," said Kincaid. "Could you give us their contact information?"

"I could," he said. "But I'd like to be able to tell them myself. They need to hear this from me. They'll be crushed," he repeated.

"Sure." Kincaid would have preferred to tell them himself, see their reactions, but they'd get to the kids before long. Kincaid wouldn't take Stanhope's word for it; in the history of mankind more than one kid had killed his parents. Still, there was no cause to prevent Stanhope from telling them first. Handing him a few business cards, he said, "Why don't you ask them to call us?"

"Is there anything else right now?"

"Not now," said Kincaid, "but we will need to talk to you again, sir. Soon."

"You can come to the house later today. I'll have my son and daughter there. You can talk to them then."

And your lawyer, thought Carlisle. "What time?"

"This evening. I'll be in touch," he said and waved them away.

CHAPTER THREE

"PRETTY SMOOTH ALIBI DROP," CARLISLE said as they walked out of the building. "We didn't even have to ask him where he was between midnight and two in the morning."

"Yeah, but it'll be easy to check out. I'm more concerned about him coaching the kids before we talk to them."

"No cause to stop him." Climbing into the passenger seat, Carlisle asked, "Where to?"

They drove back to headquarters on Fifth and Cherry to do a little fact checking on their victim before conducting more interviews and sat at opposite desks, clicking on nearly identical yellowing keyboards and taking notes on matching yellow legal pads. Carlisle's phone pinged and she read the text.

"Kyle is going to stop up in a few minutes. She's in the lab now so maybe she checked the soil samples, and can tell us if Aurora Stanhope was killed in those bushes or just left there."

The desk phone rang. Kincaid answered, spoke for a few seconds and hung up. "Our victim's son wants to see us."

"When?"

"Right now. That was the desk sergeant—he's in the lobby."

"Daddy Stanhope didn't waste any time telling him."

"*Daddy* Stanhope?"

Carlisle shrugged. "Is he coming up?"

"I told the sergeant to give us five, then bring him up."

Thanks to the world wide web, Carlisle was already sifting

through the Stanhope family details. Summarizing from her screen, she said, "Robert Stanhope. Prominent family in Washington State, from East Coast coal money, then West Coast logging, now they're the largest North American manufacturers of silicon computer chips. Aurora married into the family thirty-some years ago, but she comes from money too. One son, thirty-one, one daughter, twenty-five. And, she was a knock-out." She turned her computer screen to face her partner.

Kincaid stared at the photo, a recent society page pic of a garden party. Aurora Stanhope smiled wickedly over her shoulder. She wore a white short-sleeved sheath that showed most of her back, curved like a violin, long neck, sharp jaw, mouth curled into a dangerous smile, teeth bared, eyes glimmering, pale blonde hair.

"Wow. She looks like trouble." After a few seconds of silence Kincaid looked back at his own screen and said, "Listen to this. Aurora Stanhope also had an assault charge on her record, but no arrest because the charges were dropped. But she's loaded, so maybe it was a payoff.

"The police report says the victim was Stanhope's housekeeper, Maria Sanchez. Sanchez claimed that her boss charged her while she was cleaning the master bedroom, screaming that the tablecloth was wrong and she was expecting company. He looked at Carlisle. "*The wrong tablecloth?* What planet do these people come from? Anyway, Sanchez ends up on the floor missing a chunk of hair—we only have Sanchez's report on how that happened—and the son breaks up the skirmish."

"The same son who's waiting downstairs?"

"Only one she's got." He went on, "Sanchez goes home in tears and Mrs. Stanhope, per her own statement, entertains her guests with the help of the *other* maid.

"When Sanchez's husband comes home and sees the scratches on his wife's neck and chest and the bald patch on her scalp, he convinces her to report the incident to the police. She files a complaint, police question Mrs. Stanhope the next day and by that evening, Sanchez drops the charges."

"Sounds like a payoff," Carlisle agreed. "When was this?"

"Two years and a few months."

"Better put the Sanchezes on the list. What about the arrest?"

"A year ago, the sheriff's department charged her with reckless driving for speeding down Route 99 in pursuit of another car. A passenger in the other car called the police and gave the make and license plate number of a white Porsche that was chasing them down the highway. Troopers pulled Stanhope over to the side of the road and approached with caution.

"The report says that even after they had her out of the car for the mandatory sobriety test, she continued ranting about the other driver who, she claimed, had cut her off. She was so defiant that they finally hauled her to the nearest station, had her car towed and booked her for resisting arrest. Blood test showed no alcohol or illicit drugs in her system, but it was a while before she cooled off. Evidently her attorney reached an agreement with the state, because after a few hours in jail, they let her go pending a court appearance."

Carlisle whistled, "Nice lady. She probably got a big fine—which would be no problem for her—and the whole thing was over. Who was the other driver?"

"No idea. After the initial phone call, troopers didn't have any contact with the other car. Aurora was still driving over a hundred miles an hour when the trooper got to her so they didn't need a witness for a reckless driving ticket."

"Anything else?"

"Couple of speeding tickets—she *did* drive a race car—and lots of parking violations, all paid."

"The lady did what she wanted," mused Carlisle.

Looking over his partner's shoulder, Kincaid said, "This must be him."

A tall man with brown hair and his mother's eyes stood next to a uniformed officer at the entrance to the bullpen. DMV records put Lucas Stanhope at six-feet even, one-seventy, brown and blue. He crossed the room with good posture and a hangdog expression.

Carlisle stood and made introductions. "We're very sorry for your loss," she said and they all shook hands.

Kincaid pulled up an extra chair; Lucas Stanhope collapsed into it.

He stared at them, opened his mouth, closed it again, and finally spoke. "My dad called me. He wants me to be there when he tells my sister, but I wanted to come here first. I don't understand what happened." He sat up straighter. "I mean, *what happened?*"

Carlisle felt for him. Cautiously. The poor kid looked genuinely shell-shocked—exactly how he was supposed to look. "All we really know is that your mom was murdered sometime early this morning. Found by a jogger near the university."

Lucas looked at Kincaid as if he might be more forthcoming. "How did she die?"

"We won't know until the autopsy has been performed. I'm sorry we don't have more answers for you, Mr. Stanhope. At this point, we're still gathering evidence."

"Call me Lucas." Then he was silent for a few seconds, rubbing his temples. "We were going to have lunch on Monday. I've been out of town for months and I haven't even seen her since I got back. I just can't believe this." Rub, rub.

He looked up. "Are you positive it's my mom?" His eyes went from Carlisle to Kincaid and back again.

Hope springs eternal, thought Carlisle.

"We matched her fingerprints, Lucas," said Kincaid. "It's her." No response.

"Where were you?" asked Carlisle after a few seconds.

"What?"

"You said you'd been out of town for months. Where were you?"

"Oh." He blinked at the abrupt change in subject. "Honduras. The rainforest. I'm a research biologist and I was there to, you know, do research."

"Were you close to your mom?" she asked. But something was happening behind her that had caught his attention. She turned.

Scanning the file in her hand while walking in a straight line, Kyle didn't notice that the detectives had company until she was only a few feet away. When she finally did look up, Kyle saw Lucas and stopped dead.

"I'll come back later."

"Kyle." Lucas stood, almost knocking over his chair. "Wait." She stayed, but didn't say anything.

Finally, Kincaid said, "I take it you two know each other?"

Kyle kept her eyes on Kincaid. "We did. Look, this can wait," she said, waving the file in the air, "call me when you're finished." And then she was gone.

Lucas was still standing, staring at the door through which Kyle had just left. When he finally turned around, he said, "I have to meet my father."

"Lucas, we're going to need to talk to you."

"I'll be at the house later," he said, looking, if it were possible, even more distressed than when he had come in. "I'm sorry I barged in. I just thought…"

But Lucas Stanhope never finished the sentence. Maybe he just thought that if he came here and talked to the detectives, everyone would realize that they had made a mistake. That it wasn't his mom lying dead in the morgue. Or, maybe he just thought that if he came here, he could gain some more information about the murder. Either because he was desperate, or because he was guilty of something.

A curtain seemed to fall over Lucas's face and Carlisle knew he was shutting down. She tried to get him talking again, but eventually they let him go.

When he was gone, Kincaid turned to his partner. "Did we just miss an opportunity?"

They both knew the impromptu visit to the police station might have been a good chance to get more information out of the kid while he was still vulnerable. After he'd had the chance to compose himself and in the presence of his father, perhaps his sister, and almost certainly the family lawyer, Lucas would be more guarded. "Probably," said Carlisle, "but we'll talk to him later."

Kincaid called Kyle and less than five minutes later, she was back, looking contrite. She said, "I blew your interview."

"Yeah," said Carlisle, "you did."

"Did you bring him in?"

"He just showed up," said Kincaid.

"Was that all?" Kyle asked.

Carlisle ignored the question and said, "Fill us in."

"I should've told you when I got the ID. I'm sorry."

"Make it up to us," said Kincaid.

"We met in grad school." She told them that she had just finished the first semester of her master's program in forensics and he had been in town for winter break. "He was a PhD candidate at Stanford, back for the holiday, and we met at a party thrown by one of the teaching assistants at UW." Kyle had gone with a group of friends and as the evening progressed, had found herself drinking her second or third micro-brew shoulder to shoulder on an old sofa with a very good-looking biologist named Lucas Something.

"From that night on, we were together pretty much nonstop until he went back to California. Then we talked on the phone and emailed almost every day for months, saw each other a couple of times, but I was taking a trace evidence course at Quantico over spring break and he was going to North Carolina for a summer program in marine biology and I was only twenty-five and he was only twenty-six and, you know, we called it quits." She looked down at her hands. "And I haven't seen or talked to him since."

"Did you know Aurora?"

"Nope, never met his family." She made a dismissive gesture. "It was a whirlwind thing, and most of our relationship—if you can call it that—was long distance. Honestly, I didn't know who the victim was until we got the results from her fingerprints and even then I wasn't positive she was his mother." She looked at them. "But I was pretty sure, so I should have told you right away. I'm sorry," she said again.

Kincaid scrutinized her. "Do you need to be reassigned?"

"No." Emphatic. "I haven't seen him in years, and there's no reason I need to see him again."

Carlisle gave her a long look. "If you say it's no big deal, then it's no big deal." She nodded at the file in Kyle's hand. "Now, what did you come here to tell us?"

"Right." She set the file on Carlisle's desk. "Not much. I tested the soil samples for blood and our victim definitely wasn't killed at the site. We're analyzing the material under her fingernails, some fiber, but none of it looks like skin. That's about it for now."

After she'd gone, Carlisle leaned on her elbows, rested her chin on her hands. "What do you think?" she asked her partner.

"I don't think it's a problem. Could even be helpful if we need to throw Lucas off, because he definitely reacted when he saw her."

Carlisle agreed. "Let's go do some real police work." Looking through her email, she said, "Got records on the possibly jilted business partner. Home address in Magnolia. Business address conveniently close to the university. She's got her own company now, so maybe Mrs. Stanhope did *not* ruin her life. No police record." She looked up. "See if she's home?"

"I'm in." Before leaving the station, they exchanged Tom's Mercedes for an unmarked sedan and Kincaid crammed himself into the driver's seat. "It's just not the same, Carlisle."

Kyle Sondheim was distracted.

Of all of the relationships she'd had in her twenties, Lucas Stanhope had been a standout. A few months after they'd broken up, she'd gotten her master's degree and a job in the Seattle PD crime lab. And Lucas had effectively become part of her past.

When she'd gotten the ID back on Aurora Stanhope, it had occurred to her that seeing Lucas again was a possibility. Still, it had thrown her off to run into him at the station. If she was honest, she'd felt a prickle when she'd looked up and found him staring at her. Not that she felt inclined to be honest about it.

The prickle wasn't because she longed for his affections. Lucas had been really good sex, but good sex was not what had made Lucas Stanhope a standout.

CHAPTER FOUR

B EFORE KINCAID HAD EVEN PULLED the car out of the police lot, Carlisle's phone rang. "ME," she told him as she put the phone to her ear.

She spoke for a few seconds and hung up. "The ex-business partner will have to wait. Next stop, the morgue. Mallory has a surprise for us."

"I love surprises."

The morgue reception area, such as it was, was empty on a Saturday afternoon. But once buzzed through the security doors, the place was lively. "No rest for the weary," said Kincaid absently.

They took an elevator down one floor to the autopsy suites and followed their noses through a set of swinging doors to find Mallory standing over the clean, naked body of Aurora Stanhope.

"What do you know, doc?" asked Kincaid, his eyes scanning the uncut corpse on the table.

"What's that?" asked Carlisle pointing to the woman's neck.

Mallory's eyes sparkled. "Once we had her cleaned up and undressed, these bruises around her neck became evident. Hemorrhage in her eyes and finger-shaped bruises."

"So, she was strangled *and* hit on the head," said Carlisle thoughtfully. "Do you know what actually killed her?"

"Not yet. I should be able to figure it out once I open her up, but she was definitely alive when these marks were made and alive when she was hit on the head."

"Can you tell what she was hit with?" asked Kincaid.

"Blunt object is all I can tell you now. No apparent edges. We'll make molds of the wounds and if you find a weapon, we can see if it fits. I didn't see any obvious particulates, like wood splinters or glass fragments, but a microscope might reveal more. It could have been something made of metal, marble, stone—something heavy and solid—with no sharp edges. Like a smooth rock or paperweight."

Carlisle rolled back on her heels. "Someone bashed her head in, strangled her with his bare hands, not necessarily in that order, and then dumped her in the bushes? *Someone* was very, very angry."

"Another thing," said Mallory. "Normally with manual strangulation, we see a lot more material under the fingernails. The strangler is up close and the victim will fight like hell to pry his hands away. Scratching, pulling. There's usually significant skin and blood evidence under the nails, defensive wounds to the victim's hands and forearms, broken fingernails, bruising on the legs from kicking—but as you can see," he added, looking down at the body, "she is very nearly pristine."

"So, she may have been dazed or unconscious from the head wound when she was strangled?" asked Carlisle.

"That's one possibility. I also ran a full toxicology panel on sedatives, palliatives and muscle relaxants, in case she was drugged." He arched his brows meaningfully. "And one more thing. It appears that she had consensual sex before she died."

"Appears?" said Kincaid.

"It's not always easy to tell, detective. Vaginal swabs didn't reveal any semen, but there was a trace of standard lubricant. That and faint abrasions on her labia indicate consensual sex. I'll know more after the autopsy. Of course, if she was drugged or semi-conscious from the head wound, sex could have been forced without the usual signs of bruising and tearing. Have you found anything yet that might give me direction?"

"Only that she wasn't well liked," said Kincaid, frowning. "We still don't know where she was last night. But the husband claims he was in Portland. So, the sex was extramarital."

Mallory brandished his scalpel. "Well, unless you want to stay and watch the show, you'd better get to it."

———————————

"Time to meet Elizabeth Williams," said Carlisle on the elevator ride up to the lobby.

They left the Medical Examiner's Office on Jefferson and zipped through weekend traffic. Williams lived in Magnolia, a residential neighborhood built on a peninsula just northwest of downtown. With homes in the hills, views of Puget Sound and of the cruise ships pulling into the marina, it was a trendy commercial district—it even had a park with tide pools.

"It's not Lake Washington, but it's a pretty nice neighborhood for a single mom running a nonprofit," said Kincaid. "She can't be doing too badly since Aurora Stanhope canned her."

"Maybe," said Carlisle. "Drives a two-year-old Toyota. Grey. Sensible."

They found her house number on West Bertona Street and pulled into the driveway. A flagstone path around an attached single-car garage led to the entrance of a genuine mid-century home. Kincaid pushed the doorbell and peered through the glass foyer while they waited. The house was built into the hill and seemed to be made entirely of glass and stone. From where they stood, Carlisle and Kincaid could see straight through to the back and the open view of the Sound beyond. An expensive piece of Seattle real estate.

"Mom! Someone's here!" A child's voice filtered through a tuft of evergreen huckleberry. Almost immediately, a dark-haired woman appeared from the back of the house, waving to them as she stepped onto the path.

She said something *sotto voce* to her son and he ran ahead of them and down a wooden stairway to a terraced back yard.

Carlisle and Kincaid flashed their badges, introduced themselves, and stepped onto a planked deck running along the back of the house. Williams didn't seem surprised by their arrival. "You're here about Aurora." Carlisle nodded and she led them through a double glass door and into a bright kitchen.

Slipping out of her muddy All Stars, Williams asked, "Coffee or tea?" She stood about five-five with soft curves in all the right places of her beat-up jeans and red sweater. Twinkling brown eyes flecked with gold and olive skin gave her an exotic look despite her all-American clothes, and she had an easy smile that seemed to broaden when she looked into Kincaid's baby blues.

"Whatever you're having. This is beautiful," said Carlisle looking around. A restored low-boy divided the dining room from the living room. Everything was open and airy with high ceilings and low sofas. Books and magazines were spread casually across a teak coffee table, a fireplace had a flat-screen TV mounted above it and hundreds of Legos were scattered across a Flokati rug.

"Thanks," said Williams, peeking into a canvas bag of groceries that sat forgotten on the kitchen island. "I hope this isn't the bag with the ice cream." Another quick glance at Kincaid before she began unpacking it. "My parents bought the lot long before Google and Microsoft moved in and raised the cost of living in Seattle. They built the house and when they retired to Palm Desert, deeded it over to me. Otherwise I'd never be able to afford a place like this in this neighborhood."

Talking too much, thought Carlisle.

"Coffee or tea?" She took a deep breath. "Asked and answered. Sorry, I guess I'm nervous. Not used to being questioned."

Kincaid said, "No reason to be nervous, Mrs. Williams." But they hadn't even gotten started.

"Beth. Everyone calls me Beth." She put a tea kettle on the gas stovetop and went back to unpacking her groceries. "Have a seat," she said, indicating the stools lined up on one side of the kitchen island. "I'll check on Henry and then we can get to it."

Beth walked out onto the deck, closing the door behind her, and leaned over the railing to talk to her son. Watching her partner, who was gazing through the glass door, Carlisle said, "She thinks you're cute," and sat down.

Kincaid turned to her, smiled, then frowned. "She's a person of interest, Judy. Maybe a suspect."

She winked at Kincaid. "A little charm never hurt during a suspect interview. Just make sure you're not the one being charmed."

When Beth Williams came back into the kitchen she opened a cupboard and removed three lopsided ceramic cups so ugly that they had to be homemade. Dropping two teabags into a pot, she set everything on the kitchen island and sat down on a stool across from the detectives. "These"—she pointed to the cups—"are one of the sad consequences of my relationship with Aurora."

"It wasn't an amicable parting," said Carlisle.

"No, not at all." Beth frowned. "And I assume you know a little about it or you wouldn't be here." Silence. "Anyway, it all turned out for the best but before I got my own company going, I took a lot of therapeutic art classes at the community center. Deformed pottery turned out to be my specialty." She smiled uncomfortably.

"I read about Aurora online, but there wasn't much information. Only that she was murdered early this morning."

"We don't have a time of death yet," said Kincaid, thinking that they had better verify that the story was already in the ether. "Late Friday or early Saturday." Then he leaned forward; even seated he had to look down at her. "What were *you* doing late Friday, early Saturday, Miss Williams?"

"Beth," she said again. "I—" But the whistling kettle saved her and she got up to take the water off the stove. "Saved by the bell." No one smiled.

She poured hot water over teabags. "I don't have an alibi unless you count my sleeping child. I hired a sitter and went out to dinner last night. Was home by ten, kissed my son goodnight, and watched two episodes of House of Cards."

Carlisle said, "I love Robin Wright." But she didn't smile when she said it and Beth just stood there awkwardly.

Finally, she said, "Me too," and sat down. "Look, I don't have an adult to vouch for my whereabouts after ten on Friday, but I would never leave my eight-year-old home alone and I would never kill anyone. And I would absolutely never leave my eight-year-old home alone while I went out to kill someone."

"I understand," said Carlisle, "and normally, an alibi is just a formality. But by your own admission you and Aurora parted on bad terms. If she forced you out of her company, then you have a motive and we have to rule you out."

Beth sighed, frowned, tapped her fingers on the counter. "I guess." She passed out misshapen cups. "Let's get this over with." Leaning down, she opened a drawer in the kitchen island and reappeared with a bag of Mint Milanos.

"About seven years ago, Aurora head-hunted me away from the organization I'd been working for pretty much since grad school, promising that I would be groomed to direct the poverty relief organization that she'd started five years before. The understanding was that she would remain the figurehead and have total veto power, but I would run things on the ground. I was thrilled. It was an opportunity to lead targeted relief in parts of Africa, Southeast Asia and India that larger organizations couldn't reach. And I was way too young and inexperienced to hope for that kind of opportunity, or to be suspect when it was offered." She blew on her tea, took a drink. "So, I jumped at it.

"Anyway, I dove in, loved it, got good at it. Hard work, but we were getting real results, particularly in rural India. Then, about two years ago, Aurora *informs* me that she's taking the company in another direction and we're phasing India out. That was her word.

Phasing." She grunted, shook it off, stood to check on her son, and sat back down.

"I was shocked because, like I said, that's where we were having the most success. I didn't get it. She told me that she'd just secured a huge donation from a big manufacturing company and the condition of their sponsorship was that we back out of India. I found out later that they were setting up sweatshops in western India. They wanted us to concentrate our efforts to feed and empower people *elsewhere*. But at the time, I didn't understand. Not that understanding would have made it better. Anyway, I told Aurora it didn't make any sense to me."

With a deep breath and another gulp of tea that *had* to be too hot to drink, she went on, "What I thought was the beginning of a constructive discussion between two colleagues ended abruptly with my termination."

"She fired you?" asked Carlisle.

"She said, 'I thought you might feel that way, Beth, so I've already written your letter of resignation and prepared a compensation package.' Then she smiled at me like the Cheshire Cat.

"She'd been planning to get rid of me for a while and I never saw it coming. I felt betrayed. Not so much because she and I were at odds ideologically, although the extent surprised me, but because I considered her my friend, my family. Henry and I had Thanksgiving dinner with Aurora and her family every year. Henry called her Auntie Rora. She knew my parents. She interrogated everyone I dated and introduced me to influential people and brought soup if either Henry or I was sick." Brown eyes brimmed with unshed tears. "She was *kind* to us. And then one day she called me into her office, told me the new plan for her organization and handed me her Mont Blanc pen so that I could sign my letter of resignation. It was un-fucking-believable."

She peered inside the white Pepperidge Farm bag, offered it to the detectives. "Cookie?" When they declined, she fished one out, rolled up the top of the bag and put it back into the drawer. "I impose a two-cookie limit on emotional eating."

"What happened then?" asked Carlisle.

"I signed. What could I do? The deal she made didn't happen overnight—she must have been negotiating it for months, and she was clearly determined to get rid of me. I was already bound by solid non-disclosure agreements, the conditions of our separation were fair, the severance package was very generous, and two security guards were waiting to escort me out.

"Aurora was right to get rid of me. I never would have agreed to move out of India, but the way she did it was so cold." She got up to check on Henry again, lingering by the doors. "Do you know that by the time I got home that day, I had hundreds of emails in my inbox asking me about the press release she had put out announcing our split? She must have put it out the minute I left the building. Unbelievable," she said again.

Then she leaned against the glass and closed her eyes. "So, I have no alibi, and I probably have a decent motive for murder, but I didn't do it."

"Well, you've certainly been forthcoming," said Carlisle.

"Look, I'm happy. After I stopped feeling sorry for myself, I used all of the contacts Aurora had helped me make over the years and in six months I'd secured funding for a new organization. In a year and a half, not only are we financially viable, but we've got people on the ground. I was able to rehire everyone on the India project and add more people. If I'm conservative, the severance package I got from the EDC means that Henry and I will be okay for the rest of our lives. Not rich, but safe."

Blowing out a breath, she added, "The worst thing she did was break my heart."

They would check out everything Beth Williams had told them, but if it was all true, Carlisle didn't think she was their killer. She looked at Kincaid, who nodded, pulled his notebook from the inside pocket of his overcoat and said, "When did you last see Mrs. Stanhope?"

She considered for a minute. "A few months ago at a benefit"—she gave them the name—"but we didn't speak other than a diplomatic hello. We haven't spoken since she forced me to resign."

"Okay," said Kincaid. "We also need the name and number of your babysitter and whoever you had dinner with."

"Are you going to tell my babysitter that I'm a suspect in a murder investigation?"

"No," said Kincaid with absolutely no inflection. She looked up phone numbers on her mobile and read them off. When she named a man as her dinner companion, he said dryly, "We won't tell your date that you're a murder suspect either."

Williams's eyes flashed at Kincaid when she said, "No, you can tell him."

Though her partner kept his eyes on his notepad, Carlisle knew he was smiling on the inside.

"Anyone else who might have wanted Aurora dead?" he asked.

"Definitely. Well, maybe not dead, but I'm sure lots of people didn't wish her well."

When she didn't go on, Kincaid said, "Do you know if Aurora was having an affair?"

Beth fidgeted on her stool. "There were lots of rumors, but I really wouldn't know anything about that. I do know that she and Robert loved each other. And he would never have hurt her. Never." When she was satisfied they understood, she changed the focus, "But someone she screwed over in business? Someone other than me, of course. Aurora was exceedingly ambitious and often callous." Rubbing her temples, she added, "I thought I was the exception."

Kincaid glanced at his partner, gave her a little nod. They would come back to Aurora's infidelities when they had more to go on.

"You said that you were being groomed by Aurora. Why do you think she chose you, Beth?" asked Carlisle.

"Probably because we complimented each other. I'm more ideological and hands-on, she knew how things worked in the world of social politics, high society and trading favors. She taught me a lot in five years; I would never have been able to do the work I'm doing now without her mentorship."

She was quiet for a few seconds. "I often wonder if Aurora was secretly proud of me. If maybe she fired me because she knew I would take over our work in India, and then we'd still be covering both areas." She looked forlorn. "I guess I'll never know."

"Is that something she might have done?" asked Kincaid. "Manipulated the situation so that you could still get relief to India?"

The seal on the glass doors broke, surprising them, and they turned to see a muddy child with his mother's dark hair and a missing front tooth walk into the kitchen. He carried a yellow Tonka dump truck in both of his arms. "Wheel came off, Mom."

He set the truck on the counter. "Can you fix it?"

"This is my son, Henry," she said to the detectives. Looking at the mess her son was making on the white countertop, she told him, "Probably, but first, take off your shoes and wash your hands. Then you can say hello to our guests."

The kid said, "Okay," and trotted off to do as he was told. When he turned back from the sink, looking for a towel, Henry's eyes lit up. "Did you fix it?"

Kincaid brought the truck to the sink and rinsed the mud off, took the towel from Henry and dried his hands. "Good as new."

The boy beamed up at Kincaid. "You're super tall."

Kincaid beamed back. "You're short."

"Still growing."

"Okay," said Carlisle. "I think we've got everything we need for now. Appreciate your help, Beth. We'll be in touch."

Henry was already testing his truck on the kitchen floor and Beth led them to the front door. "I hope you find her killer," she said.

Kincaid gave her the dead-eye stare. "We will. No doubt about that."

CHAPTER FIVE

"NEXT UP: MARIA SANCHEZ," SAID Carlisle.

Pulling the car out of the drive while Carlisle plotted the quickest route to the Sanchez house, Kincaid said, "Interesting relationship between Aurora and Beth Williams. Lot of anger, lot of love, and lot of respect."

"Definitely enough turmoil for a crime of passion. But why now?"

"I don't know," said Kincaid, "but we can't rule her out."

"As much as we might like to?" she asked.

He didn't bite. "Don't want to think of a doting mother and humanitarian committing murder, but betrayal and ideology are good motives."

Carlisle turned to her partner. "Well, it was nice of you to fix her son's truck before you haul her off to jail for the rest of her life."

"He's a cute kid," said Kincaid. "It was the least I could do."

Now Carlisle wasn't even trying to hide her smile. "Cute mom, too."

Kincaid said, "She's okay."

"She's perfect. Assuming she's not our killer, of course."

"Of course," said Kincaid.

"If we find out she didn't murder Aurora Stanhope, you should ask her out."

He glanced at warily at Carlisle.

"For what it's worth, she probably didn't do it."

He sighed. "Yeah, but just my luck, she did do it. And I'd be the asshole homicide dick who fell for a killer." He scowled, made a left turn. "Where to?"

"Conveniently close to the dump site, as a matter of fact," she said, plugging the address into the car's GPS.

The Sanchezes lived on one side of a tidy two-story duplex, less than four blocks from the apartment building where Aurora Stanhope had been found that morning. Neat rows of red mums lined a concrete walkway and three recently painted steps led to a porch with two wicker chairs and a tiny table. From the back yard came the laughter and screams of children playing.

Kincaid read the names on the doorbells. "Juan Sanchez or José Sanchez?" Carlisle shrugged and rang them both. When a petite Latina in her late twenties with a third trimester belly answered, the smell of dinner cooking poured through the open door. Someone was preparing a big meal.

Her bright smile didn't fade but she looked surprised. "Hi! Can I help you?" No trace of an accent.

Carlisle smiled back, taking advantage of the woman's warmth. She said, "Hi, we're here to talk to Maria. Is she in the kitchen?"

She nodded. "Follow me." They did, but Carlisle thought someone should have a chat with her about letting strangers into her house.

An open door stood on either side of the entryway and she led them through the one on the left, past a comfortable living room and a formal dining room stuffed with two sideboards and a giant, well-used table, and into the kitchen—source of the delicious smells.

Kincaid's stomach growled. The milk in his morning coffee was long gone. Spending time around dead bodies and grieving relatives had staved off the hunger pangs, but now it was mid-afternoon and roast chicken and rice, cilantro and lime, were making his mouth water.

"Here she is—oh!" she said. "I didn't ask your names! It's this pregnancy." She patted her belly. "I'm so *flaky*!" She drew out the last word and tittered with laughter.

"I'm Detective Carlisle. This is my partner, Detective Kincaid." The happy smile faded from Maria's lips.

Maria Sanchez turned to the pregnant woman, who looked suddenly stricken, and said something in Spanish. "No, Mama, everyone is still here."

"Is someone hurt?" Sanchez asked the detectives.

"No, ma'am, no one's hurt, that's not why we're here," said Kincaid.

"*Ay dios mio*," said Sanchez, looking toward the ceiling and pressing both palms to her breast. She closed her eyes for a few seconds and then turned to the two detectives. "I thought something happened to my family!" Her accent was rich and melodious. She studied them. "But something did happen. What is it?" She turned back to her daughter-in-law. "Go get Papa and Juan." Back to the detectives. "Come! Sit." She took them into the dining room and pulled out two chairs. "Please."

They sat and Sanchez took up a station on the other side of the table, but remained standing, tapping her foot on the wooden floor. In her mid-fifties, with shiny black hair and a Cupid's bow mouth painted bright red, she was an attractive woman. Healthy and rounded with a tiny waist, her chest barely cleared the table-top when she finally pulled a chair out from the table and sat.

José and Juan Sanchez came into the room and flanked Maria, more perplexed than worried.

"Please," said Kincaid after they'd made their introductions, "let's all sit down."

They did. Juan Sanchez demanded, "What's this about?" Again, no accent. He was second generation.

"Mrs. Sanchez," said Carlisle, keeping her eyes on the tiny

woman, "your former employer, Aurora Stanhope, was found murdered this morning."

For a few seconds, no one spoke. Then Maria said, "Mrs. Stanhope was murdered? She's dead?"

"I'm afraid so," said Carlisle.

She paled and her husband went to the sideboard to get her something to drink, retrieving a bottle of water and a bottle of bourbon. "Here," he said, pouring her half a finger of bourbon and shooting the detectives a baleful look. She drank it in one gulp and the color began to return to her cheeks.

"*Gracias, amado*," she said taking a sip of water. "Mrs. Stanhope was murdered," she repeated.

"Ding, dong, the witch is dead," said Juan.

"*Basta!*" said his mother.

"You're not surprised," said Kincaid, looking blandly at Juan. "Why?"

"Because she was a bitch. No surprise someone finally killed her."

"I said enough, Juan."

"Mama, you had nightmares working there. She expected you to read her mind; she treated you like a slave." He turned to the detectives, his face red with anger. "That lunatic attacked my mother! Did you know that?"

José spoke in a quiet voice but it silenced his son. "They *do* know, Juan. That is why they are here."

Turning back to the detectives, Juan said, "You think one of us had something to do with it? That's crazy! It all happened years ago."

"Less than two years, actually. And you still seem pretty upset about it," said Kincaid.

"Of course I am. At the time, I wanted to kill her, but I didn't. But we don't have anything to do with the Stanhopes anymore, so I'm not going to go out and kill her *now*."

Carlisle stepped in. "We've read the police report, Mrs. Sanchez. It said that you accused Mrs. Stanhope of assault, but then dropped the charges."

Juan hit the table with his fist. "Not because it didn't happen!"

Ignoring him, Carlisle said to Maria, "Can you tell us what happened?"

"So that you can treat her as a suspect? I don't think so," said Juan, shaking his head furiously. "I wasn't born yesterday."

Kincaid shrugged. "You're not compelled to tell us anything. But, if you didn't have anything to do with it, why wouldn't you?"

José shut his son down with a glare and turned to his wife. "Maria?"

"I'll tell them."

José nodded. "Juan, get some iced tea for the detectives." It wasn't a gesture of hospitality—José wanted his son out of the room. Juan glowered, but left.

"How long did you work for the Stanhopes?" asked Carlisle.

"After our youngest daughter went to college and before Juan and his wife moved in," Maria began, her English slow and precise. She told an abbreviated story of coming to America and working as a housekeeper, meeting José and quitting her job when they got married, and many years later, three children born and raised and out of the nest, she had signed with a placement agency and began working at the Stanhope residence four days every week until the incident.

"That woman was horrible to Maria," said José with disgust. "But she told me nothing—just kept going to work."

Patting his hand, Maria corrected, "Not at first, José. At first, she was fine. One maid lived there and I came Tuesday through Friday from eight to four o'clock. The house is very big. Needs two people to clean." She explained that the heavy cleaning was always done during the work week and the live-in maid did lighter housekeeping in the evenings and on Saturday. No one came in after Saturday afternoon unless there was a party or some other reason the Stanhopes needed extra help.

Juan had come back with tea and stood pouring while his mother spoke.

"Maybe it's the same now. I don't know. When I worked, Mrs. Stanhope was sometimes there, sometimes not. She was very picky. Everything just so. Sometimes she told me I did something wrong, needed to do it again. But she was okay. And then, at the end, she changed, got really picky, you know? Started yelling, stomping around, watching me clean. After a while I got jumpy. Never knew when she would appear and yell. Or when she would appear and be kind. Before, she sometimes gave me the flowers to take home when the new flowers came. Gave me a fresh turkey one time when too many were delivered for Christmas dinner. She would say, 'What would I do without you, Maria?' At the end, she was still kind sometimes, but I was afraid of that too because maybe later she's angry again. I never knew."

"She was unpredictable," said Carlisle.

"Yes," said Maria. "Unpredictable. I was scared, like a cat. All the time."

"She gave my mother *nightmares*," Juan repeated.

Maria sighed. "That terrible day, I was making the bed in her room and she came in behind me. I turned when I heard her voice. 'Maria, you stupid idiot!' Howling like a coyote. I turned, but she was already there, pulling my collar, my hair. She scratched me and I fell to the floor trying to get away from her. She said the tablecloth needed to be changed, she had company coming, she wanted the *damask* tablecloth. Wasn't she generous enough, did I think I could take advantage of her kindness." There were tears in Maria Sanchez's eyes and she waved her hands as if to banish the memory. "It was terrible."

"The police report said that her son stopped the attack," said Kincaid.

Nodding, she said, "Lucas. Nice boy. I didn't know he was home that day until he came in yelling and lifted Mrs. Stanhope off of me. Just picked her right up like she was nothing. Then he helped me up and took me to the kitchen, gave me a glass of sweet red wine." She shuddered at the memory. "I couldn't stop shaking. He offered to drive me home, but I said no. He told me, go home and report it to the police."

Kincaid leaned forward. "Mrs. Stanhope's *son* told you to call the police?"

Her nod was meaningful. "Her own son."

"And what did you do next?" asked Carlisle.

"I went home. When José came home from work we called the police."

José put an arm around his wife. "She didn't even call me. I would have come home early." Another loving pat from his wife. "I found her in the kitchen. White as a ghost, stirring a pot of soup. When she saw me, her face crumpled and she was crying. Scratches on her neck, blood on her head—that woman pulled her hair out." He gently fingered a lock of thick black hair on Maria's temple. "I thought a stranger had done this. A man in the street, perhaps. I thought she could have been"—his voice trembled—"*violated* by a man. I didn't know and she couldn't tell me. She could only cry."

"I was so relieved that he was home. I finally told him what happened and we called the police station. They came here and we filed a report and they left."

"And then?" asked Kincaid. "What made you decide to drop the charges?"

Maria looked at her husband before answering. Then she shrugged and said, "The next day Mr. Stanhope and his lawyer came here and offered to make a trust in each of our children's names for fifty thousand dollars. We signed a paper and that was the end."

CHAPTER SIX

"TIME TO EAT," SAID KINCAID when they were back in their unmarked.

They drove to Little Hanoi, a strip-mall Vietnamese restaurant with the best pho in town.

Seated in a booth by the window with menus they never bothered to read, Carlisle said, "She didn't do it."

"Nope. Maybe the husband—all those emotions bubbling under the surface—and the kid's a fuckin' hothead."

"They have alibis."

"Yeah, each other. For what that's worth."

"If the evidence starts to point that way we can push them, but I don't see it."

They ordered fried spring rolls and pho, with hot tea.

"You think the payoff was enough?" said Kincaid when their waitress had gone.

"Maybe. That's a lot of money, Jerry, and they didn't seem to regret not following through with the charges. The Stanhopes are out of their lives and their kids get a hundred and fifty K between them. It's a pretty good deal." She drank some tea. "We'll keep an eye on them but in the meantime, *I'm* wondering about the Stanhope kid telling Maria Sanchez to press charges against his mom."

"He looked pretty broken up this morning." Frowning, Kincaid added, "Jesus, we're going to have more suspects than we can handle on this, Judy. We have to find motive if we're going to find our man."

"What we really need is a smoking gun."

"Right. I love it when we find a smoking gun," said Kincaid with a smirk. "It's almost as good as when the killer confesses." Their food arrived and they ate in silence until their plates were clean. When the waitress cleared their dishes, he checked his cell phone. "It's about that time." They were due at the Stanhopes' at five.

Kincaid added a big tip on top of the bill and they walked out into another eruption of heavy drizzle.

"Twenty-minute drive to strategize on how to handle the Stanhope clan," said Carlisle as they pulled out of the parking lot.

Kincaid made a few turns, then said, "While we're at the Stanhopes', we need a list of everyone on their staff over the last few years. We also need to find out how many housekeepers Mr. Stanhope has had to pay off because of his wife's bad behavior. Not to mention gardeners, pool boys, cooks, personal shoppers, employees at the Economic Development whatever. I'll be interested to find out how she treated friends and family, colleagues, other people who are not in her employ."

"All in good time. But first, I'm pretty interested in the kid. Who encourages someone to have his own mother arrested?"

"And showed up unannounced and distraught at police headquarters. You've got a bee in your bonnet about Lucas." When she just shrugged, he said, "Well, if Stanhope keeps his word, you might get your chance. Otherwise, we'll track Lucas down later." He ran a hand through his hair. "Actually, if their lawyer puts a gag on him, you might not get your chance at all. How hard can we question these people?"

"As far as they'll let us. But let's keep what we know about Lucas to ourselves for now. Might come in handy later on."

"Okay. And what about the consensual sex before Aurora was killed?"

Carlisle thought about it, then said, "On mentioning the possibility that Mrs. Stanhope had sex shortly before she was killed, not unless they mention a lover. On the assault and resisting charges? Ask what we need to and if we're shot down, regroup tomorrow."

"Don't ask about the sex? Seems important," said Kincaid.

"Probably is, but I think we want to keep the family on our side of the investigation as long as we can. If the Stanhopes are clueless, then we'd be unearthing an extramarital affair. No need to antagonize them. Not until we've got more."

They parked in the circular drive outside of the house on Lake Washington, right alongside a shiny red Audi TT.

"Nice car," said Kincaid as they stepped out of their worn unmarked sedan. "Daddy's or one of the kids'?"

"Daughter's," said Carlisle. "Dad drives a silver Jaguar."

"DMV records?"

"I peeked when we were at the station."

"So, dad drives a luxury sedan and mom and daughter drive race cars, and the son drives?" He waited for Carlisle to provide the answer.

"Psychological profiling based on automobile preference?"

"Gotta start somewhere."

"Then this will make sense. Lucas Stanhope drives a four-year-old Prius. Beige."

"The conservationist." They walked to the huge front door under the massive portico and rang the bell.

During another long wait for someone to answer, Kincaid tapped his foot and looked around. The drizzle that had begun while they were eating had turned to rain and a pleasant loamy scent emanated from the wet flower beds on either side of the entrance.

When the door finally swung open, a much more collected Lucas Stanhope stood aside to let them in.

"Lucas," said Kincaid as they stepped across the threshold.

He pointed left. "This way." As he turned, he added, "My father doesn't know that I barged into your office today. I'd appreciate it if you didn't mention it. He wouldn't understand."

They followed him through the sitting room, through a formal dining room with three chandeliers and a table the size of a handball court, down a wide, short hallway, and finally through a broad set of pocket doors and into the great room.

In every sense of the word.

French doors lined the entire back wall of the house with another row of six-foot mullioned windows above them. Stone fireplaces flanked the room and a white marble floor spanned between. Thick oriental rugs and leather furniture the color of cognac and the texture of butter made Carlisle think of men with scotch and cigars and women with gin gimlets and long-filtered cigarettes. Beyond the glass doors a stone patio and a sprawling lawn met a million-dollar stretch of Lake Washington, a stone boathouse, and a Boston Whaler bobbing alongside it.

And just to the left of the patio—Carlisle squinted a little just to be sure her eyes did not deceive—was a swimming pool, a cabana, and yes, a pool boy. A real live pool boy.

On the other side of the room, two men and a petite woman in her mid-twenties sat near a roaring fire. None of them smoked a cigar, but Mr. Stanhope held a heavy crystal tumbler one-third full of amber-colored liquid that could certainly have been scotch.

Robert Stanhope did not stand to make the introductions. "Lucas, you met at the door; my daughter, Caroline; and our attorney, Bill Thorpe. Let's all have a seat."

The two older men sat back down in matching chairs and Lucas joined his sister on one of a set of Chesterfield sofas. Curled up languidly, Caroline Stanhope looked eerily like her mother, but in miniature. With tiny bones and a small stature—DMV records had put her at five-foot-one—she had the same Valkyrie blue eyes, the same pale blonde hair and sharp cheekbones, the same straight nose and full lips. But on Caroline Stanhope's tiny body the head seemed a little too big, the sultry features almost indecent. Like a child made up for a beauty pageant.

Kincaid perched on the edge of the other Chesterfield and leaned forward on his knees. Carlisle sat back into an armchair, threw one ankle over the other knee, and straightened her shoulders. Took up space. She surveyed the group.

The lawyer was an ordinary-looking man in an extraordinary suit. He shot his French cuffs, crossed his legs and said, "I'm sure you can understand that this is a very difficult time for the Stanhopes. They want to help your investigation as much as they can, but for their sakes I'm hoping we can keep it short."

It was a gentle opening salvo; Thorpe letting them know that, ultimately, they were going to talk to the Stanhopes through him.

"Fair enough," said Carlisle, but before she could ask her first question, Caroline interrupted.

"How did my mother die?" Her body language was calm, even lethargic, but her voice cracked. *My* mother, not *our*. Carlisle studied her and let her partner answer.

Kincaid said, "We won't know until the autopsy is complete, Caroline. I know you want answers and I'm sorry about that."

"You don't *know*?" She turned to her father. "Daddy, what does he *mean*?"

Robert Stanhope moved his mouth, then just shook his head. Kincaid took a closer look at his eyes, realized this probably wasn't his first drink of the evening. Probably not his second.

Kincaid asked, "Do any of you know where Aurora might have gone last night?"

Brother and sister turned to their father. "I was in Oregon," he told them. To the detectives, he said, "As I told you, I didn't talk to her, but Annie told me she went out around eight o'clock. She didn't know where."

Kincaid turned to Lucas. "You have any idea?"

"No. Neither of us live at home." He pointed to his sister, then himself, in case they didn't know whom he meant by 'we.'

"But you both live in Seattle?" he asked.

"Yes, Caroline is downtown and I'm in Queen Anne. And I still don't know what my mother did last night."

Kincaid looked at Caroline. She shook her head. "No idea."

"When was the last time you spoke to your mother?" asked Carlisle.

Lucas thought about it. "Earlier this week, after I got back. Wednesday, maybe."

"I talked to her Thursday afternoon," said Caroline a little smugly, "but she didn't tell me whether she had plans for the weekend."

"What did you talk about?" asked Carlisle.

"Mom was having a charity luncheon next weekend and I'm invited." She paused. "Which means that I'm expected. She called to make sure I tried on the preppy outfits her assistant had dropped off for me to wear. If I *wanted* to wear any of them. Which means that I'd better."

Carlisle heard the resentment, looked at the young woman's beat-up jeans and motorcycle boots and willed Kincaid to take over. He did.

"Caroline, when you spoke to your mother, did she seem upset or anxious?"

"Yes, definitely."

Kincaid waited. Got nothing. Said, "Did she tell you what it was about?"

"She didn't have to," said Caroline. "She was upset because I told her that if she wanted me to attend some stupid ladies-who-lunch charity function, then I would wear whatever the fuck I wanted." She rubbed her forehead, still apparently upset about it.

Evidently Aurora Stanhope had tried her daughter's patience. Kincaid asked, "What was your relationship with your mother like?"

Thorpe cleared his throat. Loudly, in case anyone thought he might just be clearing his throat. "Detective, I don't see what that has to do with anything. Caroline is just expressing regret that her last conversation with Mrs. Stanhope was not more pleasant."

Kincaid hoped she would answer anyway, but she was looking at Thorpe. "Caroline?"

She turned to him. "Yeah, it was a terrible conversation. I regret it." She pulled at a lock of hair, curling it around her finger, then tried to blink a tear out of the corner of her eye. She failed.

"Your mother was upset because you argued, not any other reason?"

"If something else was bugging her, she didn't tell me."

"One more thing," said Kincaid. "Where were you from midnight to two this morning?"

Thorpe started to stand, but Caroline answered before he could protest. "Home. Alone." She shrugged, "Sorry, I can't do better."

Lucas reached over and patted his sister's ankle, then turned back to the detectives. "She was fine when I spoke to her. Just checking in with her favorite son." His expression didn't change and Kincaid had no idea how he had meant the last sentence. Sarcasm? Regret? *Is he a good egg or a bad egg?*

"Lucas, how was *your* relationship with your mother?"

"Relevance?" the attorney boomed.

"This isn't court, Mr. Thorpe," said Kincaid. "We're just trying to get an idea of how Mrs. Stanhope related to her family."

"And I'm asking why that's relevant since I'm sure you don't consider any of them a suspect."

Turning back to Lucas, Kincaid said, "Let's talk about Maria Sanchez."

"Absolutely not," said Thorpe. "Maria Sanchez retracted all allegations against Mrs. Stanhope. It was an unfortunate misunderstanding."

Kincaid wondered if Thorpe would be any less irritating if he didn't talk like a lawyer.

Lucas said, "I loved my mother, and I know she loved us, but you should know that she was demanding, stubborn. Even with us."

"Lucas, for god's sake," said Robert, irritation breaking through the booze-haze. To the detectives, with more emotion than he had shown since they'd first broken the news of his wife's death, he said, "My wife was very smart, very successful, and determined. She did a lot of good in the world. She was beautiful and charming, capable…" His voice trailed off and he looked into his crystal tumbler for solace, but found it empty.

Caroline got up, took the glass from his hand, and went to the bar to refill it.

"Do you have any idea who might have done this?" asked Stanhope as his daughter poured him another finger of booze from a crystal decanter and placed it in his hand. He looked exhausted, miserable, not like a man who had killed his wife.

"We've just begun the investigation, sir," said Kincaid. "It would help us if you could try to think of anyone who might have wanted to hurt your wife."

Caroline stifled a sound that might have been bitter laughter, Lucas looked away and Robert looked regretful.

"My wife"—he searched for the right words—"my wife was not an easy woman to get along with. She could be antagonistic." He sighed, then fell silent.

"Pugilistic?" said Kincaid.

"At times, yes."

"Look," interrupted Thorpe, "let's not beat around the bush.

You've seen Mrs. Stanhope's police record. Maybe she wasn't a perfect angel, but at least you have some direction. You should be looking at the Sanchezes, or the guy who accused her of chasing him on the freeway. Maybe he hunted her down. Road rage."

"We've already spoken to the Sanchezes," said Carlisle. "Maria and her husband and their son all have alibis that we're checking out." That they all had each other as alibis was a fact that she would keep to herself. "We read the Sheriff's report of the traffic incident and the driver of the other car was never identified. Did he trouble your wife after the event?" she asked Stanhope.

"No, as far as I knew she never even knew his name. And vice versa. They never even came face to face."

"He could have found her through her vehicle license plate," said Thorpe, giving his client a penetrating look. He clearly wanted to open the door to as many suspects as possible as long as said suspect was *not* his client. "It can't be that difficult to track someone down through their DMV records if you're determined."

Carlisle knew he was right, but to track someone down one year later and kill her for an isolated traffic offense was far-fetched. Plus, it would be almost impossible to find out who had reported her. At this point all they had was a dispatch report that indicated a male voice had called in the incident. She said, "What we really need to know, Mr. Stanhope, is whether there have been other incidents that were never reported, whether there are more people out there who might have wanted revenge."

Caroline blurted, "Anyone who ever had to deal with my mother had a reason to dislike her."

"Caroline!" said Stanhope. "Stop it."

"For God's sake, dad, be realistic. Mom made a lot of enemies, from strangers on the highway to the women she played tennis with at the club. She wasn't a saint."

"I'm not suggesting she was a saint, but I am sick of your

sniping. Let me grieve for my wife without infecting it with your bitterness. Please, Caroline."

Caroline's cheeks burned and she looked down at her hands. For a second, Carlisle thought she might cry for real. "Does anyone in particular come to mind?" she asked, interrupting the awkward silence.

When her father didn't speak, Caroline sniffled and said, "I know she had a lot of rivals on the *noblesse oblige* circuit, and Steve Lombardi and his wife hated her for almost breaking up their marriage."

"Breaking up their marriage?" said Carlisle. She thought, *Breaking up a marriage could be something.*

Kincaid wrote down the name. "Where can we find Mr. Lombardi?"

Caroline frowned and looked at her father, who was staring into his scotch, and then at her brother, who said, "Steve Lombardi is a founding partner at Lehman, Lombardi, Chance." When the name was met with blank stares, he added, "Attorneys at Law. They're a big corporate firm downtown. A bunch of senior and junior partners, at least a hundred associates doing grunt work on the lower floors and making more money than they have time to spend. Your basic John Grisham nightmare."

"And his wife?" asked Kincaid.

"Missy attends charity luncheons for a living," said Caroline with a spiteful laugh, as if it were self-evident.

"What did your mom have to do with their marriage?" Kincaid asked them, then waited.

Stanhope leaned back in his chair and closed his eyes. Checked out.

Caroline again looked at her brother. Cringing slightly, Lucas said, "I only know the story secondhand, but I think my mother told Missy that her husband was having an affair." He looked embarrassed. "That's all I know."

Robert Stanhope had gone completely rigid in his chair. Eyes squeezed shut. Carlisle knew there was more to the story, but now was not the time to ask.

"We'll check it out," said Kincaid. "Anyone else?"

Lucas cast a surreptitious look at his father, saw that he still wasn't talking, and said, "Her former business partner."

"Elizabeth Williams?" asked Carlisle.

Lucas looked down at his hands. "She hired Beth six or seven years ago and two years ago, Beth resigned. That's the story, but I think my mother forced her out." He added, "I *really* can't imagine Beth did it, but she sure had a good reason."

Robert Stanhope grunted but didn't protest.

"All right, I think that's enough for today, Detectives," said Thorpe.

"Mr. Stanhope?" said Carlisle. "We'd like to look at your wife's room while we're here. There might be something that could tell us where she went last night."

"We've already looked through Mrs. Stanhope's desk," said Thorpe. "There was nothing indicative of her plans for yesterday evening."

Carlisle and Kincaid remained silent. Stanhope finally blinked his eyes open, swirled the tumbler in his hand, and finished it off. "Fine."

"Robert," Thorpe started, but his client waved him quiet. Thorpe sighed, stood, and checked his Rolex. "I'll take you up."

CHAPTER SEVEN

T HEY FOLLOWED THE ATTORNEY INTO the kitchen and up a
back flight of stairs to the second floor. On the north side of
the house, Thorpe opened a set of double doors onto a spacious
sitting room with a balcony overlooking the lake. The room was
bordello chic, furnished with a pair of red velvet sofas, plush gold
chairs, tables and trinkets, and an elaborately carved mahogany
office set. Thorpe marched toward another set of doors, warning the
detectives that they did not have an unrestricted right to anything
they found here. "No nosing around for the sake of it. No souvenirs
in your coat pockets. And I don't want you collecting information
that isn't germane to your investigation."

The boudoir was even more lavish, with a bed the size of a
volleyball court, dozens of tasseled throw pillows and more windows
overlooking the lake. Carlisle stepped closer to the windows and
caught another glimpse of the pretty pool boy. *Nice view for Aurora
Stanhope,* she thought.

Turning back to the attorney, she nodded at another set of
doors. With a little flourish, Thorpe opened them, revealing a
master bathroom and a huge dressing room.

The detectives split up to begin their search. That way, Thorpe
could only watch one of them at a time.

"I'll start with the bedroom," said Carlisle.

"I'll take the desk."

Taking a position in the doorway between the sitting room and the bedroom, Thorpe said, "Robert said she keeps her calendar on her phone. Maybe she noted her meeting last night."

Kincaid wasn't ready to admit they hadn't found the phone. He ignored the attorney and opened a desk drawer.

Carlisle was going through the drawers of one of the nightstands. She found two fashion magazines, the latest edition of *The Economist*, a prescription for sleep medication dated over a year ago, a bottle of aspirin, a jar of very expensive body lotion, a tube of lubricant and an open box of condoms. She turned to Thorpe. "Did Mr. and Mrs. Stanhope sleep together?"

He shrugged. "I wouldn't know, Detective."

"But they don't share this room." She looked around again, seeing no sign of male occupancy. "Mr. Stanhope has his own room? Or suite of rooms?"

"I believe he does."

She filed that away and moved on to the bathroom. There were a few prescription bottles in a drawer and she noted the medications, though Carlisle was pretty certain they were hormone replacements. More bottles and jars of lotions and face creams, hair products and make-up. She opened another drawer and found another box of condoms and a pink vibrator.

She turned off the light and went to the dressing room through a connecting door.

With five hundred square feet of silk and cashmere, beaded dresses, flowing gowns and a line-up of shoes that would make the Kardashian sisters jealous, the room was a style maven's dream. A central cabinet functioned as a jewelry case and folding table. There was a huge infinity mirror on one side with a plush chair next to it. *In case she wants to relax while she surveys her choices?* Carlisle wondered as she continued to peer between hangers and riffle satin-lined drawers of baby-soft jammies and lingerie from practical to La Perla. Size small undies, thirty-six C. Nothing kinky, but lots of sex appeal.

The clothes were stylish and modern. It was the closet of a woman who enjoys getting dressed, a woman who looks good in clothes, has a lot of money and takes advantage of both facts. Some of the pieces were conservative, but Carlisle didn't see anything that justified Caroline's scornful use of the word 'preppy.'

Back in the bedroom, she inspected three scenic impressionist paintings. No pictures of her husband or children.

She joined her partner in the sitting room, where Thorpe was still keeping a watchful eye on Kincaid. Evidently, he had already gone through the desk cabinets and was now inspecting a small library of books, DVDs and magazines. He turned when Carlisle came in, removing his gloves.

"All set?" he asked.

"Yup."

"You have everything you need?" asked Thorpe.

"I think so," said Carlisle. "If not, we'll be back."

Narrowing his eyes, Thorpe said, "If you have to come back, you may need a warrant, Detective Carlisle." He led them back down the stairs to the great room. It was time for them to go.

Lucas stood, but Caroline remained seated, scowling at them. Robert Stanhope didn't get up but he did manage to call out in an imperious tone, "Keep us updated. I expect you to check in frequently."

Kincaid turned to Lucas, said, "We're going to need contact information for you and Caroline. And the names and numbers of all of the staff here at the house." He took down the cell numbers in his notebook and handed Lucas a few business cards.

"I'll have to email you a list of the staff," said Lucas and left Thorpe to walk them out.

Back in the cold Pacific rain, Carlisle asked, "So, do you think it's harder to solve the murder of a victim everybody loved, or everybody hated?"

"Same odds," said Kincaid.

"Want me to drive?"

"Nope, I want you to look at something."

As soon as he started the engine, Kincaid pulled a photograph out of his inside jacket pocket and handed it to his partner.

"It's the cabana boy," said Carlisle raising her eyebrows. "Naked."

A few seconds later, "How do you know it's a pic of the cabana boy?"

"I saw him out by the pool," said Carlisle, grinning.

Kincaid glanced at her. "When?"

Instead of answering, she said, "Where did you find this picture?"

"In the very back of her pencil drawer. Had to distract the lawyer so I could hide it in my pocket. I thought we were going to have to play detective to figure out who he is."

She laughed. "I saw him outside when we were talking to the family."

"I saw *that* guy," said Kincaid, "but I never would have recognized him as *this* guy." He pointed at the photo.

"Trust me," said Carlisle, "that's the pool boy, naked, in our victim's bedroom."

"I'm telling Tom."

"That I'm a better detective than you?"

"No, that you were checking out the pool boy."

"He was hard to miss. I can't believe you didn't know this was the same guy."

"I didn't recognize him with his clothes on."

"Get over it, Kincaid, and find out what his name is. Our pool boy has some explaining to do." She checked her phone. "Tom offered to make a late dinner. Join us."

"Nah, I'm gonna find a name and address for this guy. Besides, I might let it slip that you have the hots for the cabana boy. Rain check?"

"Anytime," she said. "We're going to have to get to the Stanhope kids on their own. They were pretty squirrely about talking in front of dad."

"Big list of interviews for tomorrow," said Kincaid, stifling a yawn.

They left the unmarked at the station and Carlisle drove her partner to his car at the Irish pub where they'd celebrated the night before.

"Call me if you find anything," said Carlisle before he closed the door.

One stop for take-out and he was home with his constant companion.

"Stanley," he said, giving the cat a scratch under his chin, "good to see you, buddy."

Pulling at his tie as he headed upstairs, Kincaid checked his phone. Lucas Stanhope had already sent him a list of names and numbers. "Reliable kid," he said to the cat. "But is he a killer?"

CHAPTER EIGHT

A NOTHER SHOWER TO RINSE AWAY the lingering aura of death, another tall glass of water to rinse away the lingering symptoms of hangover, and Kincaid felt pretty good.

Downstairs, he scooped spaghetti Bolognese into a bowl, grabbed a fork and a spoon. At the dining room table, used mostly as a very big desk, he opened his laptop.

Lucas's email included the name of the pool boy. Kevin Stoddard's official job description was 'Boat and Pool Maintenance' and alongside his name was a phone number and an address in the University District, half a mile from the apartment building where they had found Aurora Stanhope's body.

Kincaid confirmed the address with DMV records. Stoddard was six feet even, one-eighty, blonde and brown, twenty-six years old. No criminal record in Washington State. He checked Facebook. The kid had an active social life, was a student of biology at the University of Washington, Seattle campus. Born in Richland, Washington. Public pics were mostly of him around Seattle with other kids his age.

No red flags except a naked picture of you in our victim's bed, he thought, then set his almost empty bowl on the floor for Stan to finish.

Kincaid debated calling Judy, decided against it. Their best chance of catching a twenty-six-year-old college student at home on the weekend was to show up early on Sunday morning. He rinsed his dishes, left them in the rack to dry and carried his laptop to the TV room in the basement. With an old Hitchcock movie playing in the background, he did the same search for everyone on Lucas's list.

When his cell phone woke him up, Kincaid was still in the lounge chair, laptop on his lap, cat on his laptop.

"Kincaid."

"Hello, sleepyhead," said Judy Carlisle.

He groaned, "What time is it?"

"Nearly nine-thirty," she said, "way past your bedtime."

Kincaid rubbed his eyes and sat up; he'd only been asleep for a few minutes. "Second time today you woke me, Carlisle. What's up?"

"Mallory finished the autopsy. Cause of death was definitely strangulation. The blow to the head came first, probably rendering her unconscious."

"Easy to strangle someone when they can't fight back," Kincaid observed dryly.

"Indeed, it would be," she said. "He's still running a toxicology screen, but if she was out cold, that would explain the lack of defensive wounds and evidence under her nails. But that's not the reason I'm calling," she continued, and he could see her waving a hand in the air. "The reason I'm calling is because Mrs. Stanhope's stomach contents included turnips and rutabaga, duck breast and pâté du canard. Gotta be restaurant fare, right? So, I did a Google search on those ingredients and just came up with a bunch of recipes and places to buy tinned duck liver. Not useful. *But then*, in a flash of brilliance, I checked the specials at every French restaurant in town and guess what?"

"What?"

"This week's special at Gigi's Bistro on the Waterfront is braised duck breast with duck liver pâté and roasted root vegetables."

"No kidding," said Kincaid. "I'm actually impressed."

"They're still open."

Already getting up, Kincaid said, "I'll pick you up in twenty."

On his way out, he pulled a wool jacket over his sweater and jeans and laced up an old pair of brown Oxfords. He took the short stone path to his single-car garage and backed into the alley.

When he arrived at Judy Carlisle's home in the Northwest corner of the Queen Anne neighborhood, his partner was already waiting by the curb. She got in and he said, "Teenage tantrum driving you out?"

Carlisle's daughter, Janie, had turned fifteen over the summer and had transformed, like a werewolf at midnight, into a full-fledged teenage nightmare. But Carlisle was shaking her head. "No. Janie and I have declared a temporary cease-fire while the monster-in-law is here."

"Tom's mom is visiting?"

She nodded. "Pamela doesn't approve of my job or my daughter's current hair color, so Janie and I have bonded over a common enemy."

Kincaid's brow creased. "Carlisle, did you invite me to dinner tonight because you wanted me to distract your monster-in-law with my boyish charm?"

She looked at him. "I wanted you to come over for dinner. *And* I wanted you to charm Pamela."

He laughed. "I can accept that."

"Good, because you're expected Sunday evening." She smiled hopefully and swung one long leg over the other. "Unless this case requires both of us tomorrow evening, in which case—"

"In which case, I'm expected on Monday night? Okay, you've got me curious. I think I need to meet Pam."

"Pamela. *Never, ever* call her Pam." Patting her coat pocket, she said, "I printed out a few pictures of Aurora Stanhope. Hopefully someone will remember her from last night."

They drove past the restaurant on Pike Place and turned up

Stewart looking for a parking spot. "Think the department would reimburse us for valet?"

"Only if we walk in there and catch the murderer on the spot," said Carlisle. "Even then, it'll take six months."

They found a spot two blocks away, stepped out of the car into a biting wind and paid the meter. "Christ, it's cold."

Gigi's was popular with foodies and socialites. Situated on a piece of prime commercial real-estate, the bistro overlooked Elliott Bay and bordered Seattle's famous Pike Place Market. An esoteric wine list, fish fresh out of the Pacific Ocean, a seasonally-changing menu and first-class management had kept it at the top of the food chain on the Seattle restaurant scene for years.

Last year, Gigi's had also been one of the focal points of Carlisle and Kincaid's investigation into the disappearance of a local restaurateur. They had solved the case and the notoriety had made them temporarily famous, and had propelled Gigi's into an unprecedented level of popularity.

By the time they walked through the glass entrance of Gigi's, Judy Carlisle's cheeks were flushed from the October wind off of the Sound and she rubbed her hands together before approaching the host with a printout of Mrs. Stanhope's photograph.

"Yeah, I think I remember her," said the young man. "Um, let me see," he squinted closer to the sheet of paper, "hmm, she's been here a few times."

"Was she here last night?"

"Yeah, I think so."

The host didn't sound very certain. Carlisle said, "Her name is Aurora Stanhope. Maybe she had a reservation."

"Okay, maybe." He tapped a touch screen. "Yep. Reservations for two at eight-thirty on Friday night." A few patrons came to the front to collect their coats and the young host looked helplessly at the detectives. Carlisle waved him away.

"There's the guy in charge," said Kincaid, nodding toward a trim, elegant man heading their way.

"Table for two?" the man asked, smoothly taking over the host stand.

"Nope," said Kincaid. He didn't show his badge; they knew each other. Harry Cole had helped them with their missing person the year before.

The manager's smile dissolved. "An official visit? You're kidding me." One look at the detectives' grim expressions confirmed that they were definitely not kidding. He shook their hands, suggested they all take a seat in the bar.

A boutique restaurant, Gigi's seated about sixty with a small bar that brought the capacity up to eighty or so. The smells of braised meats and seared fish, sauces made with heavy cream and earthy autumn vegetables filled the cozy space with the heady ambience of a provincial tavern in Normandy, even as the posh décor spoke of a trendy bistro in Soho. Somehow, the combination was quintessential Seattle.

The restaurant was still bustling with the dinner crowd but there was an empty table in the bar. And Harry Cole, house manager extraordinaire, glided through the place like he was always meant to be there. Five-foot-ten, graceful and neat with thick black hair slicked back into a tiny curl at the nape of his neck, he wore a tailored black suit and a white-on-white tie and shirt. With a flourish, he pulled out a chair for Carlisle. She let him, taking a seat while Kincaid pulled out his own chair across from her. Cole sat between them, folded his arms across his chest and pointed at the photograph Carlisle had laid on the table.

"Did someone else go missing?" His voice was deep and resonant, belying his fastidious grooming and dancer's grace.

Carlisle told him why they were there and Harry's face fell. "Did you know her?"

He looked from one to the other. "Sort of. Mrs. Stanhope is

a regular. Plus, she was here for dinner last night." He raised his eyebrows. "Why else would you be here?"

"How often did she come in?" asked Kincaid.

"Once a month, about, but she was a presence." He sighed, then added, "So, what happened?"

"She was murdered." When he didn't react, Carlisle said, "You're not surprised?"

"Well, of course," he said without sounding surprised at all. Cole waved his hand through the air. "Beautiful woman. Confident, elegant and bewitching. When she walked into the room, everyone noticed her. *But,* she was also kind of a bitch, and in this business, it's the bitchiness that leaves a lasting impression."

He said it matter-of-factly, no resentment. "I'm being forthright about that," Harry went on, "because I figure it's the kind of thing you need to know. Not because I despised Mrs. Stanhope so much that even after her death I feel compelled to disparage her." He frowned. "Please don't tell me you think someone who works here could have hurt her."

"Did she make any of your employees that angry?" asked Kincaid.

"Of course not. I mean, she's not the only difficult customer we have."

"Is she the most difficult customer you have?" asked Carlisle.

"That depends on who you ask, Detective Carlisle. Mrs. Stanhope was probably easier on the men here than the women. She was even flirtatious with some, and she liked me."

"How much did she like you?" asked Carlisle.

"She wasn't interested in me," he said. "She liked dumb, quiet beach bodies and rich, powerful older men. I don't fit into either of those categories."

"Anyone in particular she *was* interested in?"

He glanced around the dining room. "I don't think so, but I'll ask around."

"Do that," said Carlisle thoughtfully. "Who was she with last night?"

"A man, maybe a little older than she was. Lots of hair—not just on his head. Lots of muscles."

"Any chance you got his name?"

He shook his head. "But he probably paid. I'll check our receipts from last night. Just give me a minute." Harry stood and glided past the bar and down a hall to the restaurant's office.

"Hard to imagine an angry server did that to her," said Kincaid.

The barman approached and asked whether they wanted something to drink. "We're just waiting for Mr. Cole," said Carlisle and he went away. "I'm starting to see a pattern."

"You mean, between the pool boy, her preference for male waitstaff and Cole's claim that she liked dumb hunks?"

"If she likes younger guys then maybe her dinner companion was just a friend," said Carlisle.

"Or he falls into the rich and powerful category."

Kincaid looked up as Cole approached.

"Steve Lombardi," he said, coming back to the table. Before the detectives could respond he said, "I have to check on the dining room, but I can come back in a few minutes."

"That's all right, Mr. Cole," said Kincaid. "But do us a favor and snoop around, see if anyone here really hated Mrs. Stanhope." He handed the manager a business card.

"I'll let you know," said Cole, tucking the card into his inside pocket.

They walked back to Kincaid's car in silence, huddled against the wind. When they were both buckled and the engine was on, he said, "Steve Lombardi again."

Looking at the clock on the dashboard, Carlisle said, "Almost eleven. Should we track him down tonight?"

"Nah. Tomorrow. Meantime, I'll check him out online."

"I can do that, Jerry."

"I got it. Spend some time with Tom. We've got an early morning tomorrow."

"Cabana boy?"

"First thing, if nothing else comes up. With any luck we'll get him half-asleep and hungover."

"Hard to lie when you're half-asleep and hungover," said Carlisle.

CHAPTER NINE

A s it turned out, they didn't get to the pool boy until later in the day.

By the time Kincaid picked up his partner at eight o'clock on Sunday morning they had more pressing obligations.

"The Stanhopes did a press release," said Carlisle when she got in the car. "It was on the morning news and all over social media and dispatch said the phone has been ringing off the hook. So now we have a date with Aurora's personal assistant, Karen Green. Then Lucas agreed to talk to us on his own. One-ish, his place. We'll squeeze the pool boy in there somewhere."

Green had called the police department first thing in the morning, and the desk sergeant had called Carlisle. Green was flying to Baja California in the afternoon and wondered if the detective would need to talk to her before she left.

Among other things, Carlisle and Kincaid were hoping to get mobile numbers for Steve and Missy Lombardi so that they could interview them separately instead of showing up on their doorstep on a Sunday afternoon. If Steve Lombardi had had an affair with Aurora Stanhope—had maybe still been having an affair with her— he might be more willing to talk when his wife wasn't around.

Green lived in a nice building just northwest of downtown Seattle. When they rang the bell, the Detectives were immediately buzzed in and Green offered tea which they declined. She poured herself a cup and sat down.

"Peppermint," she said, putting her nose into the steam and inhaling. "Soothing."

In her mid-thirties, Karen Green had a broad, fresh face, bright eyes and an extra ten pounds tucked into her flower-patterned yoga pants.

"What exactly do you do as a personal assistant, Ms. Green?" asked Kincaid.

She looked from Kincaid to Carlisle. Clearly neither one of them knew what a personal assistant did. "Well, I do the details. I keep her calendar, make appointments, run errands, organize parties, keep her business correspondence. You know. I take care of the crap she's too busy to take care of." She frowned. "Was." She set her cup down and said, "I can't believe she's dead. I just talked to her on Friday."

"What time did you speak to Mrs. Stanhope?" asked Kincaid.

"About four o'clock." The remnants of a mid-Atlantic accent said Karen Green was a transplant. There was still a little Baltimore twang. "I called to see if she was going to need anything before I left town. Week-long yoga retreat—*just* what the doctor ordered. She said she didn't."

"Did you actually see her at all on Friday?"

"No. I had a list of things to do and at the end of the day I dropped her dry cleaning at the house. Handed it off to Mrs. Chang. I did see her Thursday, if that helps."

She told them she'd been working for Mrs. Stanhope for nearly two years, loved her job, was well-paid with generous end-of-year bonuses and couldn't believe anyone would want to hurt Aurora.

"Right," said Carlisle. "So, you liked working for Mrs. Stanhope." Green nodded. "Did you like Mrs. Stanhope?"

A tight smile pulled at the corners of the PA's mouth. "Aurora was a really interesting woman. Smart and talented and driven." She moved her lips as if to add something but didn't.

"Miss Green," said Carlisle gently, "we know that Mrs. Stanhope was difficult to deal with. We've already found one employee who actually filed assault charges against her. Family members have told us candidly that there were a lot of people who didn't like her."

She gave that a second to settle in, then said, "We need you to help us make a list of anyone she pissed off so that we can talk to them." She leaned in close. "*All of them*. And, we need to know where you were late Friday night and early Saturday morning."

Green sighed. "I spent the night with my girlfriend on Bainbridge Island. We went to a dinner party with two other couples. You can ask them all, or check the security cameras on the ferry, or whatever you need to do because I did not kill Aurora."

Kincaid took down the numbers of Green's friends and asked for ferry times. They wouldn't check the cameras unless she became a serious suspect, but he wanted to keep her on her toes.

"I'll sift through her emails and make a list of the nasty ones, but I can tell you now that there are at least three people who should be at the top of your list." She ticked her fingers, "Steve Lombardi, Attorney at Law, his wife Missy Lombardi, and Beth Williams, Aurora's former business partner—she forced Beth out and there's a lot of bad blood there." She gulped peppermint tea, didn't appear soothed.

"And there were some ladies at her tennis club who definitely could have throttled her in a fit. *And* there were the boys on the side, if you know what I mean."

"Boys on the side." Carlisle nodded.

"Yeah. Lots of them. Aurora played the field. Men, boys, married, single. And men go nuts around Aurora; there's no telling what one of them might do when he gets dumped for someone younger and prettier, or older and richer." Another pause, as she considered. "And I'm no expert, but the daughter's a nut job." She drank some more tea, set the cup down, and said no more.

Kincaid said, "Nut job?"

"Mm-hmm. Totally unpredictable. From raging to docile in

two-point-three seconds. Really resentful of Aurora and competitive with her, but then she also seemed to want to emulate her mother. Very mixed emotions." She thought for a moment, and added offhandedly, "Very weird."

"Threatening?" asked Kincaid.

"No, not that I saw. But I wasn't often with them in the same room together. I was usually the go-between. Double-checking if Caroline was going to this or that party, or if she was joining Aurora at the country club for tennis or delivering wardrobe choices for an upcoming gala. Stuff that would probably drive any kid crazy." She laughed. "I'd drop off a two-thousand-dollar Dior suit and then she'd show up for the party in leather pants and a Katy Perry T-shirt, or whatever, and chat blithely with all the ladies and gentlemen in pearls and pinstripes. Fifteen minutes in she'd start to look contrite and follow her mother around like a desperate puppy and then she'd end up leaving in a snit. Every time." A condescending smile. "Not very self-aware."

"But no violence?" said Carlisle.

Green sighed. "No, I never saw violence."

"Did *you* get along with Mrs. Stanhope?" asked Kincaid.

Green thought for a few moments. "I'm a very good and very efficient PA and even though my duties might seem tedious, the job suits me. Aurora got me because she offered the highest salary and now that she's dead, I'll get another position without much effort. She and I would never have been friends, but we understood each other. She just wanted her life to run smoothly and I was more than capable of making that happen."

She looked at the ceiling, adding, "But I did fill my very first prescription for Xanax just after I started working for her."

CHAPTER TEN

"I DON'T THINK GREEN DID IT."

"Me neither," Carlisle agreed. "Everyone is pointing fingers at the Lombardis."

Back in the car, Kincaid said, "Who's next?"

"Unless we can get to one of the Lombardis, we'll go find our cabana boy." Armed with a list of cell numbers from Karen Green, she started dialing Steve Lombardi. "I gotta eat something," she said to Kincaid.

While she made calls, he walked up the street to a little bodega, came back with two decent pastries and bottled water. "Blueberry or raspberry?"

"Blueberry." Kincaid distributed.

"He agreed to meet us in half an hour."

"That was easy."

All it took was the threat of talking to his wife first," said Carlisle.

"Where?"

"Some place in Cascade. Near Lake Union."

Kincaid started the big engine. "Wanna run him through records?"

Carlisle gave him directions to the restaurant while she got to work on Steve Lombardi's bio. "He picked a place about as far from his house as you can get in half an hour. The Lombardis also live in a big house on Lake Washington."

"Are the Stanhopes and the Lombardis neighbors?"

"Not proximally. Lombardis are further south, but they are certainly neighbors of a socio-economic nature." She clicked a few keys. "No criminal record. No unpaid parking tickets."

They got to the little chowder shop a few minutes early and Steve Lombardi got there a few minutes late. Recognizing him from his DMV photo, Carlisle waved him over. Not a handsome man, he was just shy of six feet with a muscular build and bulky thighs that tested the seams of his chinos, a thick pelt of black hair and dark eyes. He looked like he spent too much time in the gym, which was confirmed when he took off his bomber jacket and muscles bulged beneath the short sleeves of a polo shirt. Harry Cole had been right—tufts of curly black hair stuck out of his collar and formed a dense lace over his bare forearms. Still, as he approached the table, a posture of complete self-possession and raw masculinity made him not unattractive.

Joining them at the four-top, he announced, "I'm not going to bullshit you and say I'm shocked that someone wanted to hurt Aurora—she was a real pain in the ass—but I am shocked that someone actually did it."

A middle-aged waitress wearing a gingham apron approached to take their order. "What the hell," said Lombardi, "I'll have a bowl of chowder and some fried oysters. And a beer." Kincaid ordered coffee and Carlisle diet Coke. When the waitress had gone, he added, "Best in town. It'll cost me a trip to the gym, but what the hell," he repeated.

Carlisle watched the veins rippling in his neck as he spoke and thought that Steve Lombardi could afford to skip a few days with the free-weights.

"So? What do you want?"

"Mr. Lombardi," said Kincaid, "we know that you had dinner with Aurora on the night she was murdered."

Raising an eyebrow, Lombardi said, "You know about that. I

didn't think Aurora would've told anyone." The detectives didn't offer any explanation. "She had some legal questions. We had a nice meal. Left around ten. I went straight home to my wife. No big deal."

"It was a business dinner? We've been led to believe your relationship was personal." Lombardi didn't reply. "And problematic."

"We had a few bumps in the road, but so did everyone when it came to Aurora. She was fickle."

"At one point, didn't she reveal to your wife that you were having an affair?"

Lombardi leaned back in his chair with a smug smile as the waitress put a bottle of pilsner on the table in front of him. "I was under the impression that we were going to have a friendly chat, Detective, but it sounds like it's time to call my attorney."

"That's certainly your right," said Kincaid.

The chowder and oysters arrived, but Lombardi ignored the waitress and continued to scowl at Kincaid. "She asked to meet for dinner. I thought she wanted to make"—his mouth formed a snide smile—"*amends.*" He shoved a spoonful of soup into his mouth. "Mmm, you might want to rethink lunch, Detectives. It's that good."

Ignoring him, Kincaid asked, "What did you think she wanted to make amends for?"

"For nearly ruining my marriage." He ate an oyster and chewed slowly. Took a drink of his beer, then suddenly pushed his plate away and looked at Carlisle, who hadn't spoken since she'd introduced herself. "What are the chances Missy won't find out about my dinner with Aurora?"

"Very slim possibility, sir. But *we* won't tell her unless it becomes necessary," she said.

"Why would it become necessary?"

"That depends on the real reason you met Aurora Stanhope for dinner at a romantic restaurant on a Friday night. If it was *personal*, and not all business, then your wife may have had a reason to wish her harm."

Lombardi shook his head. "Missy didn't kill anyone."

Carlisle looked at him, "Mr. Lombardi, we have to look at anyone who had motive. Aurora was brutally murdered and it's our job to find her killer. We have to talk to Missy, but we might not have to tell her that you were one of the last people to see Mrs. Stanhope alive."

There was almost no chance of that happening—when they questioned Missy Lombardi, Steve's dinner with Mrs. Stanhope would be their leverage to get her talking. But Carlisle wanted to keep up the pretense that she was a considerate cop.

Lombardi looked from Carlisle to Kincaid and back again. A vein pulsed in his temple. Carlisle counted four beats of his heart. "Bullshit. You can talk to me through my lawyer." He took a business card from his wallet and scribbled a number from his cell phone onto the back. "You can contact him, set up an appointment." He dropped a twenty onto the table and stood. "Right now, I'm going home to have a chat with my wife." He winked obnoxiously, turned and left.

A few seconds of silence. "Think we can get to Missy before he does?" said Kincaid.

Carlisle patted her partner on the shoulder. "No. But we wouldn't have gotten anything else out of Lombardi either. Lawyers always lawyer up before they tell you anything good." She picked up the business card and said, "Ronny Buccio."

"Buccio? Two Italians sticking together in a sea of WASPS?" Kincaid thought for a second. "Ronny's an ace defense attorney. No way Lombardi keeps him on retainer."

"Nope," said Carlisle, "I bet he called him the minute he found out Aurora had been murdered. He knew we'd be knocking on his door." She sighed. "At least we confirmed one thing."

"What's that?"

"Steve Lombardi was definitely sleeping with Aurora Stanhope at some point."

"Yeah?"

"Definitely," she repeated. "And he went to dinner with her hoping to start something up again."

"Make amends?"

"*Amends*." She snorted. "What an asshole."

Checking his phone, Kincaid said, "Just past noon. What's next?"

"Let's find out why Lucas wanted the maid to rat out his mom."

CHAPTER ELEVEN

LUCAS STANHOPE HAD SPENT LATE Sunday morning trying to make sense of his sister's behavior.

He'd been sitting in an overstuffed velvet chair by the sliding glass doors in her bedroom, looking over the balcony at the unlit Ferris wheel on Pier 57 when she announced, "I think I should wear this one to the luncheon," holding a navy dress at arm's length by its hanger and indicating the modest khaki-colored sheath she held against her shoulders. "Burberry. It's the one mother would have preferred.

"What luncheon?"

"The charity I told you about yesterday. These are the dresses Karen sent over."

Blink. "I thought you despised charity luncheons as much as you despised it when Mom tried to dress you."

"It's a little different now," she replied breezily, then added, "I've decided to take the rest of the semester off."

"Okay."

Caroline held the chosen dress tight to her waist, turning back and forth in front of a giant full-length mirror. "Then I'll be able to stand in at Mom's fundraisers, sort out some of the details at the Economic Development Campaign. Take care of Dad. You know."

"You hate fundraisers *and* charities, the EDC basically runs itself, and Mom never took care of Dad. Mrs. Chang does that."

"Don't be silly, big brother, Dad's a mess." She hung the khaki dress on the back of her closet door and picked up a glass holding a lot of vodka and a little orange juice, grinning at him.

"Already dancing on mother's grave?"

Her eyes flashed. "Fuck you, Lucas. Mom would expect me to be strong and to move forward."

Caroline was right—their mother would have expected them to buck up and hold forth. But he wasn't sure he bought it.

An hour later, still irritated, he was just unlocking the door to his apartment in Lower Queen Anne when his cell phone began ringing.

The caller ID didn't reveal anything but Lucas answered anyway and wasn't surprised to hear the voice of the woman detective he'd met the day before.

"We'd like to come talk to you again, Mr. Stanhope."

Closing the door behind him he said absently, "Call me Lucas."

After a pause, Carlisle said, "Do you have time today, Lucas?"

"Yeah, but…" He couldn't think of a reason to put them off. They would get to him eventually. "Yeah, why don't you just come over now?" He gave the address and ended the call.

He went to the kitchen to boil water for coffee. Lucas had been away from home for too long and for the last few days he'd been reveling in the luxurious civility of his hometown—the thick, black coffee and crispy pima cotton sheets, the towering buildings and beautiful views, the indulgent restaurants and beautiful waitresses. *Mmm.*

A grumble in his belly, loud as a thunderclap, pointed his nose to a bakery bag on the counter. He bit into the double-chocolate-caramel-nut-marshmallow brownie extravaganza he'd bought at one of Seattle's amazing bakeries the day before.

Had left forgotten on the counter because his father had called and told him his mother was dead. And he'd had to go talk to the cops. Make sure it was all real.

His belly full, he felt pretty good.

Lucas was still standing in the kitchen when the doorbell rang. After a quick check of the security camera, he buzzed in the detectives. Once their wet coats were hung in the front closet, he offered them coffee.

"Only if you're having some, Lucas," said Kincaid, and they followed him into the kitchen.

As they crossed the polished concrete floors Kincaid took in a million-dollar view of the Space Needle. From the first step through the front door, he could see straight across the apartment, through the picture windows and glass doors, over the balcony and to the city beyond. Professionally, Lucas Stanhope might be at the mercy of research grants; personally, he lived very, very well.

While Lucas rummaged around for cups, Kincaid wandered into the dining room "This is a nice place to come home to," he said.

"I like it." As he poured hot water over the coffee grounds, he caught Carlisle's look and added, "Trust me, detectives, I know how lucky I am."

They sat at the table and Lucas handed Carlisle a mug that said *Eat Shit.*

"Oh, shit. Sorry."

He tried to exchange it for another with a drawing of the Space Needle. Carlisle shook him off. "I appreciate the candor."

"Right," said Lucas. "My sister gave that to me." He handed Kincaid a cup. Bright yellow. No writing.

Carlisle asked, "You two get along?"

He shrugged. "More or less. We're pretty different and she's almost seven years younger than I am." He looked at Carlisle. "We don't have a lot in common."

"Not much sibling rivalry with the age difference?" asked Kincaid.

"You'd be surprised," said Lucas with an odd smile.

"So, Lucas, where were you Friday night?" Carlisle said.

If Lucas was surprised, he didn't show it. "I was on a date until eleven or so and then I came home."

"With your date?" asked Kincaid.

"Nope. All alone."

"Okay," said Kincaid. Thinking, *no alibi*. "Now, tell us the real story with Steve and Missy Lombardi."

He grimaced. "Yeah. I guess that could be important. The real story is that it was my mother who was sleeping with Steve. She told Missy that her husband was having an affair and that she was the other woman. Acutely hurtful because Missy and my mom had been rivals since college. From what I've heard, Missy even dated my dad once upon a time until my mom whisked him away."

"Are you positive your mom was having an affair with Mr. Lombardi?" asked Kincaid.

"Ninety-nine percent. And the one percent that isn't absolutely positive is the tiny part of my brain that still believes my mother was a decent person." He ran his hands through his hair. "I loved her so much—still do—but she wasn't very nice to people."

"Did your father know about Steve?" asked Carlisle.

"I don't know. Honestly, I would be amazed if he didn't, but I'm not going to ask him."

Carlisle nodded; she would ask him herself. Cheating was a great motive for murder. "Do you think Steve or Missy would've done this?"

"No idea." He shrugged. "Maybe Steve. Christ, I don't know. I knew them as a kid at my parents' cocktail parties. As an adult, I've seen them at country club shindigs, but I only attend those when my mother is particularly persuasive. Read coercive."

Carlisle thought that any kid who used words like "shindig," couldn't be all bad, but she didn't show it. "Did you get along with your mother?"

"I did," he said. "It was easier for me than for Caroline. My mom let my dad teach me how to become a gentleman, but it was her job to teach my sister how to become a lady. As long as I was well-behaved in public, made good impressions, and doted on her, Mom was happy enough with me."

"Doted?" Kincaid raised an eyebrow.

Lucas looked at Kincaid; his eyes sparkled and he smiled genuinely for the first time since they'd met him. "She'd have you doting on her in a heartbeat, detective, no matter how hard-boiled you were determined to be. She had that effect on men. Friends, family, colleagues, gay, straight, interested or not, there was something about her that made you hold the door open, made you want to keep her wineglass full, made you want to show up with flowers and always let her pick the restaurant. My mom was wonderful to me. I thought she was the most beautiful, the most fun, the smartest. Bigger than life."

Carlisle said, "Until?"

"Until I grew up and realized that my mother was flawed. All kids go through that at some point."

"My fifteen-year-old daughter has just begun that charming phase of life," said Carlisle.

"Yeah, well, my mom fell from the sky." He shrugged. "Suddenly I could see her very clearly."

"We spoke to Maria Sanchez," said Kincaid, "and we know that you wanted her to report the assault to the police."

He said nothing for a few seconds, then, "I guess I knew that was coming. It wasn't that I wanted my mother to get into trouble. Not exactly. But my mom was completely out of control. She needed a wakeup call." He shook his head in disbelief. "I'd never seen her like that." He looked at them. "Maria was *terrified.*"

Kincaid leaned forward. "Help me understand this. You come from a family that brought an attorney in simply to oversee an informal conversation after your mother was murdered, and yet you advised a maid to go to the police when your mother allegedly assaulted her?"

Lucas was unfazed. "My father brought Bill in, not me, and he was right to do so. I'm sure my dad would prefer I had Bill here today as well."

"But you didn't call him."

"He would have made this conversation more difficult, and I think I'm telling you things you may need to know to find my mother's killer—or at least get an idea of how many suspects might be out there. As for Maria, it was not an alleged assault. I saw it happen and it scared me. As much for my mother as for Maria. If I hadn't stepped in she could have really hurt her and the consequences of that would have been more than a payoff to Maria's family."

"You knew about the payoff?" asked Carlisle.

"Of course I knew about the payoff. I figured that's how it would play out."

"So, you never really thought there would be legal consequences."

"Nope, but I thought Maria should get something out of it and I wanted my mom to straighten up."

"Did she?"

"I doubt it. Didn't hang around as much after that."

"Did you let her know you were angry?" she asked.

"*Furious,*" he corrected. "And yes, I let her know. I told her that she'd gone way too far, that she was behaving like a common thug, that I was ashamed."

"How did she react?"

"The way I should have expected. She stopped speaking to me."

Carlisle couldn't fault Lucas for admonishing his mother, but she wondered at a kid who claimed to be furious, yet was still capable of being calculating enough to hit her where it hurt.

"That went on for a few weeks and then she forgave me. I don't know why; we never spoke about it."

"What were you doing there that day?" asked Carlisle.

"I had a date with my dad's Boston Whaler. I'd been at a climate change conference in LA for a week—about six days longer than I can stand to be in LA—and I wanted to spend a quiet day on the lake."

"And did you?" asked Kincaid.

"Nope. After my mom beat up the maid, I decided to call it a day."

"You said you'd never seen your mother violent, but she also had an episode of road rage. Were there any other incidents that you know of? Something that didn't come to the attention of the police?"

"Honestly, I just don't know."

"All right. What about Beth Williams?"

He frowned, sighing. "I shouldn't have mentioned her yesterday. Beth wouldn't hurt a fly." Carlisle gave him a look that said she wasn't going to take his word for it. "Beth and my mother were partners at the EDC until about two years ago, when they parted company. Publicly it was an amicable split, but I think my mom forced her out."

"Did your mother tell you that?" she asked.

"No, she told me they were on good terms."

"Beth?"

"She corroborated my mom's version, as far as I know."

"As far as you know?"

"Publicly. But it would have been in her best interest to keep up appearances. My mother could be a powerful enemy in a line of work where public opinion is the difference between viability and financial insolvency. Any chance that Beth had of establishing her own charitable organization would be dependent on private funding. If my mother wanted her gone, challenging that decision would have damaged Beth's chances of funding her own nonprofit. Maybe even destroyed them."

"But your mother didn't bash her publicly," said Kincaid.

"No, in fact, in a backhanded way she gave Beth a decent shot at success." He looked rueful. "I haven't had much contact with Beth since she left the EDC—when I do, she's always lovely and kind, but it's not difficult to read between the lines. Beth and her son, Henry, spent every Thanksgiving with our family for five years in a row. They came to parties, family stuff, swimming in the pool on weekends.

"Then all of a sudden, she's conspicuously absent from everything? After an amicable split? No. If she and my mom really did end their business partnership as friends, then why not maintain their personal relationship? They were close." He sighed. "Look, I'm speculating, but I'm basing it on good evidence. Ask Beth, she'll probably give you the details."

Carlisle didn't bother to tell him that they already had. "Do you think Beth would have murdered your mother for forcing her out?"

"Absolutely not. I'm telling you this to give you an idea of how my mom treated people, not to add to your suspect list. Beth has managed to set up her own organization and from what I hear, it's going well. I mean, there's a lot of uncertainty when you set up a nonprofit and I'm sure it's a lot more stressful than when she was helping to run a well-established foundation. But still, she did it. If Beth had a motive, it wouldn't have been business. But, honestly, I've always thought she was a really good person. Smart, considerate, great mom. Ambitious in her own way."

Carlisle thought, *Telling us Beth couldn't have done it because she got fired, but maybe could have for personal reasons?* She let it go for now. "Great mom," she repeated. "Where's the dad?"

Lucas looked uncomfortable. "I don't know anything about him."

"Never met him?"

"Never even heard his name."

Kincaid said, "There must've been some speculation. A little gossip to bandy about the country club? That kind of thing's gotta make the society ladies curious."

"I really don't know about that."

"Really?" said Kincaid. "An unmarried, middle-class mother partners up with a mean socialite. Attends luncheons and cocktail parties with Seattle's elite? Practically becomes a member of one of the wealthiest and most influential families in the state? And no one's talking? C'mon, Lucas."

"Okay, I mean, everyone wanted to know what was wrong with the father, what was wrong with her, and what was wrong with her kid. And everyone wanted to know what Aurora Stanhope wanted with her. I stay away from the gossip mill, but I can imagine the stories told at the tennis net."

His voice dropped theatrically. "Robert Stanhope's illegitimate daughter comes home. Robert Stanhope had an affair with Beth, Henry was the result. Lucas Stanhope fathered Henry Williams while still in college and Aurora welcomed them both into the family. Or maybe, long before there was Robert Stanhope, Aurora got pregnant and gave her baby daughter up for adoption, and the daughter, having finally found her birth mother, takes a role as protégé so as not to scandalize the family." Lucas's eyebrow twitched. "It's all soap opera shit."

"And," said Kincaid, "none of those stories is true?"

"Right," he said, "none of those stories is true. What is likely true is that Beth got pregnant and didn't want to keep the man, but she did want to keep the baby. As far as I know, the father was never in the picture."

He looked away. "One thing, I mean, one thing that fueled the gossip mill."

"One thing?" said Carlisle.

"Well, Beth *is* actually adopted."

"Really?" said Carlisle.

"Yes, really. But I'm sure it's not relevant."

"It probably isn't," said Carlisle, "unless she's your father's love-child."

"She's not."

Carlisle's eyes flashed. "I do have one more question before we go—why didn't you want us to tell your father that you'd come to the station yesterday?"

"I told you. He wouldn't have understood."

"Right," she said, "why not?"

"I don't know. Maybe he *would* understand. But I don't want him to worry that I'm running all over town having mental breakdowns."

Carlisle nodded, studied him. "I hope you know, though, that having a minor mental breakdown after a loved one is murdered is not strange behavior. It would be strange if you didn't."

"And if I let slip some terrible family secret during an emotional outburst, you wouldn't mind that either, right?"

Carlisle shrugged. "We certainly wouldn't disregard it."

Silence, then she added, "We've taken enough of your time for now." Carlisle stood.

On their way out, Lucas asked, "What's Kyle's role in this investigation?"

Kincaid had a feeling he had wanted to ask for a while. He said, "She's the lead forensic investigator on your mother's case."

Lucas thought for a moment. "So, if you need my fingerprints, she'll be the one to take them?"

Neither detective spoke for a few seconds. Then Carlisle said, "Only if every other technician working for her was, for some inexplicable reason, unable to perform the task."

Lucas turned red. "I see."

Once safely behind closed elevator doors, Kincaid said, "He wants to see Kyle."

"Maybe we'll let him. If it works to our advantage."

"Lucas seems surprisingly unperturbed by his mother's bad behavior."

The elevator doors opened onto the lobby and Carlisle said, "He was probably used to it."

"Cheating on his dad? Serial adultery? Hard to imagine getting used to that."

"Even harder to imagine that her husband would have accepted it, but we've seen it before." Carlisle squinted into the cloudy sky. "He was pretty eager to talk about Beth Williams."

"And eager to tell us none of it was relevant."

Carlisle sighed. "We have too many motives, Kincaid. And too many suspects. And, by the way, why the hell haven't we found Aurora's car yet?"

CHAPTER TWELVE

"**B**RING HER UP."

Beth Williams came into the squad room. She was wearing the same faded jeans she'd worn on Saturday and a black collared shirt was neatly folded around the collar of a black sweater. Her dark hair was shining and her cheeks were pink from the chill outside, but she looked uncomfortable as she took a seat beside Carlisle's and Kincaid's desks.

"Can I get you some coffee or soda, Beth?" asked Carlisle, standing.

"No, thanks, I'm fine," she said.

Carlisle looked at her partner, who nodded at his half-full latte. He knew Carlisle just wanted to give him a minute alone with Beth, but he didn't know if she wanted him to make their witness feel more comfortable or if she was just trying to set him up with her.

Either way, it was time to put on the charm. "Thanks for coming in, Beth, we really appreciate it."

"I don't know what I can tell you that I haven't already."

"We just want to know a little more about the Stanhope family dynamics."

"Can't you ask the Stanhopes?"

"They might not be very forthcoming at this point."

"I'll help if I can, but I was never one of them, my perspective may not be as accurate as you hope."

Carlisle came back, chipped coffee mug in hand. "You made a good choice, Beth, this coffee is wretched."

"And I thought homicide dicks living on bad coffee was just a cliché," said Beth.

"Would that it were," said Carlisle, "would that it were." She set down her mug.

Carlisle said, "Tell us why Caroline was so angry at her mother?"

She groaned. "I really hate to do this."

"Look, Beth, Aurora Stanhope was murdered in a gruesome, violent way and we need to find out who is responsible."

"All right, all right." She blew out a breath. "Here's what I always thought: Aurora was a tough act to follow and Caroline seemed jealous. Of everything. Weird stuff, even. Like, she used to complain that Aurora hadn't given her enough calcium as a kid so that she would never grow as tall as her. Caroline hated being shorter than Aurora."

Kincaid made a face. "Any chance there's some truth in that?"

"No," she said. "Absolutely not. Robert's mother and sister are very petite, so she probably comes by it naturally. If there's any nutritional reason for it then it was Caroline's issues with food as a teenager. Maybe Aurora was partly responsible for that, but she certainly didn't deprive her daughter of calcium so that she would always tower over her. That's absurd."

"Caroline had food issues?" asked Carlisle.

Beth nodded. "I didn't know her then but Aurora mentioned it occasionally and I saw pictures of Caroline when she was a teen. She was so skinny it hurt to look at—I mean, you could see the outline of her teeth through her cheek. Robert and Aurora packed her off to a treatment center somewhere but as far as I know they never did any family counseling, which probably would have helped. Aurora referred to it as her daughter's 'attention-getting phase.' In her world, eating disorders were distinctly unladylike."

"So, she wasn't sympathetic," said Carlisle. "Beth, how did this woman run a charitable organization?"

Beth laughed. "She had much more compassion for strangers than for anyone close to her. Aurora couldn't see character flaws from that far away."

Kincaid got back to the point. "Caroline must've hated her mother for that."

"I'd imagine," said Beth. "But those days were years in the past by the time I came on the scene."

"The eating disorder, but not the difference in height," he said. "You said Caroline was jealous of everything. Did that include her dad's attention?"

"Is that your detective's algorithm for human psychology at work?" She rolled her eyes. "Yeah. Probably. But not just Robert. All men, and most women, for that matter. Even at the breakfast table Aurora commanded all of the attention. She was so funny and charming and everything that was important to Aurora was important to you—even if later you couldn't remember what it was. I felt bad for Caroline. Sometimes. Most of the time she was such a snot that it was hard to have any sympathy for her. Plus, she hated me."

"She hated *you*?" said Kincaid coyly.

"Evidently, I am capable of engendering hate, Detective Kincaid. I think she thought her mom liked me better."

"Did she?" he asked.

"Yep," said Beth frankly, "but she didn't love me better."

Kincaid grunted.

"'Nother question," said Carlisle. "Who are your birth parents?"

Beth's mouth dropped open, but then she looked irritated. "Why does that matter?"

Carlisle shrugged. "It probably doesn't, but help us out so we don't have to start digging."

Beth seemed to see the wisdom in cooperating, even if she didn't particularly want to. "The short answer is that I don't know."

But she told them what she did know. Her parents had adopted her as a newborn. They'd already had two children of their own. Fraternal twins. The birth itself had been difficult—hemorrhage, emergency C-section, three weeks in the hospital post-partum. The twins were fine, but Beth's mom had nearly died.

Still, they'd wanted another child. Tubal ligation had made that impossible, especially in those days, but when the twins were ten, Beth's parents had gotten their wish, adopting Beth straight from the hospital, hours after her birth.

Beth wasn't very close to her siblings, but she loved them and they loved her. More than the adoption, the age gap and the special bond between twins were responsible for the distance. But she was part of the family, no doubt about that. A younger sibling who'd been teased and coddled by her brother and sister, who would always be the baby in the family.

Her family. The only one she had ever needed, ever wanted.

When she'd finished, Carlisle said, ""You never looked for them."

"I know who my parents are."

"Well," said Carlisle after Beth had gone, "you think Beth's parentage has anything to do with this?"

"I have absolutely no idea. Whole thing's a clusterfuck so far. Everyone Stanhope knew is a suspect. Murderer will probably turn out to be a complete stranger."

Carlisle didn't have anything to add. "Let's go talk to the pool boy."

They found Kevin Stoddard's apartment building easily enough and pulled into a parking place just down the block. As they walked up to the security door, a runner in her early twenties emerged, dressed head-to-toe in floral spandex. Carlisle caught the security door before it closed behind her and they scanned the mailboxes to find Stoddard's apartment number.

"Three-fifteen." They walked up the carpeted stairs and down the third-floor hall until they came to Stoddard's door. Kincaid banged on it. Then again. There were no sounds coming from inside, so he banged again. Nothing.

They waited, Carlisle shrugged, and Kincaid tried one last time. Finally, they heard sounds from inside, a floor creaking, the crash of someone bumping into a table or countertop, a muffled curse, and then the door opened on the young man Carlisle had seen draining the pool at the Stanhope home the previous day.

As it turned out, they hadn't lost the advantage by coming in the afternoon instead of the early morning. Kevin Stoddard looked like his day was just getting started.

In boxer briefs and a stretched-out T-shirt, his hair a mess and his summer tan fading, he wasn't exactly the Adonis he'd been in the photo Kincaid had found, but Carlisle still thought he was pretty foxy.

"Kevin Stoddard?" she said abruptly.

"Yeah? Who are you?"

"Detectives Carlisle and Kincaid." They badged Stoddard and barged through the door. "We need to ask you a few questions."

"About Aurora?" he asked stupidly.

"You know anyone else who got murdered recently?" said Kincaid.

"Huh? Oh, man. Lemme get dressed," he said and walked down the hall to what must have been his bedroom, coming out a minute later in the same T-shirt and a well-worn pair of jeans.

They followed him through a dining area with a table full of books and past a small breakfast bar that served as a room divider for a messy kitchen. "I'm gonna to make some coffee." Stoddard pulled filters and Folgers out of the cupboard and loaded up the machine. He took three cups to the dining room table and began stacking text books into piles in order to make room.

"No milk, but I have sugar."

For an unexpected visit from a couple of cops, the kid was playing a good host, and the empty beer bottles and dirty underwear Carlisle had expected to see strewn around the apartment were notably absent. Maybe there was more to this dumb hunk than met the eye. *Maybe.*

Stoddard brought the coffee pot to the table and sat down. He poured three cups and set the pot on top of a bright blue spiral notebook.

"Lucas told me it happened Friday night." He looked to them for confirmation, got none. "Did she suffer?"

Kincaid ignored the question. "Lucas told you at the house yesterday?"

"Yeah, I was draining the pool. It's terrible."

"Where were you Friday night and early Saturday morning?" asked Carlisle.

He looked a little dazed by the question, but answered anyway. "I went out for pizza with some friends, then I came home. To study."

"Alone?"

"Yes."

"And Saturday?"

"I went for a run in the morning, had brunch with my aunt, studied some more – I have an exam on Monday – and then I went to the Stanhopes' to drain the pool."

"What time?"

"I got to the house around one. Mrs. Chang was there, she'll tell you." His brown eyes looked bleak. "Am I a suspect?"

Carlisle said, "How long have you worked for the Stanhopes'?"

"Just since spring. Last spring."

"And how did you get along with Mrs. Stanhope?"

"With—good."

"And Mr. Stanhope?"

"Fine."

"Lucas? Caroline?"

"Fine. I hardly ever saw them. Am I a suspect? Do I need a lawyer?"

Kincaid leaned forward and looked Kevin Stoddard straight in the eyes. "If you want to get a lawyer, we can have this conversation at police headquarters. Honestly, I'd understand." Then he reached into his pocket for the photograph he'd found in Aurora's desk drawer and slid it across the table.

Kevin Stoddard didn't say anything for a few seconds, but the look on his face spoke volumes. In a voice cracking with nerves, he finally said, "Where did you get this?"

"In the back of Aurora Stanhope's top desk drawer," said Kincaid candidly.

With a shuddering sigh, Stoddard slumped and rested his elbows on the table, raking his fingers through thick, sun-streaked hair. "Does her family know?"

"We didn't tell them," said Kincaid. "Not yet."

"Look, I'm almost done at the Stanhopes' for the season. I have to finish closing up the pool and get the boat in. And, you know, *obviously* I won't go back in the spring, so there's no reason to tell them." Shame was turning his cheeks pink.

"Like I said, only if it's relevant to our investigation." He pointed at the photograph. "Although, if there are any more of these tucked into her belongings, the Stanhopes might find out anyway."

"Oh, Christ."

"But I'm willing to hedge our bets by keeping this between us for now. Let's just have an unofficial talk right here, while we drink our coffee." He didn't have to say, *without a lawyer*—Stoddard got it. "So, Kevin, how did you end up working for the Stanhopes?"

This should have been an easy question, so Stoddard's groan surprised the detectives.

"Lucas got me the job. Well, he suggested me and then I went for an interview."

Kincaid nodded. So, a friend of the son wound up sleeping with the mother. It added another layer of controversy to an already controversial family. "Were you friends?"

"Not really. I just met him one night. Last April, I guess it was. I knew Caroline. We were both at UW. We had a few friends in common."

"You knew Caroline too." *Yet another layer,* he thought.

"Lucas came out with her one night and he and I started talking. I told him that I worked at a beach club in San Diego before I came back to Washington for school and I needed a summer gig. He told me he knew someone who needed a guy to take care of their pool and boathouse."

"Okay," said Kincaid, backing him up a few steps, "so you met Caroline on campus? And you were friends?" Stoddard nodded glumly and Kincaid added, "Just friends?"

He shook his head, a flush spreading from his cheeks to his neck and forehead. "I mean, we met at a party last spring and ended up…" He made a gesture with his hand that apparently meant they had had sex.

Carlisle hated beating around the bush "So, you were sleeping with the mother *and* the daughter?" Before he could respond, she said, "This is a fucking soap opera."

Kincaid went on, "You hooked up?"

"Yeah, and then we went out a few times and…" He looked at them, hoping they would fill in the rest, but got nothing. "And then we just fizzled out."

"Didn't it seem strange to work for her parents after you stopped seeing each other?"

"That's the thing. Lucas never told me they were his parents."

"He didn't mention it at all?"

"I didn't know until I called to schedule an interview and the maid answered, 'Stanhope residence?'"

"Didn't that seem strange to you?"

He shrugged. "A little. But Lucas was a little drunk and I think he assumed I'd know. That Caroline would have told me. The thing is, except for Lucas, Caroline never talks about her family, and if she didn't have an expensive car and a condo downtown, you'd never know she comes from money. Especially not *that* kind of money. Lucas wrote down the number for me. Told me to talk to Ms. Green, promised he'd put in a good word. I just assumed I would be working for the *Greens*."

"How did Caroline react when you told her you got the job?"

"She didn't really. I mean, we weren't hanging out anymore and there was never anything serious between us, it was just fun for a while and then, you know, it wasn't. I ran into her once on campus and told her I'd gotten it and she just kind of smiled and said she'd figured I would."

"Did you ever see Caroline at the house while you were working?"

"No. I thought I would. I mean, if my parents had a pool and a boat on Lake Washington, I'd be out there all the time in summer, but she never came when I was there." He thought a minute. "At least, not out to the pool. She could've been inside and I'd never have known."

"Tell me, Kevin," said Kincaid, "who interviewed you for the job?"

"The assistant, Karen Green, did the interview at the house, but Aurora sat in for part of it, asked a few questions."

"Who hired you?"

"Karen called me, but I was pretty sure I had the job when I left the interview that day."

Carlisle chuckled wryly. "Mrs. Stanhope came in and gave you the nod."

Kevin rolled his eyes. "Yeah, I could tell she liked me, but I never thought it would turn into anything."

Kincaid said, "What does your job entail?"

Stoddard explained that since May, two days each week he cleaned the pool, checked chemical levels, and took care of general maintenance on the Boston Whaler, including polishing the teak and leather and filling the tank when it was low. "There's more to do now that winter is coming and I'm taking the boat out of the water and draining the pool, but then I'll be done for the season."

"Working only two days a week keeps you afloat?"

"I also work in the chem lab on campus and I took classes this summer, so two full days at the Stanhopes' was plenty. Plus, they pay really well."

Carlisle blew out a breath. "Okay kid, I think we've got the gist. Now tell us, when did you start sleeping with the lady of the house?"

Stoddard looked into his empty coffee cup. "June fourteenth."

Carlisle's brows shot up. "What, you marked it on your calendar?"

He bristled. "No, I just remember it because my dad's birthday party was that weekend and I went home for a couple of days. I was driving back to Seattle on Sunday morning when Aurora called and asked if I could come in that day." With a quick look at Carlisle, he shrugged, adding, "She said she'd pay me double."

"Did she tell you what she was paying for?"

"It wasn't like that. The only money I ever took from her was my hourly wage."

"*Double* your hourly wage," Carlisle pointed out with a mean smile.

"It was only double when I had to come in unexpectedly. After a party or if something went wrong with the pool or hot tub."

"Right, so you went in on a Sunday to attend to an *emergency* pool cleaning. And then?"

"Aurora met me at my car and walked around back with me. She asked if I could clean the hot tub first because she wanted to use it. It was a shitty day. Drizzling, overcast. Nice day for the hot tub, I guess."

"I guess," said Carlisle.

There was a long silence while Stoddard poured himself more coffee. This time he didn't offer the detectives any. "I cleaned the tub. Bunch of crap in there, flip flops, an empty champagne bottle, one of the cushions from a deck chair. Must've been a party. Anyway, she came out in a robe—"

"She went inside while you cleaned the hot tub?"

"Yeah, half an hour or so. She came out with a big bottle of Evian and took off her robe and got in the tub. I said it must've been some party the night before but she didn't respond. Just looked at me and I thought I'd offended her or something."

"At that point, had you spent much time with her?"

"Like almost none. I saw her in passing when I was working, but I never really talked to her and that was the first time I ever saw her use the pool." Stoddard had been fidgety for a while and now he got up, went to the kitchen, and returned with his own bottle of water. Safeway, not Evian.

"I just went on cleaning and a few minutes later she was like, 'Kevin, it's cold out there. Why don't you get in the hot tub for a few minutes?' I told her I'd love to, but if I got in there I'd be twice as cold when I got out again. She laughed, said I was probably right about that. Then she asked me about school, my family, you know. I told her about the surprise party we'd thrown for my dad. She asked me a million questions." Sounding a little sentimental.

"Eventually she got out of the hot tub and put her robe back on. Said she was going to turn into a prune if she stayed in the water any longer."

"Was she?" Carlisle asked.

"Was she what?"

"Turning into a prune?"

Cheeks flushed, he said, "No, she looked great."

Aurora Stanhope had asked Stoddard to join her for lunch when he was finished.

"I found her in the kitchen. They have this big old wooden table and she had cold roast chicken, fancy cheese and a tomato salad, an open bottle of red wine. It was early afternoon, but the sky was so dark that it could have been evening. She had a light on above the stove, but it didn't reach the table and we sat there eating and talking and drinking wine in the shadows."

He went silent and kept his gaze fixed on the bottle of water in his hand, but Carlisle didn't nudge him, just waited.

"It was really nice. And Aurora was so," he sighed, "amazing."

"Anyway, she made me sit while she cleaned up and then she told me that Mr. Stanhope was away for the night and that she wanted me to come to her bedroom. And that's how it all started."

"The fact that you'd already slept with her daughter didn't trouble you?" Kincaid asked. "The age difference? That she was your employer?"

"Nope. Didn't trouble me at all," he said frankly, finally tearing his gaze away from the water bottle and fixing it on Carlisle. "Aurora Stanhope was amazing."

CHAPTER THIRTEEN

Half an hour later, Kincaid circled the block while Carlisle went into a Starbucks for coffee. When she got back in the car, he said, "That poor kid."

Carlisle laughed. "I felt sorry for him too." She pulled the lid off of her to-go cup and blew on the dark roast. "I think he was in love with her."

"I think so. Might've driven him to kill her."

Kevin Stoddard had told them that the affair had lasted until two weeks ago, when Mrs. Stanhope had abruptly ended it with a phone call. "She just said it was over. I asked her why and she said that I didn't make her pulse quicken anymore. Just like that. No remorse, no sympathy, completely unconcerned about me."

"He doesn't have an alibi," said Carlisle now, "but if the kids or the husband knew Aurora was screwing the pool boy then they have a good motive too."

———————

It was late afternoon when Caroline Stanhope opened the door to her downtown condominium: another display of family money. In terms of decorating, she favored her mother's tastes—velvet, tassels, oil-paintings in gilt frames, mood lighting.

Carlisle was surprised to see that the young woman who had just yesterday complained about her mother trying to dress her now greeted them in a conservative wool blazer and creamy sweater that might have come straight out of a Ralph Lauren equestrian collection. She gave her partner a look and Kincaid raised his eyebrows; he had also noted the change.

Caroline didn't seem surprised to see them, nor was she very accommodating. They followed her into the master bedroom and were left to stand while she continued what appeared to be a comprehensive job of packing. A full set of Louis Vuitton luggage lay open and full of clothes on her king-sized bed.

"You'll have to forgive me, Detectives," she said without a hint of regret, "I'm going to stay with my dad for a while and I have a lot to do." Her closet doors stood open to reveal an almost obscene collection of black leather boots and blue jeans. *Where had she found the clothes she was wearing?* Carlisle wondered.

Blonde hair pulled into a loose bun, rosy cheeks and glossed lips made her looked healthy and wholesome despite the tight little frown pasted on her mouth.

"What can I help you with, Detectives?"

"Tell us about Steve and Missy Lombardi."

"Like what?" she asked without turning from her closet door.

"Like, could one of them have murdered your mother?"

She didn't answer. Eventually, she asked, "Haven't you talked to him yet?"

"We tried," said Kincaid.

"And he cried lawyer? You'll get a lot of that in this group of people. Nobody does anything without an attorney present. But honestly, what did you expect?"

Kincaid was wondering if this kid was always such a snot or if he just brought it out in her, but they had already decided that since Caroline already didn't like her, Carlisle would take the backseat on the softball questions and ask the hard ones later.

He soldiered on. "What do you know about his relationship with your mother?"

Caroline's eyes lit up. With excitement or anger was hard to tell. "He's a total asshole. You've seen him, so you know that he spends about five hours too many each day in the gym. I've even heard that he keeps a set of free weights in his corner office at Lehman, Lombardi, Chance. Gross. I don't know if he's trying to make up for having a small dick or what, but anyone who's wider than they are tall, for any reason, needs to rethink their self-image." She sighed. "But he's super rich, totally full of himself, and knows all the legal dirt about everyone with money in Seattle, so, of course, my mother slept with him."

Besides raising an eyebrow, Kincaid didn't react to her blunt pronouncement. The Stanhope kids seemed to take their mother's infidelities in stride, but he didn't buy the blithe attitude. "Your mother slept with him?"

"Oh, yeah. No doubt about it. No one wanted to say it yesterday in front of my dad, but she was totally the girl-half of the affair she blabbed to Missy. Anyway, I don't think he would have touched my mom. To hurt her, I mean. Missy is the one you need to look at." She crossed her legs. "Have you talked to *her* yet?"

Kincaid shook his head and smiled. "Do tell."

"Oh, she's *awful*! She's always been jealous of my mom—I heard she was in love with my dad once upon a time and then he met my mom and they rode off into the sunset together, and she got stuck with meathead Steve Lombardi. And my mom had Lucas and me and I heard Missy can't have kids. *Plus*, she always loses to my mom in tennis." She paused. "Tennis is a *big deal* at the country club. Very competitive. Also, even though she's got at least as much money as my mom, she never had the coolest car, never had the best dress at the gala, was never as pretty." Caroline seemed to take pride in this. "I mean, my mom ran an international foundation to help alleviate poverty in some of the most wretched places on earth and Missy's throws fundraisers for neglected lapdogs? Honestly. And then, she finds out my mom was sleeping with *her* husband?

And *my mom* is the one who tells her?" Her eyes were bright with admiration. "Of course she did it!"

Kincaid said, "Did what?"

"Killed my mother."

Kincaid nodded. "Huh. What do you know about Beth Williams?"

"Beth?" She looked at the ceiling. "I guess she could have done it too, but I wouldn't put my money on it."

"Why's that?"

"She has no spine. I'm sure that's why my mom got rid of her." Caroline basically reiterated what they'd heard from Lucas.

Carlisle stepped in. "You don't think that forcing Beth out of her nonprofit was screwing her over?"

As if she'd just realized there was another person in the room, Caroline blinked at Carlisle. "Well, *no*, I don't. My mother could have bad-mouthed her all over the country club and ruined Beth completely. But she didn't."

"You don't think Beth was hurt to lose your mom as a friend and mentor?"

Caroline made a face. "Beth has her own people. She's not hurting for friends and family. She's doing fine with her own nonprofit." Shrug. "No harm, no foul. Why would she want revenge?"

"Right," said Carlisle, processing the logic. She decided to change the subject. "Caroline, what is your relationship with Kevin Stoddard?"

Arching her eyebrows. "Kevin, the cabana boy? He cleans my parents' pool."

"We understand that you knew Kevin before he began working for your parents."

Her leg began bouncing. "I met him at school. We hung out a little bit."

"Did you tell him about the job at your parents' house?"

She was definitely irritated now. "No. *Lucas* did that. *I* just slept with him a few times and then I planned to forget all about him."

"Did Lucas know you'd dated?"

"We didn't *date*. We had *sex*." Clearly the distinction was important to Caroline. "But no, Lucas didn't know. I didn't even know Kevin had actually interviewed until he came bouncing over to me on campus and told me he had gotten the job. Why would he even consider it? It's so inappropriate."

Carlisle thought about that. Kevin had told them he hadn't initially known the job was at the Stanhopes' home, but he had still pursued it after he found out. Maybe it was a little weird.

"Was your mother aware that you'd had a relationship with Kevin?"

"I certainly didn't tell her. I mean, I didn't want to get him fired or make things weird for him. The guy has a right to have a job, right? I just avoided their pool when I knew he'd be working."

"And," said Carlisle casually, "did you know that Kevin was sleeping with your mother?"

CHAPTER FOURTEEN

OUTSIDE, THEY LEFT KINCAID'S CAR and found a coffee shop. There was no room to sit, so they took their cups back to the warm car. "Think she knew?" asked Kincaid.

"She wasn't shocked."

"That's not the same thing," said Kincaid.

"No, it's not. I don't think she knew."

When Carlisle had asked, Caroline's voice had broken. "No, I didn't." She'd fixed her stare on one of the open suitcases on her bed. Tears brimmed in her eyes. "I think it's time for you to go."

"I wonder if Aurora had ever done anything like that before?" said Carlisle now.

"Slept with the help or slept with one of her boyfriends?" Kincaid asked. "It sounds like she had a thing for young guys in general. Thing is, there's no evidence that Aurora knew Kevin was one of Caroline's boyfriends."

"Even if Kevin and Caroline didn't tell her, Lucas could have mentioned it." Her fingers drummed on the paper coffee cup. "But it doesn't really matter if Aurora knew. That is, apart from making her a really awful mother. The important thing is whether *Caroline* knew, and whether Aurora was in the habit of stealing men away from her daughter."

"If Aurora had done it before, even if it was just some tennis coach Caroline had a crush on when she was sixteen, then Kevin Stoddard could've been the straw that broke the camel's back."

"Could be. It's almost five o'clock," said Carlisle, checking her phone. "Should we see if they'll let us into the Stanhopes' country club?"

Kincaid smirked, "They'd be lucky to have us."

———————————

Kyle had found a clue. It might not turn out to be the clue that solved the case, but it would help.

"Hair." Kyle's voice echoed faintly in the empty lab.

"A *hair*?" said Kincaid. They'd been driving to the country club when his cell phone started to ring. He answered on speaker.

"Not *a* hair. Hair plural."

"What kind of hair?" asked Carlisle.

"Both kinds of hair," said Kyle. "And two is definitely better than one. We'll be able to get DNA, though that only helps if we get a match."

"Yeah, yeah, whatever," said Kincaid. "What color is it?"

"Light brown. Inch and a half. Wavy."

"And the pubic hair?" asked Carlisle.

"Dark brown."

"Curly?"

Kyle grunted, got off the phone, grabbed her coat and took the elevator up into the light. Such as it was in late October, in the Pacific Northwest.

Three hours until a third-date dinner with a guy named Mark who seemed like a lot of fun, but seeing Lucas had soured her excitement a little.

She needed to get home, take a hot shower, shake some sense back into herself. Her little apartment just north of downtown Seattle was warm and welcoming on this cold October day. The bundle of white lilies she'd bought herself at the market a few days earlier filled the space with a fresh perfume and welcomed her home. The minute she locked the door behind her, Kyle started peeling layers of damp wool and denim from her body, leaving a trail from the front door to the bathroom where she turned the shower on high and hot and stood under the water until her skin was pink and squeaky.

Wrapping herself in a bathrobe, she went to the small living and dining area, sat down on the sofa, and turned on the television.

Glancing at her phone, she saw that Mark had sent her a text confirming their dinner that night. She scrolled through their text messages to a very cute trio of pics she'd taken of Mark on their second date.

He was very good looking. And he was smart. And he was a lot of fun.

They'd met on one of those rare occasions when modern single woman interacts directly with modern single man. They had bypassed the online dating game by meeting in a bar.

As it turned out, Kyle had drunk just enough red wine to give her phone number to a stranger. He'd called her the very next day and asked to meet somewhere.

On their first date they'd gone to Pike Place Market, where Mark had convinced the fishmongers to include him in the famous toss. He and two professionals had thrown a decent-sized haddock around for a few minutes and afterward, he'd bought the fish.

Later he confessed that buying the fish had been a condition of throwing it to him. "For a hundred bucks."

"Mark, did you do all of that to impress me?"

"Did it work?"

"It might have, if you hadn't told me you bribed them," she'd said. "Plus, a hundred bucks for a twenty-dollar fish? You got played."

The second date had been a salsa party, and the third date… the third date with Mark might be sex.

She'd been looking forward to considering it over dinner.

And then she'd seen Lucas. And her excitement got muddled with her past.

And the past was now muddled with a murder investigation.

Looking at the photos she'd taken of Mark helped her resolve to proceed with her life as normal. Holding his hundred-dollar fish, he was just so damn pretty.

She closed the shades on the bank of windows in her living room, took off her robe, and began to dress for dinner.

———————

The country club had been a bust. The manager wouldn't let the detectives talk to the staff or the guests and he himself had evidently been deaf and blind to Aurora's antics. "She was one of our most treasured members. Generous, gracious, very popular. We will miss her. Terribly. Our sympathy goes out to the Stanhopes."

Kincaid, however, had managed to slip a few business cards to a bartender he had passed on his way to the restrooms. "Someone will call," he reassured Carlisle on their way to the parking lot.

"Yeah, yeah. That manager could guard the secrets of the pyramids."

"He's in the right line of work," Kincaid agreed.

"Much to my chagrin." When they were back in the car she said, "Let's go to your place and do some research."

"Why not yours? We've got dinner there at six, right?"

"Yes, but if we go to my house and try to work, Pamela the Terrible will distract me with her crushing disapproval."

They drove to Kincaid's house and Carlisle sat down with his laptop at the dining room table. "Beer, water?"

"Water."

Carlisle drank her water and did image searches on each of the men involved in the case. "Lucas has light brown hair, wavy. Robert is salt and pepper. Kevin Stoddard is blonde but could probably pass for light brown. Steve Lombardi's is black and so are all of the Sanchezes."

"That's something. Maybe."

"What I want to know," said Carlisle, "is who did she sleep with on Friday night and why the fuck haven't we found her car? It's not a dark-colored domestic sedan, it's a white Porsche. Someone should've spotted it by now."

Kincaid was still thinking about the brown hair. "Not enough to rule anyone out, though. The head hair could have come from anyone she had contact with since her last bath, not necessarily her killer."

Stanley jumped on the table. Kincaid said, "Hey buddy. Come here." He scratched the big grey cat behind the ears and was rewarded with snorts and purring.

"What a greeting," said Carlisle. "Sometimes I wish I could trade in my teenager for a nice fluffy cat. And Pamela. And every once in a while, my husband too."

"Poor Judy with her perfect family," said Kincaid, still scratching his cat. "But, okay, it's true. Stan really is the best."

By five-thirty, they had made a shortlist of people to interview from the list of haters that Karen Green had sent to them that afternoon. Carlisle had also tried Missy Lombardi's cell phone and received exactly the response she expected: "Make an appointment with our attorney." And she had dug out the card Steve Lombardi had given them earlier in the day and left a message for Ronny Buccio to set up an appointment for Monday. "What now?" she asked.

"Now, Judy, it's time to face Pam."

<hr />

They walked through the front door of the Carlisle home a few minutes before six. Before they had left his house, Kincaid had traded his suit and tie for a pair of crisp navy trousers and a blue sweater that made his eyes shine brightly.

"Pulling out all the stops, huh?" Carlisle had said as her partner checked his look in the mirror above the fireplace."

"I'm doing you a favor, Carlisle. Pamela won't be able to take her eyes off of me long enough to glare at you."

Now Janie practically yanked them into the living room, giving her mother a rare hug. She took Kincaid's coat and kissed him on the cheek. "Dad said you were coming." She rolled her eyes like only a teenager can. "Thank God."

"Grandma giving you trouble?"

"*Never* call her grandma," hissed Janie.

"This is very cool," Kincaid said, holding up a lock of blue hair amid her natural blonde.

Janie beamed as she hung his coat in the closet.

Tom and Judy Carlisle lived in a grey and white Craftsman on Queen Anne Hill with three bedrooms, a finished basement, and a spectacular kitchen.

Kincaid smelled butter and beef as he followed Carlisle into the kitchen.

"Jerry!" said Tom. "Good to see you. This is my mom, Pamela Carlisle."

"It's a pleasure, Mrs. Carlisle," he said with a bow that made Pamela glow with pleasure and left Carlisle shaking her head as she excused herself to change clothes. "Where do you call home, ma'am?"

"Oh, *Jerry*, do call me Pamela," she said with a lovely smile. "I live in San Diego."

"You must have come to Seattle to get out of the sun."

She tittered, her stunning white bob bouncing on the nape of her neck. "I'd bring the sunshine with me if I could, Jerry. I'm just here for a visit." She glanced over at Janie who was counting knives and forks for the dinner table and added, "Blue hair."

Janie stormed out of the room and Pamela leaned in closer, lowering her voice. "I don't know why I do it. I've been driving her crazy since I arrived." She grinned. "So tell me about this case you're on! How intriguing."

"Well, I'm not supposed to talk about it, but if you can keep a secret…"

"My lips are sealed, Detective."

Kincaid whispered, "The murder of Aurora Stanhope."

"Aurora was murdered?"

"Did you *know* her?"

"Yes. I did, sort of." She looked shocked. "When did this happen?"

"Friday night. You didn't hear about it on the news?"

"I just arrived on Friday. Haven't been paying attention to the local stories. And I suppose I don't really talk to Judy about her job."

Judy came down, Janie and Troy finished setting the table and Tom announced dinner—beef tenderloin with béarnaise sauce, boiled Yukon gold potatoes with butter and parsley, roasted carrots and fennel and a green salad, as Tom said, to cut through the fat. He served red wine and bubbly water, and, drawn together by the aromas of a Sunday feast, a warm house on a cold day, the twinkle of candlelight and the proud smile on Tom's face, thoughts of dead socialites, blue hair and unsavory career choices were put aside. The family was whole.

They ate dinner and bantered about school and San Diego. They talked about Stanley the cat and how on earth Tom had learned to cook when Pamela couldn't fry an egg and what an incredible soccer player Troy had become.

The kids cleared the table, and when the adults were alone, Kincaid said, "Pamela knew Aurora Stanhope."

Carlisle raised an eyebrow, and Tom said, "I thought her name rang a bell. Did I ever meet her?"

After her children had headed off to junior high school, Pamela Carlisle had started a small boutique flower shop called Fleur de Lis that had grown into a successful business. When Pamela retired to Southern California, her daughter, Lauren, already running the business, had bought the company outright and grown it even bigger over the last five years.

"Maybe," she said, "but I doubt it. We didn't exactly run in the same social circles." The Carlisles had always been comfortable, but never came close to the kind of wealth the Stanhopes commanded. "I knew her because we did all of her flowers. For their home, for parties, deliveries to friends. Aurora loved us. And when I was just starting out, I used to personally deliver to all of our important customers. Ask Lauren about her; they probably still do the arrangements."

Carlisle said, "What was your impression of Aurora?"

With a glint in her eyes, she held out her glass for Tom to top off and said, "Well, I don't want to speak ill of the dead, but she was very demanding."

"Demanding." Carlisle had been hoping for more.

"Last-minute changes to her orders, sending whole arrangements back and expecting replacements immediately. We always gave her what she wanted, and she was a loyal customer, but she never had a nice word for anyone. I could handle her—it was my business, after all—but she sent more than one of my employees back to the shop in tears."

Carlisle and Kincaid were thinking of the incident with Maria Sanchez. Carlisle repeated the story to Pamela who was aghast. "She attacked her? How awful. I always thought she was a snob, but she certainly seemed like a lady." Pamela shivered a little at the vulgarity.

"Maybe Aurora was just *detail* oriented," said Kincaid.

"I'll tell you, though, I can't fault her loyalty. She used us for every occasion and recommended us to all of her wealthy friends.

She was also responsible for getting us the contract with her country club, which was really the moment my little flower shop took off."

"Do you know if Fleur de Lis still does the flowers for the country club?" asked Kincaid.

"As far as I know, yes. But speak to Lauren," she repeated. "Lauren will have the answers."

"Maybe we can get an ear in the country club through them," he said to Carlisle.

"What do you need in the country club?" asked Pamela.

"Dirt," said Carlisle.

"*I* may be able to help you with that, Judy."

"Do tell, Pamela."

"My friend Evelyn is a member and I always have lunch with her when I'm in town. You could join us, Judy," adding, "We'll have to find you a nice dress to wear." She winked at Kincaid.

The kids came in with dessert and saved them all.

"Is this what you two have been working on all day?" said Pamela, delighted.

Troy carried a platter of pears baked in phyllo dough and drizzled with caramel and pecans. Janie followed with a bowl of whipped cream and a pot of coffee.

Halfway through his second cup, Kincaid's phone rang. He excused himself and a minute later, returned to the dining room with a grim look on his face.

"What is it?" asked Carlisle.

Kincaid gave a tiny headshake, nodding at Carlisle's children. Janie rolled her eyes again and said, "C'mon, Troy, let's clean up."

When they'd gone, he said, "We got another body."

CHAPTER FIFTEEN

S UNDAY EVENING, LUCAS STANHOPE ARRIVED at his parents' home on Lake Washington around six-thirty. Caroline had arranged delivery from a Lake Union deli. In fact, Lucas was pretty sure she had bought them out. When he arrived, she was standing at the kitchen counter emptying paper cartons into serving dishes. She unpacked roasted potatoes, grilled corn salad, tomatoes and mozzarella, asparagus, macaroni and cheese, sliced deli meats and three kinds of bread.

"Will you get mustard and mayonnaise from the refrigerator?" she had asked without looking up from her task.

"Hello, treasured sister," he had said and kissed her on the cheek.

"Don't be a pain in the ass, Lucas, I'm making dinner."

The evening went downhill from there. They sat their father down at the kitchen table and put food in front of him, but he only picked at a noodle salad and took a few unenthusiastic bites from the sandwich Lucas had fixed for him. Caroline kept the scotch on hand and from what Lucas could see, most of his father's calories came from the bottle.

Robert Stanhope didn't say two words at the table until the meal ground to a halt. Then, "Lucas, if you don't mind, Caroline has offered to make Aurora's funeral arrangements."

And that was that. Lucas helped his sister repackage the leftovers and tried to talk to her about their father.

"He just lost his wife," said Caroline.

"I know that, and I expect him to be in mourning, but I want to make sure that he has everything he needs."

"He does. He has me."

"I know, but what about professional help?"

"Jesus, let's give him a few days before we have him committed."

She was right, of course, it hadn't even been forty-eight hours since his dad had found out that the love of his life had been murdered. Still, he'd been so quiet since their meeting with the detectives yesterday. And he was drinking a lot. Too much.

Later, at home, Lucas decided to go back out to Lake Washington in the morning and if he was still worried, he would stay at the house for a few days. But *fuck* he didn't want to. He could hardly stand to be in that house when things were normal.

Feeling restless now, Lucas changed into sweats and running shoes and headed right back out the door. Running on city streets was another luxury he'd been missing. The cold air felt good in his lungs and he ran hard, up and down hills for an hour before he found himself, once again, in front of his building.

This time, home felt good. He took a shower, pulled on jeans and a T-shirt and sat down with his computer, fully intending to check his email, but instead he went to Instagram and typed "Kyle Sondheim."

And when her face popped up, he felt himself harden.

He hadn't thought of her in years.

Until he'd seen her yesterday at the police station. She was even more attractive than he remembered, standing there under the fluorescent lights, wearing some kind of smock, hair in a ponytail, look of shock on her face. Maybe when all of this was over, they could spend a few days in bed.

Maybe he should reach out, maybe she'd tell him what was really going on.

Detective Carlisle had made it pretty clear that he was not going to accidentally run into her again, and probably meant he shouldn't try to get in touch. Although she hadn't actually *said* that.

He clicked on Kyle's details but decided not to follow her. Not yet. Went back to her profile picture. A halo of curly hair, big hazel eyes, toothy grin.

It had been nearly six years since they'd agreed to part ways. A sensible decision at the time. They were young, their lives moving in different directions, they hadn't seen each other in months, there were so many other women in the world. And something else. A fight, maybe. He couldn't remember.

———————————

Kyle Sondheim was sitting at a little table in one of China Town's classic restaurants trying not to laugh with food in her mouth. She had let Mark order and their table was covered in lidded tin dishes of stir-fried delights. Mark was telling her the story of his first car, which he'd bought for two hundred dollars in cash and then on a dare threw it into reverse while he was driving forward.

"The transmission fell out of the car. Seriously. One big growl and then the tranny was on the pavement."

"What did you do?"

He shrugged. "Got out of the car and ran. What else could we do?"

"You left it in the middle of the street?"

"There was no one around."

"You didn't even push it to the side of the road?"

"Left it right where it was."

She was laughing so hard, all she could do was shake her head.

"I take really good care of my car now," he said with a totally straight face as Kyle tried to catch her breath. "I get the oil changed regularly. I always come to a complete stop before I try to back up."

She washed down the last of her Szechuan beef with a swig of jasmine tea. This guy was definitely coming home with her.

But it didn't work out that way.

———————

"Where?" said Carlisle as they headed down her front walk to the unmarked.

"Seattle Center. Near the Pavilion. Bunch of drunk tourists decided to take in the Space Needle on this cold and rainy night. They were crossing the park when one of them realizes she's had way too much to drink, leaves the group to puke and sees Mrs. Chang in the bushes."

"Jesus. Did she throw up on our body?"

"We'll have to wait and see."

"Annie Chang. What does she have to do with this?"

"Could be a coincidence."

"It's not a coincidence."

Kincaid agreed so he didn't say anything.

"How?"

"Gunshot to the head, according to first responders. We'll have to get Mallory's opinion on that. ID was in her purse."

Parking next to a line of police cars on Broad Street, they stepped into the fray. Someone had called the paramedics, either to deal with the drunk tourists or because it hadn't been clear that Mrs. Chang was dead. There were four squad cars on the scene, eight cops, and Carlisle counted at least that many civilians behind the police tape. Blessedly few onlookers had gathered, presumably because of the wind and cold, and they wove their way through them and badged the officer guarding the tape.

"That way," he said.

Two more cops with huge Maglites walked toward them as they approached. "She's over there, Detectives."

"Who's the ambulance for?" asked Kincaid.

"It *was* for the victim, but she's definitely dead. They stayed to treat the lady who found her. Shock. Or alcohol poisoning."

"Did they see anything?" asked Carlisle nodding her head toward the tourists.

"Nah. Just stumbled on the body."

"Did she vomit on the victim?"

"Little bit." The officer frowned ruefully. "Shot in the head, dumped in the rain and doused in some drunk chick's half-digested dinner."

"Thanks for the image," said Kincaid.

"It's not nearly as bad as the real thing," he said. "She's all yours."

"Hey, get a tarp over here," shouted Kincaid as he turned his own flashlight on the body. "Jesus, our crime scene is getting rained on."

"Yep," said Carlisle when she got close, "it's bad." The cold wind and rain mitigated the smells of blood and vomit, but it was still vile. "Do we have an ETA on Mallory and Kyle?"

"Soon."

Kyle arrived first, stepping out of the passenger side of a black Jeep and making her way across the lawn on the balls of her high-heeled boots.

"You're overdressed," said Kincaid.

"I was on a date."

"Anyone good?" asked Carlisle.

"Maybe," she said dismissively. "We're going to need shoe imprints from our drunken revelers."

Carlisle walked up. "Let's interview the witnesses, get them out of here." She sent two of the uniforms into the crowd of gawking spectators and turned her attention to the unhappy tourists.

None of them knew anything, though she and Kincaid took some extra time with the woman who threw up on Mrs. Chang.

Klieg lights shone on the death scene and a tarp had been erected above Mrs. Chang, a narrow drop cloth serving as a pathway through the mud. Mallory had arrived and stood just under the tarp watching CSIs photograph footprints around the crime scene. When he saw Carlisle and Kincaid, he shot them a baleful look. "They need a few more minutes before I can go in. I gather we're on this because she has something to do with the other case."

"She was our first victim's live-in maid."

"The maid, huh?" he said, perplexed. "Was she involved? Did she know something?"

Kincaid shrugged. "Probably."

Kyle, now swathed in scrubs, rubber shoes and a Seattle PD jacket, came toward them. "We photographed the body, scraped her nails, did a GSR test, took some trace evidence. You can get in there now if you want, Mallory. It's wet and bloody. And pukey. Hard to sift through the evidence here; my real work is going to be in the lab."

"Was there any gunshot residue on her hands?" asked Carlisle.

"No, she didn't shoot herself. I'll have to test her clothes back at the lab, though. Maybe there's something there. Under the vomit and brain matter."

Carlisle and Kincaid left a few minutes later to notify Chang's husband. They did not, in fact, live in China Town.

They lived in a small, well-maintained house in East Central Seattle. Standing on the stoop, waiting for the door to open, Carlisle felt weary. Mr. Chang opened the door already looking worried and the next ten minutes were crushing.

"Can we call someone for you?" Chang nodded and she found his cell phone, tapped the name he indicated and spoke to his daughter who promised to come immediately. This had been the second marriage for both of them and though Chang was crumbling with grief, Carlisle breathed a quiet sigh of relief when she learned that Annie hadn't had any children of her own.

When the man was breathing normally again and had some color in his cheeks he told them that his wife had been called to the Stanhopes' home that afternoon and she was supposed to be back hours ago. He had been phoning her and received no reply. He had called the Stanhopes and there was no answer.

"She always calls me," he said in an accent softer than his wife's. "She always calls."

They asked him a few questions, couldn't get much out of him but absolute bafflement and disbelief.

Chang's daughter arrived twenty minutes later. His sister was on the way. Carlisle and Kincaid gave them some numbers to call if they needed anything and left with promises to keep them apprised of the investigation.

Next stops were the morgue and the lab. Kyle had taken the clothes, combed Annie Chang's hair for fibers, and checked her body for gunshot residue before Mallory cleaned the body up and scheduled the autopsy.

"Tomorrow morning," he told the detectives. "She died between one and three this afternoon. And if nothing else killed her first, cause of death is a gunshot to the forehead. Close range. Small entrance wound, no exit, so you won't get the bullet until I open her up." He frowned. "Did you do the notification?"

Carlisle nodded. "Husband. His family is with him now."

"That's two widowed husbands in two days."

They left the pathologist still shaking his head in disgust and found Kyle in the lab standing over a blue anorak with a very large pair of tweezers. She looked up, pulled a paper mask from her mouth and said, "Why did it have to be bean burritos?"

"Vomitus?" asked Kincaid.

She gave him a look. "I've got Chang's phone over here. Two outgoing calls today, couple of texts."

"How'd you get the password?" asked Kincaid.

"No password. It's a flip phone."

"Lucky. Who did she call?" asked Carlisle.

"John Chang and Susy Chang. Husband? Children? Siblings maybe? You'll have to check that out. But the text messages are interesting." She raised and lowered her brows like Groucho Marx. "*They* came in from a contact called, 'Stanhope,' asked if she could come to the house for a few hours in the afternoon.

"What time?"

"One o'clock." She handed him the phone. "I'm going to finish a few more puke slides and then go home. Back first thing."

A few minutes later the detectives were back at their desks. Kincaid opened the evidence bag containing Annie Chang's cell phone and dumped it onto his blotter. Using a tissue, he wiped off the fingerprint dust that left a thin gray veil over the phone. It was an old model Motorola, but relatively new. He flipped it open, hit a few keys. "Now, which Stanhope sent the text messages?" he said.

"Call and find out."

He hit the send button, listened, then closed the phone. "You're not going to believe this. The texts came from *Aurora* Stanhope's phone."

Carlisle's mouth dropped open. She said, "Huh." Then, "That means Aurora's phone pinged somewhere. Why didn't the phone company let us know?"

"Non-emergency trace," he said. "We won't hear from them until tomorrow morning."

"Just as important, why wasn't Chang suspicious when she got a text from her dead boss?"

She picked up her phone, called Robert, then Caroline, then the landline at the manse, left messages on all three. "It's after midnight. I'll try Lucas too. Maybe he's staying with his father." She dialed and this time she got a real person.

"Lucas, it's Judy Carlisle." She spoke for a couple of minutes and hung up. "He doesn't know anything about Chang coming for an extra shift and he was out there for dinner at six-thirty. No one said anything about her coming by."

"You didn't tell him Chang is dead," said Kincaid.

"No, and he didn't ask why I was asking about her. That's weird, if you ask me. Anyway, it'll be all over the news tomorrow morning, so the Stanhope clan will find out soon enough."

Kincaid thought about that. "Buys us a little time to strategize." Then he said, "So someone has Aurora's phone, uses it to text Chang, gets her to agree to come out to the house for a few hours, ambushes her somewhere along the way, blows her brains out and then dumps her under some bushes by the Space Needle?"

"Again, why wasn't she suspicious when the message came from her dead boss's phone?" said Carlisle.

"The number was just labeled 'Stanhopes' in her phone. Maybe she didn't realize. Or she could have thought another Stanhope was using Aurora's phone because that's where her number was stored. Chang didn't know it was missing."

"Maybe," she said, "probably." She was quiet for a minute. "Why kill her?"

"She knew something? The murderer thought she knew something? Chang represents another female head of the Stanhope household and our killer wants to dispatch with all of them? Chang also offended our killer?"

"Okay, okay. What now?"

"Time to go home, Judy. There's nothing more we can do tonight."

———————◼️◼️◻️◻️——————

It was almost two in the morning when Kyle got home, tired and wired. There were too many things spinning around in her brain. Foreign hairs, carpet fibers, heartbroken husbands and children, puke, Mark.

Lucas.

The man who'd left a good feeling between her legs and a bad taste in her mouth.

The next morning, Kyle woke up feeling much fresher than she should. Five minutes of monkey mind in her cozy bed had apparently been enough to knock her out cold for the rest of the night. Just five hours later, she opened her eyes, gave herself a little shake, and bounced out of bed to make coffee.

Back in the lab, she had the results of the bloody carpet fiber and it turned out to be an easy database match. Fibers consistent with the textile used in several high-end models produced by the parent company Volkswagen, including the 2015 Porsche nine-eleven. Which—she checked her notes—was the same model driven by Aurora Stanhope. She called Carlisle.

"Chang might've been killed in Stanhope's car."

CHAPTER SIXTEEN

JUDY CARLISLE HAD BEAT HER partner to the station, but only by ten minutes. When Kincaid walked in, she was just getting off the phone.

"That was Kyle," said Carlisle. "The bloody fibers she found on Chang's jacket were carpet fibers from a Porsche."

While she and her partner mulled that over, she got a call phone the phone company "Whoever used Aurora's phone to text Annie Chang left it on and it's pinging in Beacon Hill."

They took the stairs down to the police lot and got into an unmarked car. Kincaid got on Interstate Five and drove south toward Beacon Hill. Carlisle's phone rang and when she got off, she said, "Near the reservoir in Jefferson Park. They'll call back with grid points."

"You think our killer is going to be sitting on a bench holding the phone?"

"Wouldn't that be nice?"

Kincaid tapped the steering wheel with the palm of his hand and grinned. Things were finally moving.

By the time they reached the park the woman from the phone company had called again, given them a street name, approximate number. Carlisle kept her on the line as they got close, but when Kincaid turned left off of South Spokane onto a residential street, she hung up. "Holy shit."

Fifty feet up on the right side sat the white Porsche Boxster, looking totally out of place with the other working-class vehicles. "It hasn't been here long," said Carlisle, watching a middle-aged man stare at the car as he made his way to his own mud-spattered Ford. "Someone would have noticed a shiny German sports car in this neighborhood." She called the lab and told Kyle she needed her and a flat-bed tow truck in Beacon Hill. "The phone must be in the car."

"That's almost as good as finding the killer holding the phone."

She patted his shoulder. "It's not even close to *that* good. But it is good."

They parked and circled the car, looking under the chassis and trying to peer through tinted windows, but found nothing amiss. "How long is it going to take them to get here?" asked Kincaid, using a gloved hand to try the locked doors.

"Forever," said Carlisle with a sigh at the heavy grey sky. They went back to the warm car and waited.

The cavalry finally arrived and Kyle did her best to print the door handles of the wet car, then had it towed.

"How'd you find it?" asked Kyle, and Carlisle filled her in.

"How long?" asked Kincaid.

"Give me some time to jimmy the lock and do the preliminary stuff."

It was after ten when they drove back to the station to check in with Dr. Mallory. "The amount of blood loss and bruising around the wound means she definitely died from the gunshot and there are no other injuries except a few postmortem scrapes, possibly from transport. On X-ray, the bullet appears to be a twenty-two millimeter. Went in and just bounced around till her brain was mush. I'm going to open her up, do the usual inspection, but I don't expect any surprises. This was a very different killing than Aurora's."

"Right," said Carlisle. "Quick and cold."

"Food," said Carlisle when they'd left the morgue. They went to a nearby diner for bad coffee and greasy eggs and by the time they were finished, it was time to check in with Kyle.

They found her in a hangar-sized vehicle maintenance bay with another technician. When she saw them, she said, "Got it open," and waved them over. "Chang wasn't shot in there, but she was definitely moved in this car."

They took turns leaning down to inspect the low interior and both pulled back, grimacing. The passenger side seat, once the color of brown sugar, was now stained with blood and brain matter, the smell of decay thick.

"Someone loaded her into the passenger seat after she was shot. Head on the seat, body in the foot well. Then they drove to the Space Needle and left her for our tourist to find."

"It takes a lot of nerve to drive around town with a dead body in the seat next to you," said Kincaid.

"In a car the cops were looking for? That's reckless." She and Kincaid thought about that for a moment.

"Aurora's prints are all over the interior. Obviously," said Kyle. "And Chang didn't leave any prints, obviously. None of the surfaces seem to have been wiped down, so if the killer's prints aren't here, then he wore gloves."

"Got the phone?" asked Kincaid.

"Over here." She took them to a workbench half-covered in evidence bags. "Aurora's iPhone and the contents of her purse. Phone was definitely wiped down and I couldn't open it. You'll have to get the password or have a techie play with it. There are two hundred-dollar bills and a few credit cards in a gold money clip. A tube of lip gloss and a powder compact."

"That's it?" asked Kincaid.

"That's all that would fit." She pointed to a hard-cased clutch, not much bigger than a sunglass case, with bejeweled brass knuckles on top.

"What the hell is that?" asked Kincaid.

"It's a knuckle duster," said Carlisle.

Kincaid arched his brows. "Is it a purse? Is it a weapon?" He threw his hands up. "And how do you know what it is, Judy?"

"Where's her driver's license?" she asked, ignoring her partner.

"It's in the glove compartment, along with a hair brush, a tiny bottle of perfume, her registration and insurance card, and a pair of cat-eye sunglasses. Céline."

Kincaid pictured Aurora Stanhope winking above a pair of Marilyn Monroe sunglasses, blonde hair hanging loose, wicked little grin, hand wrapped in the brass knuckles of her purse. "She was kind of a playgirl."

"Yes, she was," Carlisle agreed.

"I'm done with the purse and its contents, so you can take them with you; the rest is going to take a little while longer."

"What about the stuff in the glove box?" asked Kincaid.

"Haven't dusted it yet. "

Kyle didn't have much else at that point, so the detectives drove back to headquarters to go through Aurora's phone.

"When's your lunch with Pamela and her country club friend?"

"Evelyn. Tomorrow." Carlisle scowled. "I don't know what you did, Kincaid, but Pamela seems to have taken a sudden interest in my job."

"I think you just never talked to her about what you do. You sold her short."

"Sold her short?"

"Pamela's interested. You saw her light up last night when she got to pitch in."

"She got to gossip."

"Hey, we *depend* on gossip."

She looked at him skeptically. "So you solved two decades of mother-in-law rivalry with a five-minute coffee klatch in my kitchen?" She smiled. "You know it won't last."

"No." He grinned. "But it'll get you through this visit."

"You're my hero."

When they were back at their desks, Kincaid got the phone out and said, "Before we send this to the techies, let's take a shot on our own."

Carlisle agreed. They tried the kids' birthdays, the Stanhopes' wedding anniversary, Robert's birthday, Aurora's birthday. Finally, Carlisle dialed Robert Stanhope's cell phone. No answer, so she tried Caroline who answered on the second ring.

Annie Chang's murder had been on the local news that morning, but Carlisle didn't give Caroline any more details. Even when she got pissy. She told her they would need to speak to the family again that day. Then she asked about the password and listened to Caroline complain about another police visit while she went to find her father.

Pressing the receiver to her shoulder, Carlisle said in a low voice, "She's going to ask her father." A minute later, she hung up. "Zero-zero-zero-zero. Or nine-nine-nine-nine."

It was the former.

"Last communication was two text messages to Annie Chang at one o'clock and one-oh-four yesterday afternoon." Kincaid tapped the screen a few times. "Shit, Judy. You'd better take a look at this."

CHAPTER SEVENTEEN

B ETH WILLIAMS DID NOT HAVE an office as such. Her nonprofit rented a pretty nice conference room near the university for the times when she and her local employees needed to meet with prospective donors in a formal setting, but for the most part, everyone worked from home. Wherever that was. And what had begun as a sensible way to save on overhead for a start-up had turned into a permanent solution for a successful nonprofit comprised of people living in cities up and down the west coast.

Plus, Beth loved working from home. She had made a small office on the lower level of her house for her files and for times when she needed a quiet place to talk on the phone or when Henry was playing trucks and she wanted to keep an eye on him without hearing the rumbles and crashes. But for the most part, she took her laptop and cell phone from place to place as she made her way around the house.

Today, after Henry had gone to school, she'd parked herself at the kitchen island with the dregs of her coffee and a half-eaten bowl of Cheerios. She was still there at eleven when the alarm she'd set on her phone went off, reminding her to get ready for a lunch meeting in town.

Promptly at noon, she arrived at a pleasant but pompous little French bistro in Lower Queen Anne, ordered a lemonade and scanned the menu while she waited.

Two minutes later, when Missy Lombardi walked through the

front door, it was the click of her spiky heels on the parquet floor that drew Beth's attention away from the menu. Over the din of the other patrons Missy announced, in a low, almost masculine voice, "So sorry I'm late, Beth."

She wasn't really sorry, and she wasn't really late. But Beth didn't care either way because out of the blue, on Saturday afternoon, Missy had called and told her that she wanted to make a substantial personal contribution to her nonprofit. She could be late, she could be rude, she could eat with her toes, as long as she was giving the foundation money, Beth was on her side.

She stood to greet her.

Missy wore one of Chanel's iconic tweed suits in green and black with heavy gold and diamond jewelry. Her pretty face was pink from the chill autumn wind and her slightly over-inflated smile was redeemed by the most perfect button nose that Beth had ever seen. An inch shorter than Beth in three-inch heels made her just over five feet tall, and with tiny bones and white-blonde hair, she could have been Caroline Stanhope's body double.

When the waitress returned with Beth's lemonade, Missy ordered a glass of dry white wine and mussels in broth. She had obviously been here before and their server's warm "Welcome back" meant she was probably a more pleasant diner than Aurora.

In fact, this was the first time Beth had been with Missy Lombardi when Aurora wasn't also present and, over the next few minutes, the woman Beth had known as snide and pithy waxed eloquent about the weather, the wine and several items on the menu.

"You must have the *poisson en papillote*," she said. "Let's have a real meal, skip the ladies-who-lunch salad cliché."

Beth let her order for them both. They would start with the mussels, then the fish—today it was whole brook trout with Meyer lemon butter—roasted red potatoes and pan-seared asparagus for the table. "And we'll share a green salad," she said.

"Are you sure you won't have a glass of wine, Beth?"

She demurred. "You'd have to carry me home."

"One's my limit at lunchtime." She sipped. "Now, to business. Part of my family trust is an annual endowment to the charity of my choice." Beth was scrambling to remember Missy's maiden name. She should have Googled her this morning. But Missy said graciously, "Don't worry, Beth. I come from a long line of robber barons. The name isn't as important as the privilege it affords me. And one of those privileges is a discretionary pre-tax endowment, which, this year, I have decided to contribute to your nonprofit. I've done the research; my attorneys have done more research and it's settled." She slid a folded piece of eggshell stationary across the table.

Beth glanced uncomfortably from the paper to the woman sitting across from her. She wasn't sure what she was supposed to do.

"Open it."

Beth picked up the heavy cardstock and unfolded it. Inside, written in black calligraphy was a figure so much larger than Beth would ever have imagined that she nearly choked.

She looked up. Missy was grinning. "It's my pleasure and you deserve it. Your team is doing important work in India and I'm grateful to be able to contribute."

"Missy, this is incredible. I don't know what to say."

"You'll put it to good use, Beth. I have every faith in you." A busboy cleared the leftover broth and bowls of black shells from their white linen table and Beth was relieved to see that Missy had dripped as much as she had. "Now," said Missy as their waitress delivered the main course, "let's eat and you can tell me all about your little boy and life as a single mom in our fair city."

Beth was happy to sing for her supper. Missy's generosity and warmth had disarmed her, made her wonder if she had short-changed Missy in the past. When she'd taken Missy's call on

Friday, she hadn't been looking forward to sitting down to the same spiteful one-upmanship she'd always seen between Aurora and Missy. Not that it would have stopped her from accepting the invite. A contribution is a contribution, no matter what kind of asshole is offering it. But as it turned out, Missy Lombardi was good company.

She had met Henry once, a few years earlier at an Easter Egg Hunt at the country club. Aurora had invited Beth and Henry. "What a charmer!" she said now.

"He has his moments," Beth agreed.

Inevitably, the conversation turned, as it always did when she spent time with married country-club types, to Beth's relationship status. "I have to ask, Beth, are you dating?"

"Oh, here and there," she said, not so comfortable with this topic. "I don't have a lot of free time."

"You're quite a catch, Beth. You wouldn't have any trouble attracting an eligible bachelor."

Beth knew she was quite a catch, though she wasn't entirely sure what made her one. In any case, she'd had plenty of offers. She flashed on Detective Kincaid's twinkling blue eyes and bouncing red pompadour. She'd liked that detective. Right off the bat.

Though, if she ever saw him again, he would probably be coercing personal information or arresting her for murder. She pictured a windowless room, a blinding floodlight aimed at a single folding chair.

"Beth?" said Missy, amused. "I lost you for a second. You must be distracted by Aurora's murder. What an awful thing." But she was still smiling with one side of her mouth. Missy Lombardi had not limited herself to one glass of wine. She was now sipping her third glass and despite the big lunch and flourless chocolate raspberry ganache extravaganza she'd ordered for dessert, the wine seemed to be loosening her up.

"Have the police come to talk to you?" she asked.

"Saturday afternoon," said Beth.

"And what did they say?"

She gave a very abbreviated summary of her conversation with Detectives Carlisle and Kincaid two days earlier. "They just wanted to know why Aurora and I stopped working together."

Missy Lombardi's eyes flashed crystal clear and the smile vanished.

"And what did you tell them?"

Beth leveled her gaze on Missy. Not so tipsy after all. "I said that she and I agreed it was time to part ways, that we would do more good focusing our efforts in different arenas."

"Right," said Missy, her eyes losing focus again.

Beth wanted to ask whether the police had been to the Lombardi estate, but she didn't want to jeopardize the big fat donation check coming her way.

Finally, Missy signaled their waitress for the check and turned back to Beth. "I want you to know, Beth, that just because Aurora is gone, it doesn't mean that you don't have powerful friends in Seattle. Come to me if you need anything at all. And that includes a criminal defense lawyer if those two detectives get pushy."

Beth wondered briefly if Missy thought she'd killed Aurora. *Could be.* Then it occurred to her that Missy knew there were two detectives going around asking questions. Maybe they had been out to talk to the Lombardis. She dropped the train of thought. Didn't want to overthink that pile of money.

When they left the restaurant, a car was waiting out front for Missy. She slid elegantly into the back seat, giving Beth a little wave. "My lawyers will arrange everything this week." She suddenly looked at Beth with an uncomfortable familiarity, as if she knew her through and through. "And remember, Beth, anything you need."

Then she was gone.

Beth walked to her car, both exhilarated and disoriented,

wishing she could delete the last fifteen minutes of conversation. Missy's final glance had nearly made her skin crawl.

She couldn't and wouldn't say no to Missy's contribution. But it was hard to shake the feeling that Missy Lombardi wanted to step into the space that Aurora had vacated. That she would soon come calling for her again. So soon after Aurora's murder, an offer of friendship and aegis had felt like an oddly intimate overture from a woman Beth hardly knew.

She got into her car and checked the dashboard clock. Time to pick up Henry at school.

CHAPTER EIGHTEEN

L ATE MONDAY MORNING LUCAS STANHOPE had been sitting at the dining room table with a pot of coffee and his laptop, watching a news story about Annie Chang's murder. There were no details, just that she was found by the Space Needle.

His phone rang and Caroline announced that they would all need to be questioned about Annie at the house that day.

"When?" he asked, feeling sick to his stomach.

"I don't know, just get over here as soon as you can."

Lucas promised to head over within the hour but it was a few minutes before he made any effort to move.

Eventually he stood, stretched and went to his room to pack a bag. He was going to stay at the big house tonight.

When he arrived, Lucas found Caroline reading a book by the fireplace in the great room. Two men he'd never seen before stood on the dock by the boathouse. "Who are they?" he asked after kissing his sister on the cheek.

"They're going to dry dock the boat."

"Where's Kevin?"

"I told Kevin we didn't need him."

"Why? Wasn't he almost finished for the season?"

"Yes, he was."

"Why did you let him go early?"

"Because he was fucking our mother."

Lucas's jaw dropped. He looked around to make sure their father wasn't in the room. "What the hell are you talking about?"

"Those detectives told me when they came to my place yesterday."

"You didn't think to mention it last night?"

"I was still processing," she said, strangely circumspect.

He sat in a chair facing her. "Does Dad know?"

"*I* certainly didn't tell him." She sat up and tucked her legs underneath a blanket. "But that doesn't mean he doesn't know." She shrugged. "He's got to know she fucked around on him."

Lucas thought to protest, but what was the point? "I'm sorry, Caroline."

"For what?"

"About Mom and Kevin. I had no idea."

They sat for a few minutes in mutual disappointment for their mother. Then Caroline said, "I don't think *she* knew that Kevin and I had gone out."

"Does that make it better?"

"Ever so slightly." She went to the bar and pulled a bottle of water from the refrigerator. "But it probably wouldn't have mattered. She was a total narcissist, Lucas. Everything she did was to suit herself. Everything."

His sister's tone was flat but he could see rage in her eyes. He noticed how she was dressed: pink cashmere sweater and pinstriped trousers, tan leather boots. With her hair tucked up into some sort of twist, she looked just like their mother. But smaller. It was creepy.

"How's Dad doing?" Lucas asked uncomfortably.

"He's going to be fine, Lucas. Everything is going to be fine." She walked to the French doors and stood staring through the glass. Lucas got up to find his father.

Taking the back stairs two at a time, he hurried to his father's rooms on the second floor, knocked but didn't get a response, opened the door. The sitting room was empty and so was the unmade bed. He checked the bathroom, the dressing room, finally looking through the balcony doors. Robert Stanhope stood at the railing in his shirtsleeves, wind billowing the wet broadcloth at his back.

"Dad?"

His father turned, cheeks and forehead red from the cold, damp hair hanging low on his brow, but he didn't look sad. Robert Stanhope's face was twisted with anger.

The expression vanished so quickly that Lucas wondered if he had seen it at all.

"Come inside, Dad."

Once he'd gotten his father's promise to change clothes and come downstairs for lunch, Lucas went to the kitchen. Unloading yesterday's deli cartons onto the counter, he stuck spoons in each and called it a buffet.

Caroline came in from the great room and frowned at the cartons, but didn't say anything. "Where's Dad?"

"He said he would come down." Already regretting his promise to stay, Lucas wished he could leave this house. He was angry. And sad. And sick of them all. He hadn't been prepared for Caroline's revelation, or the look on his father's face as he stood dripping on the balcony, or the agony of breaking bread with these two raging, lost souls.

When his father came down the tension in the room shot up a few notches. He was dressed in dry clothes and he had toweled his hair. Eyes bright and clear, and empty. He greeted his children with a nod and filled a plate from which he started eating before he even got to the table.

After a few bites, he said, "Caroline, will you make arrangements for another live-in? I don't want you to have to worry about meals."

"Of course." They had another woman come in to do the heavy

cleaning, but in addition to constantly tidying up, Mrs. Chang had taken care of meals, morning coffee, bedtime snacks, and all of the household details from stocking the bar to accepting deliveries to berating the gardener when he took too many breaks, and Robert Stanhope didn't want to go too long without a replacement.

"Will you be able to train someone new?"

"I'll take care of everything, Daddy."

"I called Jim. He can be here whenever we need him. Have you heard back from those detectives about when they're coming?" When Caroline shook her head, he frowned. "Well, I suppose it doesn't matter. Are they coming to ask us about Mrs. Chang or your mother or both? Both," he answered his own question.

After lunch Caroline went back to her book, Robert Stanhope disappeared upstairs and Lucas collected his bag from where he'd left it in the front hall, went to his room and fell asleep.

Steve Lombardi's attorney had been putting them off all day.

Carlisle hit end on her phone and looked at her partner in exasperation.

"Steve called Aurora at eleven-fifty-five on the night she was murdered. We need to talk to him. God, that man is so smug. I wish we could just haul him in and rough him up a little."

"It's not enough to arrest him, Judy."

She rolled her eyes. "I know that. We have to get him to come in on his own or we have to find more evidence and he's been dicking us around *all day.*"

"Look," said Kincaid, "we have to talk to the Stanhopes today and they want their lawyer present, so let's set that up and then check in with Kyle and see if she has anything for us. Maybe Lombardi left a print in the car."

"Even if he did," said Carlisle, "we don't have his prints on file.

In fact, none of the players' prints are on file, *except* our victim, which isn't helpful to us anyway."

Kincaid made the call. Three-thirty at the Stanhope estate. They walked to the lab and found Kyle in the hallway, tapping on her phone with one hand and eating a very dry-looking sandwich with the other.

"Yum," said Kincaid.

She dropped the phone into a pocket of her lab coat, tossing the rest of her sandwich into a trash can. "Day-old peanut butter and jelly."

"My partner is teetering on the edge," said Kincaid. "Please tell me you have something for us."

They followed her into the lab, where she washed her hands and opened a window on her oversized computer screen. "I found several sets of prints that don't belong to either of our victims, at least one set from a man, but they're not in the database, so you'll have to find the owners on your own."

"Of course," said Carlisle in disgust.

"Yeah, sorry," said Kyle. "Also, I found more hair. Mostly blonde. Several strands are shorter than Aurora's, but there are dozens of reasons that explain the different lengths. Still, we'll have them tested for DNA."

"DNA only helps us if we ever make an arrest," said Carlisle. "First we need to get a defendant into the courtroom." She looked at Kincaid. "Caroline has light-blonde hair, Missy Lombardi too."

"The prints might help rule some people out. Or in."

"If we can get them," said Carlisle. None of this was improving her attitude.

"What about the family? Surely they let you print them."

"I don't think their attorney will let us print them." She looked at her partner. "Actually, Lucas asked about getting printed."

"Yes, he did," said Kincaid.

"Lucas," said Kyle.

"Yeah," said Kincaid. "He wanted to know if *you* would be the one taking his prints." He smiled. "And Carlisle told him that your entire team would have to come down with West Nile disease before that happened."

"Aha," said Kyle. "And now? Now you're thinking it won't take West Nile?"

"If you could convince him," said Carlisle, "maybe the other two would agree."

In the car ten minutes later, Kincaid said, "Try for DNA too."

"Right. How am I supposed to do that?"

"Just, you know," said Carlisle, "whip out your swabs like it's nothing and if he protests say something like, 'Oh, Lucas, I guess I thought we were doing DNA too, but if you don't want to...' wink, wink."

"What?"

"Flirt with him."

"Is *that* how you flirt, Judy?"

"You know what I mean," said Carlisle. "He likes you—take advantage of that."

"Is this okay with you?" said Kincaid.

Kyle smiled. "Absolutely," she said, then asked, "Do they know you're bringing me?"

"Seemed better not to mention it," said Kincaid. "Right now, we have no leverage and they've been really cooperative, but they're a family with money and power and one of the best attorneys in Seattle who's not going to let us slip anything past him. If it doesn't work, fine, but it's worth a shot."

They spent the rest of the drive filling Kyle in on the investigation. When they made the turn into the Stanhopes' drive, Carlisle asked, "Have you been here before?"

"A couple of times. Lucas was staying at his parents' for winter break when we met."

"But you never met his family?"

"No. The sister went with his parents to St. Bart's or somewhere after Christmas. I had a roommate, so." She left it at that.

"So, you had the run of the place," said Kincaid.

They parked, went to the front door and waited. Eventually, Robert Stanhope opened the door looking grim.

"Come in." He didn't seem to notice that there were three of them as they followed him to the great room. "Were you able to access my wife's phone?" he asked, but didn't seem interested in the answer.

They walked through the wide doorway and turned toward the group of people by the fireplace. Lucas said, "Kyle."

Stanhope glanced over at Kyle, indifferent, but Thorpe inserted himself between his clients and the newcomer.

"You know her?" Caroline asked, lips curled in a scowl.

Carlisle stepped in and made the introductions.

"And why, Detectives, did you bring a crime scene technician to a friendly meeting?" asked Thorpe.

"We're hoping the Stanhopes will give us fingerprints, Mr. Thorpe. For elimination purposes only."

"We both know what that means" he said coolly. "

Carlisle didn't react. "We found Aurora's car and handbag this morning and it's full of hair and prints that don't belong to Mrs. Stanhope. We need to find out if any of them came from someone who had no business being in that car."

"You found the Porsche?" asked Caroline. "Is that where she was killed?"

"Jesus Christ," said Stanhope and slumped into a leather chair.

Lucas was still staring at Kyle. Caroline was still waiting for an answer.

Finally, Thorpe put a hand up. "You should have contacted me about this beforehand, Detectives."

"Hey," said Lucas. "What happened to Annie Chang?" It was

the first time anyone had mentioned the murdered housekeeper and it silenced the rest of the family.

Kincaid gave them the abridged version, but didn't mention that she had been transported in Aurora's car.

"Yesterday afternoon, Mrs. Chang got a text from Mrs. Stanhope's cell phone asking her to come in for a few hours. The text indicated that in the aftermath of her death, the family needed some extra help. She agreed to come in at two o'clock."

Before anyone could respond, Thorpe said, "The Stanhopes have no knowledge of any such request and Mrs. Chang has not been to the house since Saturday. I understand you spoke to both Caroline and Lucas at their homes yesterday afternoon. Caroline arrived here shortly after three-thirty, Lucas joined them for dinner in the evening and Robert was here the entire day. I hope you're not suggesting that a family grieving for the loss of a wife and mother, a family, I'll add, who has gone out of their way to accommodate you even against the advice of counsel," he shot the Stanhope children a sharp look, "an upstanding family in the Seattle community who should be grieving," his voice had reached its crescendo, "that this family," he gestured with a sweeping motion that included the three remaining Stanhopes, "had anything to do with the murder of their *maid.*"

Kincaid rolled his eyes. "We're not in court, Mr. Thorpe. We're just here to see whether the Stanhopes can help us make sense of Mrs. Chang's murder."

"You're fishing."

"We're just trying to figure out who killed Mrs. Stanhope and what Chang has to do with it."

"*And* get elimination prints," said Thorpe irritably.

"And hair samples," said Kincaid.

"*And hair samples?*"

"For Christ's sake, Jim, let's just answer their questions," said Lucas.

Thorpe looked at Robert Stanhope, who nodded. "Fine, have a seat," he said.

Kyle remained standing, doing her best not to look awkward. This was the first time she'd ever been included in a witness interview and she wasn't sure of her place. Then Lucas stood. "Kyle," he said and indicated his chair, taking a coffee cup from the low table next to it and going to sit next to his sister on one of the Chesterfields. "You can set your bag on the table."

Kyle took the seat, nodded at Lucas with a professional smile and tried to look more confident than she felt.

The detectives asked standard questions: had Mrs. Chang been behaving differently lately, how close was she to Mrs. Stanhope, had the family had any contact with her after she left on Saturday, was it possible that someone who worked at the house, or made deliveries to the house, would have had a grudge against either victim, and so on.

"You mean, like the gardener or the guy who delivers groceries?" asked Caroline. "How would we know?"

"Maybe your mom said something to you? Or to you, Mr. Stanhope?" said Carlisle.

Stanhope shook his head. "I really have no idea. Aurora took care of those things."

"Perhaps you can make us a list of your service providers?" asked Carlisle gently.

"Of course." He frowned. "Is there any chance that this is all about Mrs. Chang and that my wife was... you know."

"Collateral damage?" said Carlisle, understanding why he couldn't. "We'll certainly look into that, Mr. Stanhope."

When they had exhausted that line of questioning without learning anything new, Carlisle said, "Let's move on. Do any of you know why Mrs. Stanhope was having dinner with Steve Lombardi on Friday night?"

Lucas looked like he'd been sideswiped. Caroline let out a disgusted breath.

Robert Stanhope was furious. His jaw tightened and he bolted out of his chair.

Thorpe said, "None of the Stanhopes has any comment about that dinner."

"Understood," said Carlisle. "But can any of you shed some light on her relationship with Lombardi?"

"Enough!" Stanhope was clutching the edge of the bar and glaring at Carlisle. "Take your prints and leave. Caroline will make a list of service people and you can start asking if any of them killed my wife." He turned to Kyle. "How do we do this?"

After that, Thorpe kept a tight lid on the questions, and an eagle eye on Kyle, who had set up shop at the bar. Once she'd finished printing Stanhope, she pulled an oral swab kit from her bag and when Thorpe looked like he would intercede, said quickly, "Your DNA will help us a lot, Mr. Stanhope."

"Dad, please," said Lucas.

Kyle took prints, took swabs, and after Robert Stanhope had stormed off and Caroline had retired to her room, Lucas took his turn and the mood around the bar grew decidedly more intimate. Thorpe was sitting with the detectives around the fireplace, doing his best to glean more information about the investigation. The detectives, for their part, were trying to glean more information about the Stanhopes.

———◆———

Kyle was quiet on the drive back to Cherry Street while Carlisle and Kincaid plotted their next few moves.

When they arrived at the station, she headed to the lab with her new samples and they went to their desks. Kincaid called Lombardi's attorney again and left another message with his secretary.

"What do you think?" asked Carlisle.

"About Robert Stanhope? Aurora and Steve Lombardi? First sign of anger. And he's pissed."

"Good thing I didn't ask if he knew who she'd had sex with that night."

"Might've sent him over the edge."

She rolled her eyes. "He knows she was sleeping around. He knows exactly what it means that his wife was dining with Lombardi. He's outraged. Maybe he killed her. Have we heard back from the airlines?"

"Thursday, Stanhope flew to Portland on Delta and Saturday at eight in the morning he flew back."

"It's what? Two and a half, three hours' drive from Portland to Seattle. He could've driven home, killed her, dumped her, stuck her car somewhere until he could move it and then gone straight back to Portland. Do we know where he stayed? We can get keycard records for his room."

"He stayed in a corporate apartment. No keycard."

"Damn."

Kincaid's phone rang and while he talked, Carlisle called Mallory. They both got off at the same time. And spoke at the same time. "You go first," said Carlisle.

"That was one of the massage therapists at Aurora's country club. She has some information for us."

"When?"

"Hour, Capitol Hill."

"That gives us enough time to talk to Mallory and fight rush hour."

Dr. Mallory was in his office when they arrived at the morgue, studying a framed photograph. When they came in he turned it to face them. A recent picture of Mrs. Mallory, big smile, as Dr. Mallory laid a kiss on her cheek.

"I don't know what I'd do without her." Mrs. Mallory was about the same age as Mrs. Stanhope and Mrs. Chang. Put the three side by side and that was probably the only thing they had in common, but Carlisle got the point.

"Too close to home?" asked Carlisle.

"Don't know what I'd do without her," he repeated. "Two men prematurely widowed in as many days."

"Before you get too sentimental," said Carlisle, "one of those men may have widowed himself."

"*Touché*," he said. "Well, no surprises with Chang. She died of the gunshot wound to her head. No signs of pre- or peri-mortem injury. Time of death was probably between noon and four yesterday afternoon."

"We've got a text sent at one that says she planned on being at the Stanhopes' home on Lake Washington at two," said Kincaid.

"Did she make it?"

"Stanhopes say no."

He made a note. "So, time of death between one and four. She was in the car long enough to develop some livor mortis in that position, but it really got started in the park. She was probably out there for a few hours before our tourist found her."

He flipped a page in the chart he'd been consulting. "I removed the bullet. Definitely a twenty-two caliber, bounced around in her skull. Would've killed her instantly. I sent the bullet to ballistics two hours ago. Kyle will get the results when they come through." He looked up at them. "Pretty straightforward assassination. I'm sorry I don't have much for you."

"Fair enough," said Carlisle.

"Do you think it was the same killer?"

"Probably," she said, "though it's a very different kind of death."

"A lot of rage with Stanhope," Mallory reiterated his earlier observation, "nothing here but cold efficiency."

They left him and drove to a soup and sandwich place in Capitol Hill.

"What's her name?" asked Carlisle from the passenger seat.

"Kelly."

"Kelly what?"

He grinned. "Kelly Deepthroat."

"She wouldn't give you a last name? Doesn't she know we can find it in ten seconds?"

"Apparently not." He winked. "Kelly Sorenson, twenty-seven, brown, brown, five-foot-four, no criminal record."

Kelly was already there when they arrived. Introducing themselves, Carlisle nodded at her lidded paper cup. "Would you like anything else?" She wouldn't, so Carlisle went to get coffees for herself and Kincaid.

Kincaid sat down. "Thanks for getting in touch, Kelly. We need all the information we can get to solve this case." He asked a few mundane questions about her work at the club until Carlisle came back with drinks and then they got down to the nitty-gritty.

"Lance Bremer." They waited. "He's one of the pro tennis coaches at the club. You know. Made the circuits, wasn't good enough to be a real champ, and those who can't..." She looked at them expectantly. "Teach. Anyway, Lance was sleeping with Mrs. Stanhope."

"Really?" said Kincaid.

"Really," she said lasciviously. "I don't know how long it had been going on—at least six months—but when it was over, she switched coaches, which didn't look good for Lance."

"She'd been sleeping with her tennis coach for the last six months?" he asked, wanting to clarify.

"No, they broke it off last spring."

"Ah," said Kincaid, "and you think Lance was angry about it?"

"I *know* he was because I overheard them arguing about it in the spa. He said that she was making a mistake and she said that she *never* made mistakes. He had her by the arm and she shook him off and said that he'd lost *those* privileges and that if he couldn't get over it, then he didn't belong at the club anyway and she would have him fired." Deep breath. "*Then* he said that he never knew she was such a bitch and she laughed and said it wasn't personal, she was just tired of him, or bored with him—something like that." She stopped, didn't go on.

"And?" asked Carlisle.

"And then he just walked away. Stormed off. And she went to change for her massage. Not with me, with Sven."

"You have a masseuse named Sven?" asked Kincaid.

"*Masseur*," she corrected. "No, but that's what we call him because he's tall and blonde and the women at the club love him.

"What do you think Mrs. Stanhope meant when she said that Lance didn't belong at the club if he couldn't get over it?"

Her eyes flashed and she let out a mean chuckle. "She meant that if he thought an affair with a club member was anything more than that, then he should get his head out of his ass."

Carlisle studied the young woman. She was clean cut with a healthy, athletic body, broad, flat chest, strong arms and shoulders under a white cotton turtleneck. Her brown hair was all one length and pulled back into a two-inch ponytail and her face was very, very plain. She asked, "Is that sort of thing common at the club? Members sleeping with the staff?"

She shrugged. "Not really, but it happens. I mean, there's a strict policy against it, *plus*," she laughed, "you'd have a lot of angry husbands and wives dropping their memberships if it happened a lot."

"So, Mrs. Stanhope and Lance should've been pretty discreet?" Kelly nodded. "Arguing in the spa seems kind of careless, doesn't it? Was the argument you overheard the first you knew of their affair?"

"Well, no, I suspected something."

"What made you suspect?"

"Just the way they were together."

"Kelly," said Carlisle, "what's your relationship with Lance Bremer?"

Turning red, she said defensively, "I just work with him."

"Will that be the answer Lance gives us when we ask him?"

"You're not going to tell Lance I talked to you?"

"Will that be his answer, Kelly?"

She looked down. "We had a thing."

"When?"

"Last year."

"Before Mrs. Stanhope came along? Is that why he ended it with you?"

"No! And there was nothing *to* end. A bunch of us went out after work and got drunk. It was just once. Anyway, that's not why I'm telling you about Lance. He's hated Mrs. Stanhope ever since, always bitching about her when we're all at the bar. He can't believe she went with a different coach and he's not surprised that she was shitty to the new cocktail waitress and wasn't it about time she got a boob lift, and so on. Typical rejection backlash."

"Did he ever talk to the other staff members about their affair?"

"Oh no," she said vehemently. "It was bad enough that she dumped him as a coach. Lance's ego is way too big to admit that she dumped him as her boy toy. Besides, if anyone blabbed to management, he'd get fired."

They questioned Kelly Sorenson for a few more minutes and when she'd left, Kincaid went back to the counter for sustenance and more coffee.

Over corn chowder and a BLT, they discussed Kelly's revelations. "She might be spiteful, but I think she was telling the truth," said Carlisle.

"Could give *her* a motive to kill Aurora."

"A year after the fact? And why would she kill Mrs. Chang? I don't think so."

"What about Lance?" said Kincaid. "And—*Lance*? A tennis pro at a country club named *Lance*? Didn't those preppy names go out of style with the eighties? I feel like we're in an episode of *Murder, She Wrote.*"

"Jessica Fletcher would have this case done and dusted by now."

"We'll have to talk to Lance." Kincaid pulled out his phone. "Let me see what I can find." He pulled Bremer's records, checked with the DMV, scribbled something in his notepad. "Two unpaid parking tickets. I've got an address; let's pay him a visit."

They finished their soup, brought the trays to a trash can and headed to Lance Bremer's apartment in the University District. "Another lover living in the vicinity of the dump site?" said Carlisle. "Coincidence?"

"Or just an indication of Aurora's penchant for young men," said Kincaid. "Only time will tell."

Lance Bremer lived in a decent condo at the back of the building. He buzzed them through the security door without asking who was there and answered his door in jeans and a polo shirt that showed off his muscles.

"Who are you?" He looked surprised.

Kincaid pulled out his badge. "Homicide. We want to talk to you about Aurora Stanhope."

His jaw clenched. "I don't know anything about that."

Carlisle saw the wallet in his hand. "Expecting dinner? Let's get this over with before your pizza arrives."

He stepped back from the door and led them to a dining room set straight from the low-end side of the Ikea showroom. He was tall and strong but not bulky with sun-streaked blond hair, blue eyes and skin still tanned from a long summer on the tennis courts. He looked like a Lance. "I don't know anything," he repeated and sprawled in an armchair.

Kincaid didn't like him. "How long had you been sleeping with her?"

"Hey, I was just her tennis coach."

"Right," said Kincaid. "let me lay it out for you. We know

you were sleeping with her, we know that she dumped you in the bedroom. We know that she dumped you on the tennis court. We also know that you were pissed about it. Two days ago, Aurora Stanhope was murdered by someone who was also pissed and we're here to rule you in or out. The quicker you accept those facts, the faster we can get out of your hair. Unless you did it, of course. 'Cause if you did it, you just landed in the middle of a life-long shit storm."

Lance started talking.

CHAPTER NINETEEN

KYLE RAN THE PRINTS; ALL four Stanhopes had been in the Porsche at some point. No surprise there. Who wouldn't want a ride in a shiny white racecar? She had identified and labeled several different hair samples and marked them for DNA testing if they ever got a viable suspect—the city probably wouldn't spring for a fishing expedition.

In the meantime, she checked the hair samples under a microscope; they all matched but one—a blonde hair she'd found in the hinge of Aurora's sunglasses. She labeled it and put it with the others, making a note to mention it to the detectives.

Ballistics had come back and the bullet had probably been fired from a Ruger revolver, but it didn't match anything they had in the system.

Mid-afternoon and she was done for the day.

Mark had already sent her two text messages. He wanted to meet for a drink and she couldn't go, needed a few days with this case and a few days to consider her past relationship with Lucas and whether it was at all relevant now. Carlisle and Kincaid were going to grill her at some point, and she wanted to have an opinion ready beforehand.

She hadn't sent Mark a reply because she wanted to go, was trying to think of a way to fit him in between now and bright and early tomorrow morning.

But Lucas was in the way. She gave up, called Mark, made a date for the weekend and hopped in her car.

———— ┥■━□┝ ————

Home at last, showered and dried, stirring frozen peas and carrots and a generous squirt of sriracha into a pot of boiling ramen noodles, Kyle was warm and comfy in a well-worn hoodie and shearling slippers. But not quite relaxed. The memory of Lucas Stanhope's hand in hers, the way he'd looked at her, spoken to her, left Kyle unsettled.

Good thing she'd been wearing latex gloves. She did not want to remember the feeling of his skin on hers. Because, although skin on skin had been the best thing they'd had going for them, the physical stuff was at complete odds with the sentiment.

Theirs had not been a good break-up. And after today, Kyle wasn't even sure Lucas realized it.

The afternoon at his house had been bizarre. Walking past the dining room table where they'd had sex, into the great room where they'd had lots of sex. And there he was. Sitting on the sofa upon which they had also had lots of sex.

When it had been his turn for prints and samples, she had said while opening a cheek swab, "I'm really sorry about your mom, Lucas. Open."

He had smiled first, then gave her a sad look and opened wide. "You look wonderful," he'd said tentatively while she took his prints, and she hid her cringe at the tenderness she knew was false.

Then his big hand had wrapped around hers and one finger had awkwardly sought the bare skin above her wrist and she'd nearly jumped. "I want to see you, Kyle, and I know now isn't the right time, but maybe when this is over..." He had left it at that but had stared into her eyes for far too long before Kyle broke her gaze away and began repacking her equipment.

In the past few hours, she had relived the moment dozens of

times. Felt the same repulsion that had been there when they'd broken up. Even years later, grown up and over it, she didn't want him near her. Those feelings usually faded, but with Lucas they seemed to have intensified. Maybe it was the circumstance. Murder didn't put a pretty spin on anything.

She thought about their break-up. An event previously filed neatly in a clean slot in her emotional history labeled, *better off.*

She thought of Mark. No reluctance there.

Still, she didn't know if what she was feeling was just in her head, or a grown-up response to what'd happened six years ago. A weekend in San Diego, Lucas so full of himself she could hardly stand him. Lucas, standing on a bar table announcing he was god. Getting kicked out, the bartender assuming he'd had too much to drink. Kyle knowing he'd had exactly one beer.

At one point, he had thrown her on the bed, holding her down, tickling her maniacally. She hadn't been able to move. Panic had taken over and she'd fought hard while he'd howled with laughter. Then, just like that, he'd let her go—distracted by something else.

Later, finding him on the bathroom floor, scared of his own shadow, calling an ambulance.

He'd obviously had a breakdown of some sort. Not his fault. Right?

She didn't know how Carlisle and Kincaid would interpret it. Didn't want them to grill Lucas about his mental health. Didn't know if she should just tell them anyway.

Kyle decided that if they asked, she would tell them and they could judge. Otherwise, she'd just see what happened in the investigation.

Settled.

She poured the entire pot of noodles and broth into a big bowl, grabbed a fork, a spoon and, optimistically, a set of wooden chopsticks still wrapped from her last take-out. Then two—no, three—paper towels.

Kyle took her dinner to the coffee table in her living room, sat cross-legged on the floor and pulled up Lucas's Instagram page on her laptop.

———————

Lance's pizza arrived, cooling on the table while Lance Bremer sang.

He admitted to having an affair with Aurora, admitted to being angry when she broke it off, but vehemently denied hurting her in any way.

"What was in it for you?" asked Kincaid.

"What do you mean?"

"I mean, did she buy you things, pay your rent? Why were you sleeping with a rich, married woman a quarter century older than you?"

Lance was offended. "Hey, man, I'm not a gigolo. I didn't get anything. Not even dinner in nice restaurants because she wouldn't be seen in public with me." He scowled, sniffled. "Aurora was exquisite. I mean, I couldn't resist her. Gave me these looks across the court like she knew everything about me. Like a cat. Laid out the rules and told me I could take it or leave it." He sighed. "Such a bitch." His eyes widened. "But I did *not* kill her."

"Why did she end it?"

"I don't know. She didn't even bother to make up a reason." He looked for sympathy, got none. "I asked. She just gave me a patronizing smile."

Kincaid thought that sounded about right. "So, she dumped you and didn't even bother to tell you why? Just like that, she didn't want you anymore. And then she fired you? A quarter century older than you and she just doesn't want you anymore? That's humiliating, man." Kincaid smiled. "Embarrassing."

Bremer's cheeks were dangerously red. "You should be talking to her husband."

"Oh?" said Kincaid.

"Aurora flirted with everyone and I'm sure that if she was fucking around with me, she was fucking around with other guys too."

"Like Sven, the masseur?" asked Kincaid.

He rolled his eyes. "Man, his name is Mike and he's gay. But she flirted with him anyway. And the bartenders and the other coaches, but the one who really pissed off Stanhope was Steve Lombardi. They used to all play doubles and I swear, Stanhope was shooting the ball straight at Lombardi's crotch."

"Robert and Aurora Stanhope played against Steve and Missy Lombardi?" asked Carlisle.

He looked relieved that they already knew the main characters. "Yeah. Huge rivalry."

"And Aurora flirted with Steve?"

"Way beyond flirting. There was something going on there."

Carlisle said, "So, it was okay to openly flirt with her friend's husband, in front of her own husband, but you didn't even get dinner and a movie?"

"Dude," said Bremer, "I was just the help."

CHAPTER TWENTY

AN HOUR LATER, KINCAID STOOD in front of his open fridge, contemplating. A grey paw reached out from the floor and he looked at his cat. "Hungry, Stan?" Pulling a carton of eggs and a block of Wisconsin cheddar cheese from the top shelf of the fridge, he set to work.

After they'd left Lance Bremmer, Carlisle had said, "Big bruised ego, but he didn't do it."

"Nah." Kincaid had agreed. "And if his alibi checks out we can sideline him." Bremer had claimed to be in Phoenix for a tennis match over the weekend. It would be easy to verify.

"Let's see if Kyle got anything and then call it a day. If something comes up we can head out again after dinner."

Kyle had already left for the day, but had sent them an email. She'd found some blonde hair that didn't belong to Aurora or Caroline. Ballistics were back. Ruger revolver, probably. Nothing that couldn't wait until tomorrow, so the detectives had gone to their respective homes.

While his eggs were cooking, Kincaid fed Stanley his kibble and cut up a fat tomato, dressing it with olive oil and kosher salt.

Bachelor's supper in one hand, cutlery in the other, he sat down at the dining room table with his cell phone and laptop and started eating. It had been a long day but Kincaid's mind was racing.

Where had Aurora Stanhope and Mrs. Chang been killed? They still hadn't found the primary crime scenes for either murder; they had no idea where Aurora had gone after dinner at Gigi's; they had no idea what had happened to Mrs. Chang on Sunday between one in the afternoon and landing under the Space Needle with a hole in her head.

He made a note to check in with Harry Cole, ask if he'd heard anything from the waitstaff at Gigi's, though it wasn't likely Aurora had been murdered by a disgruntled busboy. They kept hearing testimony that Robert Stanhope had not only been aware of his wife's infidelities, but that he had also been really angry about them. Not surprising, but their first take on him had been studied ignorance and blind adoration.

Still, despite being out of town, he'd had time to drive back from Portland and murder his wife, and he had the money to hire someone to do it—though the method said rage, not a professional.

And Chang? How had she gotten caught up in this? Was it possible she was complicit in Aurora's murder? That she had been a loose end?

Other than a worried voicemail from her husband, she hadn't received any calls or texts after the one requesting her services at the Stanhopes', so how had she detoured into the hands of her killer? Maybe she had gone to the Stanhopes. Maybe she had arrived and Caroline or Robert or both had taken her out. Maybe Lucas was lying about when he arrived at his father's house and the three of them had done it together. A family affair?

But *why?*

Tuesday morning was dreary but warm and balmy.

Carlisle and Kincaid were both at their desks by eight-thirty. They'd finally gotten a sit-down with Steve and Missy Lombardi in their lawyer's office and they had an hour to plan a strategy.

"I wish we could interview Missy on her own," said Carlisle. "I have a feeling if we bring up the affair between Aurora and her husband, Buccio will throw us out." She peered inside her coffee cup and walked off to get more. When she came back, Kincaid was eyeing her.

"What?"

"I can see your legs."

"So what?" She rolled her eyes. "Today is lunch with my mother-in-law and her country club friend. Pamela made me wear a dress."

"Did she take you shopping?"

"For your information, this was hanging in my closet next to many other dresses." Carlisle was wearing a gabardine sheath dress the color of ripe plums and grey suede heels that matched her grey flannel suit jacket.

"Are you wearing a necklace?"

"Jesus, Kincaid, is this the first time you looked at me today? Not very observant for an ace detective."

"Did you let Pamela pick out your outfit?"

"Maybe. The only thing she criticized today was my hair." She pointed to the dark blonde mess she had tucked into a short ponytail.

Now her partner's eyes went wide. "Earrings? Are those diamond studs?"

"Half-carat," she said. "I did borrow these from Pam."

"*Never* call her Pam," said Kincaid, checking out her legs again. "You should wear a dress more often."

"*Anyway*," said Carlisle, "while I appreciate the attention—especially from you—"

"What does that mean?" said Kincaid with a happy gleam in his eyes.

"It means you spend more time at the tailors than Pamela."

"No reason to waste this physique on an ill-fitting suit."

"Can we get back to it?" she asked impatiently.

Kincaid acquiesced. "We have to ask about the affair. It's the whole reason we're talking to Missy Lombardi."

"What I don't get," said Carlisle, "is why Steve wants to talk in front of his wife. He knows we're going to ask about the affair and he knows we're going to ask about dinner on Friday night. Is he that big an asshole that he doesn't care what she hears?"

"Probably, but he also knows she'd find out anyway. We would've talked to her eventually and we would have asked if she knew about the dinner. He's a lawyer; he knows the play."

"I guess so, but why discuss it in front of her?" She shook her head. "The big issue is going to be how fast Ronny Buccio throws us out of his office."

"We'll have to play real nice." Kincaid's cell phone rang. "It's Harry Cole," he said, brows raised.

Carlisle went back to her internet search of Missy Lombardi. When Kincaid was off the phone, she said, "We thought the Stanhopes were rich, but Missy Lombardi puts them to shame."

"Family money?"

"*Big* money. Warren Buffet money."

"What about Steve?"

"He's no slouch—he makes a lot of money at his firm, but he's no Arabian prince." She looked at him. "Did Harry get anything?"

"He said he asked around. The waitresses all agreed that Aurora was a pain in the ass, the waiters all agreed she was a flirt, but he didn't detect anything suspicious."

"What about Friday night? Does anyone remember anything strange?"

"He said the most memorable thing that happened Friday night was that the bartender got some lady's wedding ring as a tip."

"A wedding ring? Did she have a fight with her husband?"

"She was alone with her iPhone."

"Jesus. That's some tip. I bet she'll be back for it."

"Harry said they put it in the safe. Evidently that's not the first time a woman has handed over her valuables to get back at her husband. He said that last month, a lady gave her floor-length mink coat to the hostess. Her husband came back for it twenty minutes later."

Carlisle laughed incredulously. "I'm so lucky to have Tom."

"And Tom is lucky to have you," he said. "Now let's get going."

------■-■-□-■------

Promptly at nine-thirty, Carlisle and Kincaid announced themselves to the receptionist at Ronny Buccio's law firm. Twenty minutes later, they were shown to his corner office.

Buccio wasn't actually handsome, but he was compelling. Thick, very dark brown hair about two inches too long for a white-collar criminal attorney, brown eyes surrounded by smile lines, a healthy flush of self-satisfaction. As he approached with his hand out he took a second to give Carlisle the once-over.

No introduction was necessary. Ronny Buccio knew every detective in Seattle PD.

"Detective Carlisle. Good knees," he said with a wink. "Kincaid." He introduced them to Missy. "You've already met Mr. Lombardi."

They all sat around a small conference table. Buccio said, "Ask your questions."

"Thank you for taking the time," said Carlisle, looking at Missy, ignoring her husband's smug smile. "First, a few routine questions." She asked them about Aurora Stanhope: how long had they known her, did they know her husband, children, did they spend time at her house, did they know whether anything was bothering her lately.

"When was the last time you saw or spoke to Aurora?" she asked.

Missy looked at their attorney who nodded at her. She said,

"The week before last. At a planning meeting for a silent auction benefiting the Humane Society."

"Did you talk to her?" asked Carlisle.

"Only to say hello. There were ten of us and we spent an hour or so discussing menu options, high-end donations for the silent auction, how many attendees we were each responsible for. That kind of thing. Just business."

"Mrs. Lombardi, how long have you known Aurora Stanhope?"

She looked at the ceiling, apparently thinking back. "We met in our first year of college. We were pledging the same sorority."

"And did you consider Mrs. Stanhope your friend?"

Missy smiled ruefully. "At times. But there was an underlying competitiveness that kept us from ever becoming close."

"So, frenemies?."

With an arched brow, Missy said, "Sometimes competition creates a stronger bond than trust."

"But you weren't really friends, yet you've maintained a relationship all these years?"

"I may not have liked her, and she certainly wasn't the person I would turn to in a crisis. She did terrible things," she said, throwing a meaningful glance at her husband, "but, for whatever backward psychological reason, I was glad she was in the world. And I'll miss her presence now."

Carlisle didn't buy it for a second. She turned to Steve. "What about you, Mr. Lombardi? You last saw Mrs. Stanhope on Friday night, correct?"

Lombardi shifted in his seat, pulled his gaze away from Carlisle's long legs. This time the glance that Missy threw him was baleful, but she wasn't surprised, neither by his leering nor his rendezvous with Aurora Stanhope. Steve had told his wife about the dinner. "Yes," he said without elaborating.

"What was the purpose?" asked Carlisle.

"Other than nourishment?" Carlisle didn't bother to respond. "I told you, we met to talk about a legal matter."

Carlisle played along. "What legal matter?"

"You know Mr. Lombardi can't violate client confidentiality," said Ronny Buccio.

"But she's dead," said Carlisle, still looking at Lombardi.

"Next question," said Buccio.

"Why schedule a business meeting on a Friday night at a romantic restaurant?" she asked.

"Gigi's is romantic?" said Lombardi. "*I* just go there for the food. And Aurora and I have known each other for a very long time. She came to our wedding," he said, managing to nod at his wife while strategically avoiding her glare. "We played tennis at the club, we're in the same social circle. She asked for a dinner meeting and I obliged. Nothing more to it than that."

Kincaid stepped in. "Mr. Lombardi, were you sleeping with Mrs. Stanhope?"

"No," he said so calmly that it could have been the truth.

"Did you *ever* have an affair with her?"

"We went through this on Sunday. Absolutely not." Real conviction.

Turning to Missy, Kincaid said, "Did Mrs. Stanhope ever tell you that your husband was having an affair? With her or with someone else?"

"Tread lightly, detective," said Buccio, but he nodded to his client to answer.

"Yes, she did. In fact, she insinuated that *she* had been having an affair with my husband."

"Total bullshit," said Lombardi.

Missy looked at him flatly then turned back to Kincaid. "But it wasn't true and it was years ago. Long forgotten."

Carlisle looked at Steve. "It wasn't true?"

"Asked and answered," said Buccio.

But Lombardi answered anyway. "Absolutely not."

Turning back to Missy, Carlisle said, "*I* wouldn't be able to forget something like that."

"Maybe not forgotten," Missy agreed, "but in the past. If I paid too much attention to the malicious rumors and innuendos that people make, I would lose my mind. Anyway, you can imagine that the incident put a damper on any trust I may have had for her in the past. To say the least," she added with a smirk. "But Aurora was ubiquitous on the Seattle social scene, and therefore unavoidable. I had to find a way to make my peace with her bad behavior or move to a different state. I chose the former."

"And you, Mr. Lombardi," said Kincaid, "that must have been upsetting for you too."

"I was outraged," he said, looking like he was still outraged, "but as my wife said, I had to make peace with it. Aurora could be unpredictable and when she was angry, nothing was verboten. Still, she had good qualities and, in some ways, those helped balance the bad."

"Why do you think she made the accusation?"

"*Why?*"

"It's a spiteful thing to say. Was she angry with you? Either of you?"

Missy spoke up. "She was angry with me. I had recently joined the board of one of her favorite charities and we disagreed over some of the allocation of funds."

"So she told you she had been sleeping with your husband?" Kincaid asked with incredulity. "That seems extreme."

"It *was* extreme, Detective, but not at all out of character. I think her logic was that I would either be so distracted by marital issues, or be so humiliated that I would quit the board and she would once again be king of the hill."

Kincaid said, "Is that what motivated her? Being king of the hill?"

Nodding, Missy replied, "And not just the hill, Detective Kincaid, Aurora wanted to be king of the whole mountain."

Carlisle said, "Mr. Lombardi, what time did you and Mrs. Stanhope leave Gigi's on Friday night?"

"Around ten. A few minutes past."

"Did you leave together?"

"No, she took her own car. We parted at the valet stand."

"Then what did you do?"

"I went home."

Carlisle looked at Missy, who nodded. "He came home around ten-thirty, ten forty-five."

"And why did you telephone Aurora at eleven forty-five that same night, Mr. Lombardi? Did you have something to add to your *business* discussion?"

Lombardi looked baffled. "I didn't call her."

"Mr. Lombardi, we have a record of a call from your cell phone to Aurora's cell phone at eleven forty-five on Friday night."

This time Ronny Buccio stepped in. "*If* there was a phone call then it was a continuation of their dinner conversation, which was a legal matter and is thus confidential. Move on."

"For the record," said Carlisle, "you deny calling Aurora Stanhope after you had dinner on Friday night?"

"Nothing here is on the record," said Buccio. "We're just having a friendly chat."

"What about Robert Stanhope? Do either of you know him well?" asked Kincaid, backing off before they got themselves thrown out.

Missy looked away, but Steve answered, "I've known him as long as I've known Aurora. He's a good man. Good businessman, good father."

"Good husband?"

Lombardi looked at his wife as though it was her job to field such questions but Missy just regarded him blankly. Finally, he said, "Of course he was. Let's face it, Aurora was tough and he stuck with her."

"Any indication that he was seeing someone else?"

Lombardi looked as if the thought had never occurred to him. "I've never heard anything." Again, he looked at his wife.

"Neither have I," she said.

"Although," Steve added, "he does travel quite a bit for business. He could have someone on the side and we'd never hear about it."

Carlisle hid her disgust at the adult rumor mill that ran in this social circle. She asked, "And Mrs. Stanhope? Was she seeing anyone else?"

Lombardi smiled maliciously "She was seeing *every*body else."

"Except you," said Carlisle.

Lombardi glared. "Right."

"So, Mrs. Stanhope fooled around a lot?" Kincaid asked Missy.

She flashed him a sly smile. "Indeed, Detective. At least, that's what I heard. But I heard it over and over again and as they say, where's there's smoke…"

"Did Mr. Stanhope know about her extracurriculars?"

Missy shrugged. "Not that I could tell."

"Blind devotion," said her husband.

Missy nodded, adding, "At least until recently."

She said it casually, as if she were commenting on an unexpected change in the weather. Kincaid took the bait. "What happened recently?"

"They'd been arguing."

"How do you know?"

Noncommittally, she said, "I could tell. And, Aurora said something."

"At the board meeting?" asked Kincaid.

"I asked after Robert and she said he's male menopausal. Then she laughed and told me that after all these years he was developing a jealous streak."

Kincaid wanted to ask why Aurora would have confided in Missy, given their relationship, but didn't think it would accomplish anything. "Anything else?"

"No. I would've thought it was just her sense of humor or her mood that day, but I'd been noticing little things. Like Robert sort of following her around the club. Keeping an eye on her. And I saw them arguing about her tennis lessons—Aurora chooses her tennis pros by their proportions, if you know what I mean. Just little things like that." She looked from Kincaid to Carlisle. "It was all very subtle, but when you put it together…"

"Where there's smoke?" said Kincaid and Missy nodded sagely.

"Could Robert Stanhope have murdered his wife?" Carlisle asked bluntly.

"No, no. I can't imagine that. I only meant that their marriage might not have been so rosy lately. But Robert wouldn't hurt anyone." She added, "Besides, Robert was in Portland that night. He couldn't have done it."

"And how do you know Robert was in Portland on Friday night?" said Carlisle.

Missy Lombardi rolled her eyes and said, "Because it's all over the country club, Detective. Haven't you learned anything by now?"

There wasn't a lot to say after that and Ronny Buccio shut it down a few minutes later.

"They've told you everything they know, Detectives. If you need more, contact me directly and we can make arrangements. In the meantime, please don't contact my clients without speaking to me first."

Standard legal proviso. They nodded ambiguously on their way out the door.

In the elevator, Carlisle said, "Did you buy that about Robert's alibi being all over the country club?"

Kincaid shrugged. "What I don't get is why she doesn't dump Steve. I had the feeling she's barely tolerating him."

"Didn't Lucas tell us she was interested in Stanhope way back when?"

"And Aurora took him away?"

"Maybe Missy killed her," said Carlisle.

"To get Stanhope back? After thirty years?"

"Just revenge." She sighed. "Yeah, after thirty years, it doesn't seem very likely."

"It's more likely that Robert Stanhope had finally had enough and choked her to death, then took out the maid because she saw something."

"Or," said Carlisle as they made their way to the unmarked, "in a shallow postmodern version of the Elektra Complex, Caroline knocked her mother out with a paperweight and then strangled her in a rage so that she could take her mother's place in Seattle society."

"*Or*," said Kincaid, starting the ignition, "Steve Lombardi did it in a fit of jealousy and then whacked Mrs. Chang because she never passed his phone messages along."

"Or!" Her ringing cell phone interrupted the thought. "Carlisle."

They'd been driving back toward the station, but she told Kincaid to turn around. "Patrol have Chang's car. She was definitely killed inside it."

"Where?"

"A few blocks from the Stanhopes' house. It was in a neighbor's driveway."

"Since when? They didn't notice?"

"They're out of town. The gardener was scheduled to work this morning. He saw the car when he drove up. Looked inside, saw blood and brains and called the cops."

Twenty minutes later they arrived at the scene on Lakeside Avenue. Kincaid interviewed the gardener before joining his partner where she stood talking to Kyle beside a white Buick Lucerne.

"Bad news is that the gardener didn't do it."

Dressed in a Tyvek suit and paper cap, Kyle looked like an alien amidst the greens and golds of the trees. "Looks like Chang pulled in here, wound down the window and was shot right in the driver's seat. The killer let her bleed out inside of the car and then dragged her"—she pointed at some bloody marks on the body of the car around the driver's side door—"over the pavement to here and then picked her up, probably to put her into another vehicle. Lucky for us, the trees protected the drag from the drizzle."

"She was dragged, not carried? Maybe a woman?"

"Yeah. But with all of that blood and brain tissue, maybe the killer could've lifted her, but didn't want to get that close."

"Hey, Detectives!" a uniform called to them from outside a solarium attached to the eastern side of the house. An impressive oversized Dutch Colonial, the home would've been dwarfed by the Stanhope manse, but sat perfectly on this generous lot. "I think you need to see this."

Kyle followed behind them with a handful of extra nitrile gloves. When they got a look through the window at the orchid garden inside, she started handing them out.

Flourishing, but for half a dozen broken pots on the floor, the greenhouse was eerily beautiful. But something violent had happened here between the slat tables and shelves that held the delicate flowers.

Kincaid turned to the uniform. "Find out where the owners are." He pulled his phone out and made a call to the DA's office, spoke for a minute, ended the call. "Exigent circumstances for the greenhouse," he told his partner.

"Rest of the house?" asked Kyle.

"Not without permission or evidence."

A sticker on a side door told them an alarm was going to sound when they broke in. Kincaid called the company.

"They never wired the solarium, only the house is alarmed. Just put the sticker there as a deterrent." He tried the door and it fell open—the latch had already been broken.

"Whoever got in here must've known that," said Carlisle, adding, "or got really goddamn lucky. Security company is going to notify the owners?" Kincaid nodded.

Kyle stepped inside but Carlisle and Kincaid remained at the door looking in. A fist-sized rock covered in blood sat amid shards of clay and scattered soil.

Kyle snapped some pictures, and the detectives walked back to the Buick.

"We got our primary crime scene for Chang, probably for Aurora too," said Kincaid. "Security company says the owner is Andrew Shermann, out of town from October twelfth until the middle of December. So they probably have nothing to do with what happened here. Nice thing to come home to," he grumbled. "Whoever did this knew that no one would be here."

"Our killer lures Aurora here, hits her over the head, strangles her in the conservatory."

Kincaid picked it up. "Then lures Mrs. Chang here and kills her in the Buick with the revolver." He turned to Carlisle. "Why?"

She looked at him and shrugged. "Chang *must* have seen or heard something incriminating. Why didn't she tell us when we came to the house?"

"We didn't tell her Aurora was dead. If she was suspicious about something, she might not have wanted to talk to us before she talked to the lady of the house."

"She could have seen something on Friday night. Maybe Aurora even came back with someone that night and then left again."

"Right. So, let's assume Aurora was killed here too. It's three minutes from the Stanhopes' place. Aurora might've gone home and left again, or she could've been diverted on her way home."

Kyle emerged from the greenhouse in paper booties, holding the rock. "Bunch of blonde hair stuck to the dried blood."

"Did it come from this property?" asked Carlisle.

"No idea."

"Probably a weapon of opportunity," said Kincaid. "Which doesn't fit at all with the theory that she was lured here to be murdered."

"Could've been lured here for sex? A lovers' tryst gone wrong?" Carlisle mused. "It wouldn't be out of keeping with what we know about her."

"Or she could've been knocked out somewhere else and then murdered here," said Kincaid. "Not lured at all. Killer dumped the rock in the greenhouse, forgot about it."

"Is there any indication that she knew the owners or had any ties to this house?"

Looking up at the main structure, Kyle said, "We can't go into the rest of the house, right?" She looked at Kincaid for confirmation, said, "And the door from the greenhouse is locked up tight, so we can't accidentally go into the rest of the house either."

Carlisle rubbed her temples. "Whoever got in here knew the greenhouse wasn't alarmed, knew the owners were away." She looked at Kincaid. "Let's find out if the Stanhopes and the Shermanns have any friends in common. And let's find out where Chang worked before her gig at the Stanhopes."

"Want to have another look inside before we start removing evidence?"

They stepped inside. There wasn't much sign of struggle—which fit with the lack of injuries to Aurora's body. A white comet orchid had a single drop of red blood on one of its petals and there was a dusting of soil around the broken pots. Even so, the scene was creepy.

"Mind if we step out for half an hour?" Kincaid asked Kyle.

"Nah. We're just going to be bagging and tagging for a while."

He turned to Carlisle. "Let's pop over to the Stanhopes'. Since we're in the neighborhood."

"I like your style, Kincaid," said Carlisle, smiling for the first time since that morning.

A few minutes later, they stood at the front door of the Stanhopes' home, a few streets up and one very expensive block to the east of the Shermanns'. She checked her phone before slipping it back into her coat pocket. "I have about forty-five minutes before I have to leave for lunch with Pamela."

The door opened and Robert Stanhope stood unhappily in the foyer. "Do you have news?" he asked with absolutely no hope in his voice.

Kincaid said, "We have a possible lead, Mr. Stanhope. We'd like to ask a few questions."

"Right," he said, looking more than a little frustrated. "More questions." But then his eyes alit on Carlisle's bare knees and smooth calves and, as if without his own volition, Stanhope let them inside.

But not beyond the foyer.

Carlisle got right to the point. "Did you or Mrs. Stanhope know an Andrew Shermann?"

"I don't think so," he said uncertainly and the look in his eyes was telling—Robert Stanhope was afraid they'd found another of his wife's lovers. "Who is he?"

"We believe we've found the site of your wife's murder, Mr. Stanhope, a few blocks away on Lakeside Avenue. At the home of Andrew and Edith Shermann."

"The Shermanns' house?"

She nodded. "But there's no indication it had anything to do with the Shermanns. They've been away for a week and there's no sign she was ever in the actual house." They'd done a quick background check on Andrew Shermann and discovered that he lived with his wife of forty-five years in the house on Lakeside Avenue. The Shermanns were in their mid-seventies and had no criminal background. "Unless you can tell us otherwise, we're thinking the scene was opportunistic."

Looking relieved, Stanhope said, "Oh. Well, I don't think I

know them, but Aurora knew so many people through her charities. I can ask around."

"We'd appreciate that, sir," said Kincaid. "We'd also like to know how you came to hire Mrs. Chang. Was she referred to you?"

Now Stanhope laughed wistfully. "No one was ever referred to work for Aurora. Even before Mrs. Sanchez, my wife had a reputation. I think she went through an agency. Just"—he looked up the stairs—"just give me a minute."

He took the stairs slowly, like a man much older than his fifty-eight years, and headed down the hallway and out of sight. When he came back, Caroline was walking ahead of him. Dressed in a pencil skirt and blouse, she looked ready to go out for the afternoon and the expression of impatience on her face suggested she had other places to be.

She bounced down the curving stairs on stockinged feet, shoulders back, chin high, and handed Kincaid a folded slip of paper. "That's the name of the agency that sent us Mrs. Chang, and will, hopefully, be sending us another housekeeper sometime this week." She reached for her father's hand as he finally took the last step onto the marble floor. "We can't go much longer without good help." With a reassuring squeeze she let go of her father's hand.

Gross, thought Carlisle.

"Caroline, do you know Andrew or Edith Shermann?" asked Kincaid. "They're an older couple, mid-seventies, live a few blocks away?"

"Never heard of them. Why?"

Kincaid glanced at Stanhope, a little surprised he hadn't filled his daughter in on the latest development. "We believe your mom was murdered in their conservatory while they've been out of town."

Caroline looked appalled. "In a greenhouse?"

"We're trying to figure out why she was there. If you think of anything, let us know."

Back in the car, Kincaid said, "She moved right into her mother's place."

"Pretty weird," Carlisle agreed. "but Daddy Stanhope doesn't seem to mind."

"I'm not sure *Daddy* Stanhope has noticed. He's pretty out of it."

"Maybe."

"Maybe?"

"Have you forgotten his rage yesterday when he found out Aurora had dinner with Steve Lombardi? And remember what Missy said about the recent change in attitude toward his philandering wife."

"I don't know," said Kincaid, "he seems wrecked."

"It could be an act, it could be guilt, it could be regret; it could even be true. But he had motive and opportunity and he's the beleaguered husband so he's still a suspect. Now, I have to get to my lunch."

"Drop me at the crime scene. I'll ride back with Kyle."

———————◆—■◆□—◆———————

Promptly at one o'clock, Judy Carlisle walked into the dining room of a seafood restaurant on Lake Union. She gave the host her wool coat but kept the blazer on to disguise her gun and shoulder holster then walked across the room to a bank of windows and joined her mother-in-law and Evelyn, her country club friend.

When she slid into the booth and unbuttoned her blazer, Evelyn let out a delighted gasp and stage-whispered, "Is that your gun? Oh, Pamela, this is so exciting."

Nodding indulgently, Pamela sipped a white wine spritzer and said, "My daughter-in-law lives an intriguing life."

They ordered lunch and made small talk. Evelyn had not been close to Aurora Stanhope, but she did know her. "*Every*one knew Aurora. She was infamous at the club."

"Not a very nice woman, from what I've gathered," said Carlisle.

"Not at all, though she did some very good things in the

world." She made a face. "But on a personal level, she was selfish and arrogant."

"A real bitch, huh?" Carlisle could tell this woman appreciated the direct approach.

Pamela let out a disapproving sigh, but Evelyn giggled. "What do you want to know?"

"I want to know who she was sleeping with."

Eyes glowing with amusement, Evelyn said, "*I* think she might've had something going with one of the bartenders, but it might have just been playful flirting. Put her in front of a handsome man and she turned into a cat with a mouse. Popular wisdom is that one doesn't fool around in the country club. Too incestuous, too much chance of getting caught. But Aurora didn't seem like the kind of woman who worried about getting caught." She considered. "I did hear she had an affair with Steve Lombardi once upon a time, but that it was long over. Not that his wife would ever forget it."

"Missy didn't like Mrs. Stanhope?"

"No. And she didn't hide it. She went rigid whenever Aurora entered the room. Once, during a club tennis tournament, they were playing women's doubles against each other and Missy aimed a backhand right at her in the quarterfinals. Hit her so hard in the shoulder that Aurora was out for the rest of the tournament. Missy isn't so great in singles because she's so tiny she can't cover the court, but she's a winner in doubles, killer backhand. Absolute ace. She meant to hit Aurora. I'd swear to it."

"Aurora must not have been Missy's biggest fan either."

Shaking her head, Evelyn said, "Aurora was breezier about it; she mostly pretended that Missy didn't exist, but you could tell that Aurora knew it drove Missy crazy. The only time I saw her really mad was when Missy hit her with that ball. She called her several names you don't often hear at the country club. Very graphic."

"Could Missy have killed her?"

"With the tennis ball?" She giggled. "No, no, I can't imagine that." She shook her head. "No."

"What about Robert Stanhope? How was their relationship with the rumors of her infidelity?"

"You've never met a man more in love with his wife." She paused for effect. "At least until recently."

CHAPTER TWENTY-ONE

BACK AT THE CRIME SCENE, Kyle had found something.
A bit of torn cloth. Hardly even that, actually, but it was a trace—perhaps a trace of the killer.

"Kincaid," she called, walking out of the solarium with a sealed evidence bag.

He took the bag, looked at her, then back at the bag, squinting. "What is it?"

"It's thread," she said. "Four pieces of thread. But if they match the fiber under Aurora Stanhope's fingernails, then we've got something."

He examined the evidence again. "White. Can you tell me anything about it now?"

"Let me get it under a microscope first. It might only help us if we find the clothing these belong to. Unless," she said with significance, "the material is unusual."

"Some of these country club guys might have their shirts custom made," said Kincaid.

"I'll look for proprietary matches." Kincaid was still frowning "It looks to me like it might have come from a torn button, so we're searching for the button too."

Kincaid didn't look impressed. "It's *something,* Kincaid. Keep your chin up—we're not done yet."

He kept his chin up for another ten minutes, then had one of the uniforms drive him back to the station and got on the phone with the DA, who confirmed there was no way they could compel fingerprints and a DNA test on the Lombardis.

He considered Steve Lombardi's reaction when they had asked him about the call from his cell phone on Friday night. His surprise had seemed genuine. Besides, why wouldn't he just cop to it? What was the big deal when he had already admitted, in front of his *wife*, to having dinner with Aurora? Buccio had suggested that the call, if there had been a call, was a follow-up. But Lombardi had flatly denied making the call.

And if Steve hadn't made the call, then who had? Missy would've had access to her husband's phone after he'd gotten home that night. Maybe she had checked his recent calls? Hit redial and bitched at Aurora for luring her husband away? Again.

Kincaid didn't buy the story that Aurora had invented an affair between her and Steve just to piss off Missy. Did Missy buy it? He didn't think so; she was too smart and her husband was too slimy.

When Judy walked into the squad room a few minutes later, Kincaid was surprised to see that almost two and a half hours had passed since she'd dropped him back at the crime scene.

"Have you solved it yet?" she asked, kicking off high heels under her desk and reaching down to rub her feet. "If we have a late night, I'm going to have to go home and change."

"I don't know, Judy. That outfit is already working for us; Stanhope and Lombardi couldn't take their eyes off of your legs."

"Whatever," she said, though she had always been proud of her legs. "So, what do you know?"

"Kyle found a clue."

Carlisle's eyes went wide. "What is it?"

"Several pieces of thread."

"Thread? And?"

He explained the significance of the thread and Carlisle shrugged. "Lot of 'ifs' in that scenario."

"Best I got. What did you learn?"

She ticked off a list on her fingers. "Aurora was a big flirt, may or may not have had a fling with one of the bartenders at the club, is rumored to have had an affair with Steve Lombardi—once upon a time—and you've never met a man more in love with his wife than Robert Stanhope, but lately he hasn't been on the scene as much."

"So, nothing new?"

"Correct. But Pamela was thrilled that I came and Evelyn got to feel like a confidential informant and she will definitely volunteer to be our spy if their country club ever comes up in another murder investigation."

"A Seattle socialite for a CI? That's something."

"Oh, there was one other thing. Missy once got so mad at Aurora that she nailed her with a tennis ball during a doubles match, and our Aurora got so mad that she swore."

"She *swore*?"

"She said things on the tennis court that no gentle ear should hear," she said. "But all kidding aside, it sounded like Missy actually hurt her. She had to bow out of the tournament."

"Let me ask you this," said Kincaid, "if Missy could go after Aurora on the tennis court, do you think she could've killed her?"

Carlisle blew out a heavy gust of air. "I don't know. Why? What are you thinking?"

"I'm thinking that the smart thing for Steve Lombardi to do during our interview would've been to cop to the phone call and claim client confidentiality."

"He did."

"No, his attorney did."

Carlisle thought about that, then nodded. "So if he didn't make the call, then who did?"

"Missy," said Kincaid.

"Why?" said Carlisle. "Hey, you know what we need? We need some goddamn evidence. Where are the telltale signs of struggle?

The scratched necks and skin samples? The fingerprints and eyewitnesses?" She rubbed the back of her neck. "Two murders in less than three days and we've got nothing definitive. This case is a nightmare."

"Buck up, partner," said Kincaid, not without sympathy. "Now tell me what you think about Missy Lombardi murdering our two victims."

"She doesn't have an alibi. Normally manual strangulation would rule out a woman, but Aurora was already incapacitated when she was strangled, so it could've been her. Chang was shot—no gender bias on guns . Our victims were lured to an empty house. Easier for diminutive middle-aged woman to do that because one look says Missy isn't a physical threat. She also hated the victim."

"See?" said Kincaid. "Now we're cookin'."

"Okay, but here's what *I'm* thinking," said Carlisle, warming to the subject of suspects. "We have two independent witnesses who say that Stanhope's affection for his wife was cooling of late. He's got motive, no alibi, *and* the murder site is four blocks from his home. Not only that, he's most likely to get caught by Mrs. Chang doing something suspicious."

"And there's the motive for killing her too."

"She would have been the first to know if they were fighting."

"And the first to know that Aurora was sleeping with someone in her own bed."

"Semen stains and used condoms," said Carlisle. "The inelegant remains of the day."

"But he has an alibi for the time Chang was killed."

"His daughter."

"True."

"Have you called the agency that sent Mrs. Chang to the Stanhopes'?"

"Not yet," said Kincaid, searching the desktop for his trusty notebook.

"What the hell were you doing the whole time I was gone?"

"You mean while you were out having a fancy lunch on Lake Union? *I* was contemplating our case, searching my memory for nuance and subterfuge." He located the notebook, pulled out the slip of paper Caroline Stanhope had given him. "Seeking possibilities not yet considered."

"Blah, blah. Make the call."

He did.

Carlisle could tell from the expanding smile on her partner's face that he was learning something good and by the time he hung up, she was anxiously tapping a pen on her blotter. "Well?"

"Before she went to work for the Stanhopes, Mrs. Chang spent three years at the Shermann household on Lakeside Avenue. She left when the Shermanns started wintering in Palm Desert and only needed her part of the year. Stellar employee, no complaints."

"She's the link," said Carlisle, her eyes lighting up. "She told the killer no one would be home *chez* Shermann." She thought a moment, then went on, "If she hadn't ended up dead, she'd be a prime suspect."

"She still could have killed Aurora."

"I guess she could have, but I don't think so. Let's not get distracted by that just yet."

"Agreed," said Kincaid. "The same killer took them both out but in radically different ways. Aurora was personal, Chang was clean-up. Chang knew the killer and told him—or her—that the Shermann house was vacant and the solarium wasn't alarmed. Maybe didn't even know the killer was going to *kill her*"—he winked at the pun, got a big eye-roll—"found out she was dead on Saturday, confronted the killer, agreed to meet on Sunday and gets murdered herself."

"But she's on her way to the Stanhopes'. How does she end up at the Shermanns'?"

"Killer sends a text using Aurora's phone hoping Mrs. Chang

won't think anything of it. It works; she's on her way to the Stanhopes' and the killer stops her along that ridiculously long driveway, says they have to talk."

"If killer hung out at the end of the Stanhopes' driveway, no one would have seen him from the house or the road," said Carlisle.

"Or the killer is Robert Stanhope and he simply waits for her at the house, takes her to the Shermanns' under some guise—"

"—or, if Chang objects, our killer just brandishes the gun and carjacks her," said Carlisle.

"One way or another he gets her there, shoots her. Neighbors don't notice the shot because it's cold out and they're all locked up tight inside of their well-insulated houses on their big expensive plots of land surrounded by trees and hedges. Killer stuffs Chang in the Porsche to be disposed of after dark and what? Goes home?"

"If it was Stanhope, he only had to walk a few blocks," said Carlisle.

Kyle called and asked them to come down to the lab.

On the elevator, Carlisle said, "This had better be something we can use."

Kincaid laughed, but it was true. They needed a break in this case and it had to be good enough to get them a warrant. They needed evidence.

When she looked up and saw them come through the doors, Kyle didn't mince words. "The threads from the greenhouse match the fibers under Aurora's fingernails *and* I know where those threads came from." She looked at them expectantly.

"And?" said Kincaid.

"Robert Stanhope's custom-made shirts."

Kyle explained that the thread was a cotton and silk blend imported from India by a fabric company in New York City. "It's very expensive and very exclusive and there is only one tailor in the Pacific Northwest that has ever ordered it."

She had called the tailor and instead of running into a brick wall when she said that she was with the police department crime lab and needed a client list, she'd said simply that she wanted to order several shirts in that fabric and could they tell her whether it was in stock. The friendly woman on the other end of the line had asked if they were for Mr. Stanhope. If so, they already had his measurements on file and could get started on an order right away.

"Evidently, he's the only customer that orders it. I told her he had gained a few pounds and would have to come in for new measurements before we placed an order. Easy as pie."

Kincaid beamed. "That'll get us a search warrant."

They were back at their desks and on the phone with the DA's office in less than five minutes. "He's going to chase down a judge before quitting time and try to get back to us tonight."

It was five o'clock and they decided to break for dinner at Carlisle's house. When they arrived, Pamela was drinking tea and doing the Sunday crossword puzzle at the kitchen island.

"New York Times?" asked Kincaid. "I'm impressed."

"Don't be," she said with a wink, "I started it two days ago and when I don't finish by next Sunday, I'll recycle this one and start all over again."

"Well," he said, "your perseverance is even more impressive."

Judy Carlisle had detoured to the dining room to make sure her children were doing their homework and now she greeted her mother-in-law. "Hi Pamela. Pizza and salad for dinner." She had already called the family's favorite pizza place and ordered the usual.

Pamela said, "I suppose I can't complain if I don't offer to cook."

Carlisle sighed and went to change clothes.

As soon as she was gone, Kincaid said, "Why do you do it?"

Laughing, Pamela Carlisle said, "I can't help myself, Jerome.

It's just so easy to get under her skin. But I'll fix the salad to make up for it."

She offered him a drink and he accepted a glass of peach-flavored sparkling water. "Gotta go back to work soon."

"Oh?" said Pamela, pulling spring greens and grape tomatoes from the refrigerator. "Has there been a development?"

"Well," he said conspiratorially, "some trace evidence has finally pointed us in the direction of a suspect and we're waiting on a search warrant."

"How exciting," she said. "I won't ask who it is." She chopped arugula and added it to the bowl of greens. "It's one of the Lombardis, isn't it?"

He grinned. "Now why would you think that?"

"Didn't Judy tell you what we learned from Evelyn at lunch today? Rumors that Aurora had an affair with the husband? The long rivalry between her and the wife? The dreadful incident on the tennis court? It's a veritable hotbed of resentment and jealousy."

Kincaid raised his eyebrows, but said nothing.

"Seriously, though, Jerome, I know you can't tell me; Judy already laid out the rules. But I think it's the Lombardi woman."

Carlisle came down in a sweater and black trousers. "Thanks for making the salad," she said to Pamela suspiciously. A few minutes later Tom came in the back door and a few minutes after that the pizza arrived.

They sat at the dining room table and ate salad with Green Goddess dressing and thin crust pizza with lots of toppings. The kids talked about school. The adults did not talk about work.

Kincaid had eaten many dinners at this table and felt like part of the family, but tonight he also felt a little pang of envy. He found his thoughts were on Beth Williams and her son Henry, but the spell was broken when his phone rang. Kincaid excused himself and walked to the kitchen.

A minute later, he stood in the doorway and said, "That was the

DA. We got a warrant for both master bedrooms, the maid's room and the laundry room." Carlisle doled out a few kisses to her family, Kincaid thanked them for dinner, bade them farewell and then they were out the door and on their way back to Lake Washington.

By design, they arrived a few minutes ahead of Kyle and her team, pulling into the circular drive right next to Caroline's Audi. Carlisle was happy to be out of heels and into her leather oxfords as they trod across the cobblestones and rang the doorbell. This time it took three rings and five minutes to get an answer. The face on the other side of the door was clean and elfin and full of contempt.

"What now?" Though it wasn't quite seven o'clock, Caroline was wearing navy blue silk pajamas, her face scrubbed, her fine blonde hair pulled into a bun.

"We need to speak to your father," said Carlisle.

"Absolutely not."

"What do you want?" asked a husky voice from the top of the stairs. Robert Stanhope was still in business attire—minus the jacket, and he looked irritated.

"Sir, we have a warrant to search the premises," said Carlisle, brandishing three sheets of paper she had printed out before leaving her house.

"Caroline," said Stanhope, "get dressed and call Jim."

"Daddy—"

"Go." He turned back to the detectives and reached for the warrant. As he stood reading it, the crime scene van pulled into the drive and Kyle got out, directing her team on what to bring in with them.

"Mr. Stanhope," said Kincaid, "take all the time you need with that," he said, pointing to the warrant, "but we're going to get started. Is there anyone in the house besides you and your daughter?" Stanhope shook his head without looking up from the warrant.

The next few minutes were chaotic as the crime scene technicians took their first steps across the Stanhope threshold.

Robert Stanhope was indignant but let them through. Caroline reemerged in jeans and a baggie sweater that had probably come from her mother's closet. Kyle marched in with three forensic technicians and a lot of equipment, and finally, four uniformed officers joined the party to keep an eye on the Stanhopes and anyone else who might show up during the search.

Kyle sent one tech to find the laundry room and one to Aurora's suite. Then she followed Carlisle and Kincaid straight to Robert Stanhope's bedroom.

Stanhope's rooms, identical to Aurora's suite, were about as far away from his wife's as you could get and still be in the same house. Carlisle wondered if they had always had separate bedrooms, or if it had simply become convenient when the Stanhopes' relationship changed. They turned to the right at the top of the stairs and followed the corridor to a set of closed double doors.

Apart from the layout, Stanhope's side of the second floor had nothing in common with Aurora's. The sitting room was furnished in shades of bachelor beige, tartan plaid and tweed. The walls were lined with shelves of books and antiquities. There were two framed photos of his children. A much larger one of his wife.

Kyle went to the closet and sent another tech to start on the bathroom. Carlisle and Kincaid gloved up and started going through the desk and file cabinets.

Ten minutes later, Carlisle said, "Here we go."

She'd been flipping through a drawer of hanging files when she found a blacked-out tab. Opening the file across the desk for her partner to see, she flipped through a short stack of eight by ten photographs of Aurora Stanhope, the first few had been taken at least twenty years ago judging from the styles and surroundings. In them, Aurora was with a handsome man the detectives didn't recognize. The pics were of them kissing in the front seat of a car, entering a hotel somewhere on the coast. Next came a similar series of four-by-sixes with Steve Lombardi from another decade. Several more were of Aurora with various men, some younger, some contemporary, some older. In the back of the file was a short stack of digital printouts, featuring the cabana boy lounging naked in her bed.

"I don't see the tennis coach," said Kincaid, blowing out a breath. "Jesus, that's a lot of pain."

"Stanhope knew about all of this, all these years."

They stood in astounded silence for a few seconds.

Kincaid said, "This must have been killing him."

"It did kill his wife."

CHAPTER TWENTY-TWO

CARLISLE LEFT THE REST OF the desk to her partner. She and Kyle went to the maid's quarters on the first floor behind the kitchen and walked single file through a narrow door. There was an old wardrobe, a dresser and a writing table supporting a nineteen-inch television and cable box. A twin-sized bed with decent linens sat under a row of mullioned windows. The bathroom had a small claw foot tub with a shower extension and pedestal sink. Compared to the rest of the house it was like a monk's cell, but it was comfortable enough.

"Anything specific I should be looking for in here?" asked Kyle, pulling on a fresh pair of gloves.

"Complicity," said Carlisle.

"Right." They got started: Kyle in the bathroom, Carlisle in the wardrobe.

Three identical black uniforms hung side by side along with half a dozen white aprons. Two thick cardigan sweaters, a shawl and a pair of black pants with an elastic waistband were the only civilian clothes hanging above a good pair of boiled wool slippers and black nurse's lace-ups. No smoking guns, no blackmail notes, no voodoo dolls.

In the top dresser drawer, she found six pairs of clean cotton briefs in pastel shades, several pairs of support hose, black and white socks and one modest cotton bra, thirty-four B. The next drawer held a few long-sleeved and turtleneck tops, two flannel pajama sets and a pair of chinos, also with an elastic waistband, all folded with military precision.

A stack on top of the dresser featured several Chinese-American newspapers and a romance novel.

She turned on the television. TLC, My Big Fat Gypsy Wedding. "Jesus."

Carlisle was sure that Chang had told the killer about the Shermanns' empty property, but had she done it unwittingly or was she part of a conspiracy?

"Anything?" she asked Kyle.

"Hair, fingerprints, fluids…" She shrugged. "Lots of stuff."

"Relevant?" asked Carlisle.

"No idea. All of the hairs I've found are coarse black and grey, consistent with Chang's. Eyeballing it, I'd say a few drops of urine and a few drops of blood but no semen. No condoms or lubricant or ball gags hiding in and amongst her paper products, so I don't think anything shocking happened here. She had normal toiletries, nice but not high-end. Sunblock, moisturizer, lip balm. Some no-make-up make-up—blush, pressed powder, black brow pencil. No surprises."

"When you're done, take a look in the other room, especially for blood or fluids. I want to make sure nothing happened in here. In the meantime, I'm going to talk to Caroline and check in with Kincaid."

Down the corridor and through the kitchen, Carlisle wound her way back to the great room and found Lucas alone by the empty fireplace. Someone must have called him.

"Where's Caroline?" she asked.

He startled. "Her room, I guess."

Sitting in the chair closest to him, she said, "You got here quick."

He looked at his feet. "You can't really believe my dad did this."

"There was enough evidence for a partial search warrant, Lucas.

You're going to have to come to terms with that." He didn't look like he was going to come to terms with that.

"How long is this going to take?"

"Could be a long, long time, Lucas. Maybe you should go home."

"I don't think so, Detective Carlisle." He rubbed his eyes. "Maybe Caroline should go."

"She certainly can if she wants to. At this point, so can your dad. But he can't go far."

He gave her a mean look. Then his face went slack and he said, "My dad didn't kill my mom, Detective. I know he didn't."

———————

A few minutes later, Lucas checked his sister's room, still furnished as it had been when she was in high school. He found her curled up at the end of the bed.

"What's happening?" Caroline asked, her eyes bloodshot and dry.

"Dad will be fine. We'll sort everything out." But the burdened look in Caroline's eyes made clear that platitudes would not do.

In a harsh whisper, she said, "What if he did it?"

Lucas stared at her. He closed the door behind him. "He *didn't* do it, Caroline. I can't believe you would say that." His mind racing, he repeated, "He didn't do it, Caroline."

But she was frantic. "Last night he fell asleep downstairs watching TV and I went to his room. Lucas, he knows all about her affairs. There's a whole file in there with pictures of Mom and other men." She clawed at her skinny knees and rocked back and forth on the edge of her bed. "I thought about taking the folder, getting rid of it, but then I figured he'd notice and be pissed, or embarrassed, or sad. He doesn't think we know." She moaned. "I should've taken it. I'm sure the cops found it." Her face crumpled.

Lucas tried to soothe his sister, patting her on the back, giving her a half-hearted hug. But the gestures didn't come naturally, and they weren't comforting.

When the tears had run their course, Lucas left the room, closed the door behind him and exhaled. He and Caroline functioned on different wavelengths. He felt for her but didn't really understand her.

He wandered downstairs, suddenly hungry.

In the kitchen, staring into the fridge, he realized that hunger did not translate into appetite. He pulled a block of cheddar cheese from one of the drawers, got a knife and started eating.

"You're supposed to sit down while you eat," said Carlisle, emerging like a specter from some dark corner of the kitchen.

"I'm not eating, I'm refueling."

"Running on empty?" she asked, without sympathy.

He shrugged. "Want some?" When she shook her head no, he wrapped up the cheese and put it away, poured himself a glass of orange juice and finished it in one go.

She was about to ask whether Caroline had decided to stay when she saw his face change and knew that Kyle had come in behind her.

———————————

Kyle took Carlisle back to Chang's room, picked up an evidence bag and showed her the wrinkled white shirt inside, the blood soaked into the shoulders, chest and arms, the missing button from the cuff.

"In a gallon zip-lock bag, tucked in between the clean towels."

Carlisle found Kincaid in Robert Stanhope's bedroom and updated him. Then she called the DA, who got an expanded search warrant to include the rest of the house and started work on an arrest warrant for Robert Stanhope in case they needed it.

Halfway down the stairs, Carlisle and Kincaid watched the front door fly open and Jim Thorpe storm through. He scanned the foyer, looked up and barked, "What the hell do you think you're doing?"

"We're searching the house," said Carlisle calmly.

"You'd better not be searching all of it," he said. "Robert read me the scope of your warrant and if you step one foot outside of it, I'll have your ass."

Carlisle didn't react; it was a lawyer's job to bluster and threaten. "It's been expanded."

Thorpe blinked but didn't miss a beat. "Show me."

She did.

"Fine," said Thorpe. "Where is he?"

He was in the great room, pacing. Caroline and Lucas sat at opposite ends of a sofa, silent.

Before Thorpe could open his mouth, Carlisle said, "We need to question your client at the station, Mr. Thorpe."

"On what grounds?" said Thorpe.

Carlisle rolled her eyes. "We've applied for a warrant, but at this point, we have enough evidence to arrest your client without one. Either way, he's coming to the station. Just depends on how you want it to play out."

Lucas and Caroline stood, shocked. Caroline said, "Daddy?"

Stanhope said nothing.

"Up to you," Carlisle said to Stanhope.

Stanhope turned to Thorpe and said, "Follow us to the police station."

───────

"My client is willing to answer your questions, Detectives, as I advise."

"What I really want to know," said Kincaid, tossing the open file of photos onto the table between them, "is why it took you so long to kill your wife?"

Stanhope spoke before Thorpe could object. "I didn't kill my wife."

Kincaid ignored him. "Because those photos are graphic. And there are a lot of them. I mean, you've known for years—decades—that she was fucking around behind your back—no, right in front of you—and you kept it inside. Honestly, I'm amazed you held it together for so long."

He looked at Thorpe, who was looking through the pictures, trying and failing to hide his surprise. "Oh no. You didn't tell your lawyer about the photo file, did you?" He shook his head. "That's a bad move. You have to tell your lawyer everything."

Stanhope was turning red. Thorpe said, "I need a few minutes alone with my client."

"You've had plenty of time alone with your client already," said Kincaid.

"I can shut this down right now, Detective."

Carlisle said, "Let's get some coffee."

When they were out of the room, Kincaid said, "Why didn't he tell his lawyer about the photos? He had to know we'd find them eventually."

"Denial? Hope? Who knows."

Ten minutes later they were back in the interrogation room.

"The photographs are circumstantial," said Thorpe, "and if anything, they prove that he loved his wife in spite of her indiscretions. As you said, why would he do it now when he's known all along?"

"*Why*?" Kincaid started reading from a list of names he'd copied from the back of each photograph, then added the tennis coach and the pool boy. "And those are just the guys we've found so far. I'm sure there are plenty more."

Stanhope glared at Kincaid.

Thorpe said, "My client was in another state when his wife was murdered. If knowledge of his wife's affairs is all you've got, then we're leaving."

Carlisle knew everything they had was circumstantial. But they had a shitload of it, enough for an arrest. Still, a man like Robert Kincaid would very likely be out on bail in the morning. The shirt, though, the shirt was a big deal—even without DNA proof that the blood on it was Aurora's—with everything else, it was definitely enough for an arrest.

She needed him to give up hope. She needed Stanhope to realize he was fucked. She needed him to confess.

Carlisle leaned across the table, looking Stanhope straight in the eyes and delineated the evidence against him. "And that's just what we have so far. We haven't finished searching your house and we'll get a warrant to search the company apartment in Portland, too. See, we figure you could easily have driven back from Portland, killed your wife, and snuck into your house to clean up before driving back to establish your alibi. No one can testify that you were in that apartment all night on Friday night. We've only got your word for it, and that might have been enough except that Mrs. Chang found your bloody shirt and when she found out that Aurora was dead she asked you about it and you killed her too."

Stanhope stared at her. "I didn't kill my wife." He leaned back in his chair and folded his arms across his chest. "Tell them, Jim."

———————

"Goddamn it," said Kincaid, slapping his desk with an open fist.

"We still have to check it out."

"Why the hell didn't he give us his alibi right away?"

"Because his alibi is an expensive hooker," said Carlisle. "He didn't think he'd have to tell us, so why would he?"

"He could be paying her to lie."

"Could be. We'll check that too."

Kincaid sighed heavily. What Jim Thorpe had told them was

that his client had spent late Friday evening and all night with a Russian woman named Tara Petrovitch whom he had met through a very exclusive matchmaking agency called Celia Rose. "Look it up," he had said smugly, "Tara is under the leggy blonde tab."

Carlisle was already online. She turned her screen so that he could see. The Celia Rose homepage was tasteful as far as those things went. "Says we have to log in or register to go any further." There was a telephone number listed at the bottom of the page and she used her mobile to call it while Kincaid marched back to the interrogation room to ask for Stanhope's login.

When he came back to his desk, Carlisle rolled her eyes at him. She was still getting the runaround from a woman with a posh British accent that was probably fake. He nodded and she said, "Never mind," into the phone and hung up. "He gave it to you?"

Handing her a slip of paper, he said, "Anything to get him out of here faster."

"Huh," said Carlisle after she had logged in as Robert Stanhope and clicked on his account history. "It's just like Amazon." Indeed, Stanhope's recent "dates" were listed, as well as the day, time, duration and his rating of the experience. He'd had three dates and they were all with the same woman.

"He likes Tara," said Kincaid. "And according to this, he booked her for an overnight on Friday."

"Who wouldn't like Tara?" said Carlisle when she had opened Tara's profile page. Brigitte Bardot hair and five miles of legs sticking out of a short black dress. She wore a little too much make-up and a sly smile. There were several more photographs, showing Tara in a variety of scenarios: pencil skirt and fitted jacket, a roller-bag trailing behind her as if she had just returned from an important business trip; swathed in an oversized man's shirt, sexy librarian glasses on the tip of her nose, reading the LA Times in a hotel suite; big black Jackie O glasses and a barely-there Saint Tropez one-piece, lounging on the edge of an infinity pool. "She's gorgeous, *and* at home in any social situation."

"And she's a diplomat." Kincaid read a few lines of her bio out loud. "'I'm happiest when you're happy. I love to dress up or down, and sometimes I don't like to get dressed at all. Whether we're at an important cocktail party, dining in a French restaurant, or just spending a day alone on the beach, I'm right at home.'"

"Aurora's polar opposite," said Carlisle.

"Something tells me her agreeable good personality wasn't his top priority."

"We're not letting him go until we've got her on record giving him an alibi."

Kincaid started making calls and Carlisle continued to read through the profile. Tara had a minimum two-hour booking at eight hundred dollars an hour. She thought back to her days as a beat cop, when she'd pulled hookers off the street who were selling themselves in fifteen-minute increments for ten bucks. Of course, Tara Petrovitch was in a whole other league. Expensively dressed and beautiful from head to toe, *clean*, she claimed to be a college graduate, to speak three languages—English, French and Russian— and to be a lover of both French philosophy and English romantic poetry.

When he was off the phone, Kincaid said, "They're going to contact Celia Rose, but it might take all night." He looked at his phone. Midnight. "We're going to have to let Stanhope go."

"We could hold off till morning; we're already gonna be in deep shit for bringing him in," said Carlisle, musing.

Kincaid ran his fingers through his thick red hair, grunted unhappily.

"*But*, we'd be significantly deeper in shit if we try to arraign him in the morning, knowing that he has an alibi."

She looked at her partner, picked up the phone and called Kyle.

"I've got my techs sweeping the basement and outbuildings

with a black light, but I don't have anything right now that would help."

"Okay," said Carlisle, "wrap it up."

She hit end, turned to Kincaid. "She's done with the house. Cut him loose."

———————◆—■—◆—◆—◆—■—◆———————

Kyle was loading a plastic bin full of evidence bags into the back of the crime scene van when she heard footsteps on the cobblestones behind her. Turning, she already knew who it was.

"Lucas," she said, "I can't talk to you about the investigation."

"I don't want to talk to you about the investigation."

She looked at him. He had just lost his mother. His father was being questioned for her murder. He looked exhausted and she felt a wave of pity wash over her.

"I don't want to talk about that, Kyle. I really don't. I just want to know, when this is over, can I call you?"

"Call me?" She was dumbfounded. This guy really didn't remember how things had ended between them. Or, was it possible, he hadn't realized it even then?

Lucas half-smiled, his eyes burning with something Kyle couldn't decipher. "Just think about it." He turned and walked back inside.

CHAPTER TWENTY-THREE

THE NEXT MORNING, KINCAID GOT to his desk just before eight o'clock. The escort service had confirmed Stanhope's appointment with Tara Petrovitch as well as his payment for the entire night. Portland PD had talked to *Tara*, aka Janette, who had confirmed the date.

Carlisle came in a few minutes later with two paper coffee cups in her hands.

"You brought the good stuff," said Kincaid, almost managing a smile.

"Thought we might need it."

"Did you get the call?" he asked.

"You mean the one where our lieutenant rants and raves about the fact that we interrogated an upstanding member of the community even though he had an alibi? Yeah, bright and early. I tried to tell him that Stanhope had failed to mention his alibi during several interviews and that we had good grounds to pull him in, but if his repeated use of the word *idiocy* is any indication, I don't think he cared." She raised her hands in resignation. "Anyway, after he calmed down he agreed we should keep our eyes on Stanhope—if we do it with delicacy."

"Right. Let's go back to Chang—she could be the key to all of this. I'm going to call her husband. We need to know a little more about the maid." He got voicemail, left a message.

Carlisle gave him an unenthusiastic thumbs-up and turned to her computer.

He opened his notebook. *If Stanhope didn't kill his wife and his housekeeper then who did?* He flipped through the pages, read the names and stopped when he came to Caroline Stanhope.

She was an odd kid.

Taking over her mother's duties two days after she was murdered. Carlisle had even thought she was wearing Aurora's clothes. And she hadn't seemed too shaken up about her mom's death.

And she was definitely a daddy's girl.

"What are you thinking?" asked Carlisle.

"Caroline Stanhope doesn't have an alibi, she had access to her father's shirts, she knew Mrs. Chang and knew she would come out on Sunday when the family needed her. There was no love lost between Caroline and Aurora. And her behavior is bizarre."

"You think she would frame her father? Because if it wasn't Stanhope, then whoever did do it left us a trail leading straight to him."

"That might not have been her intention. Maybe she had one of her dad's old shirts—"

"And just happened to be wearing it when she murdered his wife? And left it where Chang could find it?"

"Hear me out. She only lives a few blocks from Gigi's. It's a happening place, maybe she just pops down for a drink, maybe she's walking by on her way somewhere else and sees Aurora with Steve Lombardi. She's furious, knows her dad is out of town and goes back to their house to wait for her. Confronts her before she even gets inside."

"And while she's waiting, she slips into one of her father's bespoke button-downs. White? And why doesn't Mrs. Chang notice her?"

"First of all, one of those shirts would practically cover her whole body—if she was planning to kill her mom, one of her dad's shirts wouldn't be a bad choice. Why white?" He gave her an exasperated look. "How the fuck do I know? Maybe it was the first thing she grabbed from the laundry.

"Second, maybe Mrs. Chang did notice. She could have seen Caroline take the shirt, didn't think anything of it until Aurora ends up dead, finds it somewhere and stashes it for later use."

Carlisle looked skeptical, but she said, "So Caroline hits mom over the head, gets her back in the Porsche, drives to the Shermanns', strangles her, dumps her by UW, drives the car back to the Shermanns', walks back to the mansion and changes clothes. Then, the next day, Chang goes sniffing around after she finds out Aurora is dead, discovers the bloody shirt and hides it in her bathroom for leverage."

"Isn't that what I just said? Caroline leaves the car through the weekend because she doesn't know what to do with it. In the meantime, Chang confronts her with the shirt."

Carlisle raised her eyebrows. "Then, Sunday afternoon, Caroline kills her too, stuffs her in the Porsche, leaves her at the Shermanns'. And Sunday night she gets rid of Chang and the Porsche, and leaves Chang's car behind."

"Yeah, something like that," said Kincaid.

"Fuck."

Kincaid's cell phone rang. He listened, said, "Thanks for getting back to me, Miss Chang." To Carlisle, he mouthed *daughter*. They spoke for a few minutes and then Kincaid turned to his partner.

"Did she know anything about the Shermanns?" Carlisle asked.

"Nope. But she found twenty-five thousand dollars in cash, packed into a zip-lock bag and wedged behind a pile of clean linens."

Carlisle was shocked. "Well, that's definitely something. Any idea where it came from?"

"No, and she says her father was as shocked as she was, swears he has no idea where it came from. But she says it's been there a while—long enough to collect dust. Definitely longer than Saturday."

"Kid should be a cop." Carlisle tapped her fingers on the desk. "We gotta send someone to pick up the bag," she said. "Actually, we'll go ourselves. The daughter probably went gently on her dad, having just lost his wife, but he must know something."

Kincaid nodded "They always know something."

"All right, let's go," said Kincaid.

"Yep. Then we'll take a photo of Caroline down to Gigi's. See if anyone recognizes her from Friday night."

They took the unmarked to Northeast Seattle, driving mostly in silence, and found themselves once again feeling the weight of grief as they stood on the Changs' stoop, under the heavy November clouds, waiting for someone to open the door.

The twenty-something face that appeared in the window of the heavy wooden door belonged to Chang's daughter. She invited them to sit in the living room. The extended family seemed to have cleared out, leaving a stack of folded blankets and extra pillows on one of the recliners.

"I'm Susy. I called you this morning." Her voice was strong but her gaze was despondent. "Everyone else left this morning." She looked like she might cry, held it together. "The money is on the kitchen counter. I put it in a paper bag."

"How did you find it?" asked Kincaid.

"I was putting the extra bedding away. The money was sitting in the back of the linen closet. I didn't notice it yesterday."

"And you have no idea where that money came from?" asked Carlisle.

Susy shook her head. "My parents don't have that kind of money and if they did, it would be in a bank."

"We need to see him," said Kincaid and she reluctantly stood to get her father.

At the base of the stairs, she halted. "My stepmom wouldn't have done anything bad. Wherever that money came from, it wasn't because she did something bad."

The detectives didn't say anything, gave an appeasing nod. Whatever that money had come from, it definitely wasn't because Mrs. Chang had done something good.

They heard the slow heavy tread before they saw Mr. Chang's feet on the stairwell. He made his way to a recliner, sat down. "I don't know where that money came from, detectives. Really."

"Actually," said Carlisle, "we'd like to know how your wife was behaving when she came home on Saturday?"

"The same as always," he said, shrugging. "I noticed nothing out of the ordinary."

"The thing is," said Carlisle, "your wife had just found out that her employer had been murdered. It's hard for me to believe that she wasn't upset."

Chang looked puzzled, shook his head. "Annie didn't know that Mrs. Stanhope was dead when she came home on Saturday. Not until Sunday, when the Stanhopes asked her to come in for a few hours. She said that's why they needed her to come back. They needed help."

"Your wife didn't tell you that Mrs. Stanhope had been murdered until Sunday?" asked Kincaid.

"She didn't know, not until Sunday. They called, told her, said they needed help. She was upset, said she wanted to go to them."

"She did know," said Carlisle. "Your wife knew Aurora Stanhope was dead. She knew on Saturday."

Carlisle looked at him, saw realization wash over him and take form.

She felt like they had just beaten a broken man.

"That was bad," said Kincaid when they were back in the car.

"The worst."

"Why do you think she lied to him?"

"I think she lied to him because she had realized that whatever she did to get that twenty-five thousand dollars had helped Aurora's killer. She was freaked out, maybe felt guilty, maybe she was scared, maybe she was planning to shake down the murderer for more money. In any case, she needed a minute to think about it before she told her husband. It wasn't in the news until Sunday, easy enough to put off."

"That's one hell of a poker face if she thought she had abetted a murderer."

Carlisle agreed, but added, "You saw the way she stonewalled us on Saturday. Annie Chang could've won a poker game with God."

Putting the car in drive, Kincaid pulled out into the street. "Gigi's?"

"Yep. I'm hungry," she said.

"To show the photo of Caroline, not for a candlelit lunch."

She flicked him off. "I meant after."

"It's a good thing my eyes are glued to the road, or I would've seen that," he said.

When they got to Gigi's there was nowhere to park. "Goddamn parking," he said as they walked along Elliott Avenue, tucking their chins to avoid the cold wind off the bay.

It was eleven-thirty and the restaurant had just opened for lunch. The hostess was seating a four-top of paunchy middle-aged men in expensive suits and two more parties were already waiting for tables. Carlisle and Kincaid bypassed the line and went to the bar. Discreetly flashing his badge, Kincaid asked the guy stocking wine if Harry was around.

"Somewhere. I'll get him."

They waited a minute and Harry came out looking like a Paul Smith model in a deep purple suit with the telltale stitching.

"Detectives," he said, "don't suppose you're here for lunch?"

"We should be so lucky," said Kincaid. "In fact, we're here on business." Carlisle brandished a printout of Caroline Stanhope from her Facebook page. "Was she here on Friday night?"

Harry took the photo and studied it. "Is this the daughter? They look a lot alike."

"This one's seven inches shorter and half as wide," said Carlisle. "Very petite."

Harry was thoughtful. "I can't say. She looks so much like her mother I feel like she would've stood out just for that, but if she was in the bar, or some corner that I overlooked..." He blew out a breath. "Can I keep this? Ask around?"

"Please," said Kincaid. "Anything else come to mind about Friday night?"

"Nope, sorry." Then he flashed a cheeky grin. "Except the woman who tipped our bartender with her wedding ring came back for it. She traded it for a twenty."

Carlisle smiled. "You called it."

"They always come back," said Harry, shaking his head.

When they were back on the street, Carlisle said, "Let's go to the market for lunch."

"Twist my arm," said Kincaid happily, and they walked down Pike to the market, where they picked up meat and potato piroshkies and lemonade.

———————— ◆■▪◆ ————————

Kyle Sondheim had been sifting through evidence since nine-thirty that morning. She hadn't gotten to bed until almost three and now she was running on four cups of stationhouse motor oil and a supermarket bagel she'd found in the break room. When Carlisle and Kincaid came into the lab with treats from the market she nearly swooned.

Kincaid filled her in on the cash found at Chang's house. "Is that what's in the big bag?" she asked and took a swig of lemonade. "Let's take a look."

Kyle dusted the zip-lock bag with a wispy fingerprint brush, scanned the prints and matched each and every one to Mrs. Chang. "Well," she said, "if you had any doubt who hid the money." She pulled out several bundles and began dusting those too, but found nothing helpful.

Carlisle's shoulders moved up and down heavily, more like a relaxation technique than a shrug.

"If it's any consolation, I found plenty of prints at the Stanhopes'."

"Anything useful?"

"Maybe."

"Yeah?" said Kincaid.

"Aside from Chang's prints in her room, I found both Robert's and Caroline's prints. None from either Aurora or Lucas. Also, Caroline's prints were all over her father's rooms. Bedroom, bathroom, closet, desk, you name it. And they were clear, fresh prints. In other words," she said, in case they didn't get it, "she's been in there digging around. Recently.

"Also," said Kyle, "I checked the hairs I found in Aurora's sunglasses against the sample I took from Caroline and they're a match. An out-of-court match, that is. I won't have DNA back for a while. But under a microscope they're the same color and texture and they are the exact same thickness, down to a ten thousandth of a micron."

Carlisle didn't look at her partner but she knew he was thinking the same thing.

Caroline Stanhope was getting interesting.

CHAPTER TWENTY-FOUR

W EDNESDAY MORNING, CAROLINE HAD WOKEN in her own
bed in her parents' house feeling hungover. Sometime in the
middle of the night, her father had come in to tell her he was home.
Everything was all right. Then she'd drifted off again.

She didn't even remember going to sleep the first time, but here
she was, still dressed, gummy mouth, gummy eyes, bottle of water
next to the bottle of her mother's Ambien on the bedside table.

She washed up and then made her way down the back stairs to
the kitchen.

Halfway down, she stopped. The door at the bottom of the
stairs was open a crack and she could hear her father and brother
talking. Arguing, really

"How the hell should I know how her blood got on my shirt,
Lucas? I didn't kill her."

"I know you didn't kill her, Dad, but it doesn't look good."
There was a clatter of porcelain and she smelled coffee.

"And why was your shirt in the housekeeper's room? Did Annie
say anything to you about it?"

Caroline thought her brother sounded nervous. Her father just
sounded exasperated.

"Of course she didn't. If she had… well, I don't know what I
would've done, but she didn't."

"Why did they let you go? I mean, how did you get out of
there?" Lucas was definitely freaked out. He stammered and

Caroline flinched. The last thing they needed right now was for him to lose his shit.

"I got out of there, Lucas, because they didn't have any proof that I hurt my wife. Not only that, but I was in Portland the night she was murdered, a fact that those detectives seemed to have forgotten when they dragged me to the police station."

There was a long pause and then she heard her brother say, "Dad, I know about the photos you have of Mom."

Fuck, fuck, fuck, thought Caroline. Lucas could never keep his mouth shut.

"For Christ's sake. How the hell would you know anything about that? Did you go through my desk?" Silence followed during which Caroline could only imagine her father had realized Lucas would never have gone through his desk.

Footsteps; she waited a few seconds, then peered through the door. Lucas was alone in the kitchen so she stepped in.

Her brother took a look at her, then held up the coffee pot. She nodded, scowling, and said, "Traitor."

He glanced at her. "Still listening at the door?" He sighed. "Caroline, he's obviously not telling us everything. I had to call him out on it. He was almost arrested. Besides," he added, "I didn't tell him how I knew about the pictures."

"Did you notice that pregnant pause when he asked if you'd been snooping? That was dawning awareness. It took him two seconds to figure out how you knew."

"Your reputation precedes you, Caroline." He handed her a cup of coffee, smirking. "Sugar?"

"Fuck you, Lucas." She took a sip. "Are you gonna stick around today?"

"For a bit," said Lucas.

Caroline bristled. "You can't sell me out to Dad and then take off."

"Grow up, Caroline," he said. "Just tell him you had no idea and he'll think I found the pictures."

"He'd never believe *you* were going through his files." She was already plotting how to spin it. Looking for some reasonable explanation. She'd been looking for something. Paperclips, masking tape. Then it came to her—she was so very, very worried about her father that she had riffled through his things to make sure there wasn't *something* there he could hurt himself with. Equivocation was the key here. And then she would cry. She'd been so frightened when she'd stumbled upon the pictures that she had told Lucas. Please, please, forgive her, Daddy.

That would do it. She looked at her brother. "Do what you like," she said, and went to find her father.

———————

Carlisle's cell phone rang. "It's Lauren, Tom's sister."

Kincaid nodded and turned back to Caroline Stanhope's Instagram page. He didn't get Instagram. Thought it was basically just Facebook without the excessive blah, blah, blah. Actually, now that he thought about it, maybe that was better. Maybe he *did* get Instagram. Carlisle got off the phone and he turned to her. "Anything good?"

"Hard to say. Apparently, Pamela left her a message this morning, thought she'd facilitate a follow-up on their flower deliveries to our relevant parties."

"And?"

"And Lauren said that we could come by and talk to the people who deliver to the country club and the Stanhopes'. And she told me Fleur de Lis also delivers to the Lombardi manse. I think we'll at least get some dirt. Nothing else to do right now. C'mon, let's take a ride down to the docks."

———————

Lauren Carlisle sat behind a desk in a windowless utilitarian office that would have been charmless but for the penetrating scent of flowers and eucalyptus. She looked up from her computer, glanced around her at the dingy file cabinets and stacks of invoices, and frowned. "Let's not talk in here."

She stood and gave her sister-in-law a hug and greeted Kincaid warmly, then led them to some folding chairs at a cutting table in the main warehouse. Here the décor was even more minimal, but they were surrounded by hundreds of plastic buckets holding buds, blooms and greenery bathed in grey light filtered through a corrugated plastic roof. An industrial-size greenhouse.

A few years older than Tom, Lauren Carlisle radiated contentment. Her skin was make-up free and her cheeks were rosy from health and happiness. Blue eyes twinkled when she pointed to an open package on the table. "Fig Newton? It's all I got."

"How about some gossip?" said Carlisle. "We're treading water."

"Got it," said Lauren and walked away.

"She's prettier than I remember," said Kincaid.

"And happily married. Again. You missed your chance, Jerry."

When Lauren came back she had a burly man in his early thirties in tow. "I just deliver the arrangements," he said when they asked. "The staff at the country club checks the invoice and sets them out. I barely even get in the door."

"Nothin'," said Kincaid when the guy had gone.

Next up was a woman about the same age with a broad open face. She was dressed to go hiking, including a pair of beat-to-death leather lace-ups the same color as her polar fleece vest and everything about her would have seemed drab except for the million-watt smile she turned on them once she was seated.

"I can't believe Aurora was murdered. You never think you're going to know someone who was murdered, right?" she added vaguely. "Anyway, she could be tough. Wanted everything just so, but I carry a bucket of extras in the van with me and I could usually fix whatever she thought was missing, or not full enough, or not fresh enough. I've been delivering there for years and I think it was kind of a game for her. Trying to trip me up. But she was always happy when I left."

"You deliver to the Lombardis too?" asked Kincaid.

"Yeah, I pretty much follow the yellow brick road around Lake Washington. It's crazy."

"Crazy how?" asked Carlisle.

She shook her head. "So much money and so much beauty and most of the time, the only people I ever see in those big houses are the help. If I lived there, I would never leave." She gave the detectives a mild smile and shrugged. "It seems like a waste."

Carlisle nodded. "But you saw Mrs. Stanhope frequently?"

"Like I said, she liked to be there when I arrived. Give me a little hell, through a little bitch my way. I kind of liked her."

"Ever see Mrs. Lombardi?"

"Another grown-up debutant. *She* never complains, though. Always friendly and agreeable. She always says how spoiled she is to have fresh flowers each week." She looked at them. "She just says it to relate. But it's a nice sentiment."

"Anything else?"

She laughed a little. "The words you've been waiting to hear. Drum roll, please." Their half-hearted smiles didn't dampen her enthusiasm when she said, "And she always asked if Mrs. Stanhope had given me hell. And I always said no."

"That it?"

"That's it. I figured they had some kind of rivalry, except that it seemed pretty one-sided because Mrs. Stanhope never once mentioned Mrs. Lombardi." She thought for a minute. "Honestly, they're all kind of weirdos. The seriously privileged. Maybe it's just because I'm not part of that world, but it's like they all live in a bubble full of their own rules and they're own distractions, and for someone like me, it all seems a little petty. Mrs. Stanhope and

Mrs. Lombardi never struck me as unusual, relatively to each other. Relative to my world, they're all freaks."

Carlisle knew what she meant, but it wasn't particularly helpful. "Ever talk to Lombardi about Mrs. Stanhope?"

"*Nooooo*. That would be a quick way to lose my job and I like working here. Lauren's the best." She winked at Carlisle. "Feel free to tell her I said so."

On their way out, Kincaid asked Lauren, "Ever run into Caroline Stanhope during your endeavors to make Seattle a more beautiful place for the rich and corruptible?"

Lauren smiled wryly at him, then wrinkled her nose. "Don't tell anyone I said this, but that kid is a nightmare. We did her sweet sixteen party and high school graduation. She wasn't as bad for the grad party, but Caroline wanted what she wanted for that birthday, and she was a rabid bitch about it, like her first taste of adulthood had released the monster within. Fought like hell with her mother, ordered me and everyone here around with blatant contempt. No respect." She gave a little shudder. "Mom was still here then, but she put me in charge of it and I swear, she knew exactly what she was doing." Lauren gave her sister-in-law a look. "Trial by fire."

"I know how that goes," said Kincaid as they moved toward the exit. "Just curious, who took care of the grad party?"

"Aurora chose the arrangements, but someone else, a younger woman who worked for her, ran interference with the kid. After the birthday, I think Aurora decided an intermediary was in order."

"Between you and Caroline?"

"No such luck, between Aurora and Caroline."

Carlisle considered, tried to remember how long the PA had said she worked for Aurora. "Was the woman's name Karen Green?"

"No. It was Beth something. Beth… something. Anyway, I saw her at Aurora's corporate party planning summits. It's been a while since I stopped doing deliveries, so it's been a few years since I've seen her, but Beth seemed to run a lot of interference for Aurora at those too. Bit of a diplomat."

"Right. Hey, thanks for helping out. I appreciate it."

"Anytime. We all still on for dinner this weekend?" Carlisle nodded and they embraced warmly. Then Lauren turned her gaze on Kincaid and gave him a once-over. "You look good in that suit, Jerry. Maybe you should join us at dinner?"

Carlisle laughed out loud. She knew Lauren was mostly joking, but her sister-in-law had enough Marlene Dietrich in her to keep you guessing.

"I heard you got hitched again, Lauren," said Kincaid, all smiles.

"Just a formality, Detective."

Back in the car, Carlisle said, "Stop flirting with my in-laws; they'll start liking you more than me. Hey, how'd you know she'd done Caroline's grad party?"

"I didn't for sure, but Caroline has a whole Facebook album devoted to her graduation party and the flowers were very nice."

"You're a true detective, Kincaid. Tried and true."

"So, are we gonna start seriously looking at Caroline for this?" said Kincaid.

"Well, she had every opportunity that Robert had to kill Aurora and plenty of motive; she could have strangled her mother if Aurora was already incapacitated. Means, motive, opportunity, but it would be a long shot to prove in court and there's no way the DA's office is going to let us haul in another Stanhope unless it's a slam dunk. And I can't blame them; if Stanhope decided to flex his muscles, he could fuck up a lot of people politically. Besides, we'll look like assholes if we keep harassing Stanhopes willy-nilly."

"Don't want that," said Kincaid mirthlessly. "But let's keep digging."

"Maybe someone at Gigi's will recognize her from Friday.

That would help." She narrowed her eyes. "And I wanna talk to Beth Williams again. We didn't ask her nearly enough about the Stanhope family the other day."

"Agreed." Kincaid pulled out his phone, dialed a number from his notepad. "Miss Williams, it's Jerome Kincaid. Beth, right." He gave Carlisle a look, talked a minute, ended the call. "She said she'd come to us. Business meetings downtown today."

———————◆———————

"So, what now?" asked Beth. "I'm not the person to talk to about Robert. Most of what I know about him is filtered through Aurora anyway."

Carlisle and Kincaid just looked at her.

"Isn't Robert your prime suspect?"

Carlisle looked at her partner, exasperated. They had kept Stanhope's question and answer session at the precinct out of the papers, but evidently not out of the gossip mill.

"Hey," said Beth, "high society in this town talks. But if you arrested him, why are you asking about Caroline?"

"We didn't arrest him, Beth," said Kincaid.

"But you searched his house?"

"Do you think Robert Stanhope killed his wife?"

"No. I think he loved her very, very much, in spite of the fact that she took him for granted sometimes."

"Love can be a powerful motive for murder," said Kincaid.

She frowned. "That's terrible."

"You say she took him for granted," said Carlisle, "but in fact, she cheated on him. A lot. And from what I understand about your relationship with Aurora, you *had* to know about it."

"I believe I already mentioned that."

"You said that you'd heard she was unfaithful to him but as far as you knew, it was just rumor. But now we *know* that she screwed around. *A lot.*" She let that sink in, then said, "Robert may have loved her and been furious with her at the same time."

"I suppose," she said, "but it was all more complicated than that... And Aurora implied that he wasn't totally innocent either. I don't know if that's true, of course, I mean if Robert was fooling around then he was a lot more discreet than she was. But I think they had an understanding."

"Why didn't you mention this before, Beth?" asked Kincaid.

"Because it's all conjecture and I don't think it's relevant anyway. And I hate gossip."

"Not relevant because you don't believe Robert Stanhope killed his wife?"

"Because he didn't seem that troubled by her affairs and would therefore have no reason to kill his wife."

"Ah," he said. "And you think he was okay with it because Aurora told you so?"

Beth eyed him. "Touché, Detective."

Carlisle didn't want this to become antagonistic—not yet anyway. She changed the subject. "We had a chat with Aurora Stanhope's florist, and she told us that Caroline Stanhope could be a chore."

Beth's eyebrows rose. "Caroline? Yeah, she *was* a chore, probably still is. We went over that already." Eyebrows raised. "Is she a suspect?"

"No, no," said Carlisle. "We're asking about everyone." Beth didn't buy it, but Carlisle didn't care. "So, Lauren—the owner—said that Caroline and Aurora argued a lot."

"I can corroborate that. I *have* corroborated that."

"Exactly," said Carlisle with a broad smile, "and now we'd like you to *elaborate* on that."

Beth shook her head, said, "But Aurora was strangled and Caroline is just a tiny slip of a thing. And Aurora would never have let her do it."

"Strangled?" Carlisle had hoped the cause of death wouldn't have leaked yet, but she was wrong.

"Wasn't she?" Beth read the truth on their faces. "Detectives, you can't keep secrets from these people. Aurora's murder is like the Kennedy assassination for Seattle high society. The crème de la crème are calling on every campaign donation they've ever made to find out what happened. I might not be one of them, but I'm on the periphery. And I hear stuff."

Carlisle didn't doubt it, but she didn't like it. "And if I told you Aurora had been poisoned, would you believe Caroline could have done it?"

Beth sighed. "Maybe, yes. But listen, I can't imagine it."

"Is that because you can't imagine someone committing murder or because you don't think Caroline could murder her own mother?"

"Both. Mostly the latter."

"Any reason to think Caroline or Lucas knew about the affairs?"

"Aurora's affairs? They would've heard the same rumors everyone else did, although Lucas was away at school by the time I started working with Aurora. Obviously from what I saw, Caroline was closer to the logistics of her parents' relationship than he was, why aren't you asking her these questions?" Beth peered closely at the detectives. "Surely not because you're concerned about upsetting her?" She raised an eyebrow. "You can't really think she did it? No. No. Killing her mother to protect her father would've just hurt him. I mean, I'm sure Robert is crushed by Aurora's death."

"What if," said Carlisle, "Caroline found out that her mother was sleeping with one of her boyfriends?"

"One of whose boyfriends? Caroline's?" She stared at Carlisle. "*Nooooo.* I don't believe it."

Over the next fifteen minutes Carlisle and Kincaid managed to get a pretty clear picture of a bad-on-bad mother-daughter relationship.

What they had thought was rebellion and resentment on Caroline's part seemed to be real animosity, even hatred, and that was reason enough to take a really close look at her.

But what Beth said next nearly made the detectives' eyes pop out of their heads.

"So, was it Jonathan? The boyfriend Aurora slept with?"

Kincaid played it cool. "What makes you think it's Jonathon?"

"Well, actually when you first said it, I couldn't believe she would do that to Caroline. But now that I've thought about it, I can kind of imagine. He was around so much."

Carlisle was thinking that Beth had turned out to be a much better gossip than she gave herself credit for. She let Kincaid take the lead.

"And Jonathon came to mind right away?"

"Caroline lived at home her first year in college and he was always around. I think they were together the whole year. In college that's a big deal."

"That's a big deal anytime, if you ask me," said Kincaid affably.

"Maybe, but in college a year feels like the beginning, the end, and love eternal in between. Caroline was totally in love with that guy."

"Can you give us a little chronology?"

Beth considered. "Honestly, I don't remember a lot of detail, but I do remember the break-up, because it was bloody awful. End of the summer, I think before her sophomore year? She lost weight—which was scary because of her history—took a leave of absence from school and divided her time between weeping and plotting his death."

"Plotting his death?" asked Carlisle, eyebrows raised.

"Not seriously," said Beth, backing up. "It was kid stuff." She blinked. "I can remember planning brutal revenge against an ex-boyfriend or two at that age."

"Any idea why they broke up?" asked Kincaid.

"Oh. Absolutely," she said. "Jonathon cheated on her, then told her about it, then dumped her. One fell swoop." She looked at Carlisle. "He could've at least had the decency to let Caroline dump *him*. Right?"

Carlisle grinned. "Yeah, I guess I can see why she would have wanted some revenge. So, you think the affair he had was with Aurora?"

Now Beth looked wary. "I didn't. Not until you said she'd slept with one of Caroline's boyfriends." Carlisle didn't correct her, but they hadn't actually said it, just asked if it were *possible*. "Aurora was hell-bent on getting rid of Jonathon and I never really understood why. Not so much at first—at first, she didn't pay them any attention. But later, when she thought they were getting serious—marriage serious—she made it clear to me that *this* guy was *not* going to marry her daughter."

"Did she make it clear to Caroline?"

"No way. Aurora was too clever for that. And she was right— if she had told Caroline that she didn't like her boyfriend, she probably would've flown to Vegas and married him the same day." She shook her head. "To the young couple, she was all charm and good will. Well," she amended, "maybe not the latter, but only because she wasn't that type of person. My point is that you'd never have known that she didn't approve of the relationship unless she told you plainly."

"And she told *you* plainly," said Kincaid.

"She did."

"But if she didn't like him, why would you think she had an affair with him?" asked Carlisle.

Beth shrugged. "I guess it sounds funny, but just because she didn't want him to end up marrying her daughter doesn't mean she didn't want to fool around with him. Or maybe she disapproved because she had slept with him? I didn't mention it before, but some of the rumors about Aurora involved younger men. And Jonathon was a seriously good-looking guy. Dark hair, dark eyes."

"Rich?"

"I don't think so. But don't quote me."

"Anything else that makes you think they were sleeping together?" asked Carlisle.

"I don't know, but when you said it..." She went quiet for a few seconds; Carlisle waited her out. "There were lots of furtive looks on his part. I came to the house a few times and he was there but Caroline wasn't. You know, she was always on her way or had just stepped out. I figured he was using the pool or mooching out of the Stanhopes' overstuffed cupboard. But if he was sleeping with Aurora, then it makes sense he was there so much." She squinted, thinking about something. "And from what I saw, the only thing worse than Caroline's rage at Jonathon after they broke up was her rage at Aurora."

"She was angry with her mother after her boyfriend dumped her?"

"Furious. Unrelenting. The thing is, she was always pissed at Aurora, always snotty, and I figured that after they broke up, Aurora had told her she didn't like Jonathon anyway and she was better off and that had added fuel to the fire between them. I even wondered if Aurora had had something to do with it. Had a 'talk' with him, if you know what I mean. Maybe paid him off. But if he told her that he'd been having sex with her mother, well, that would explain everything. She would have blamed her mother for the breakup."

"You think he might have told her?" asked Carlisle, thinking he'd have to be an idiot.

"Don't you? I mean, it would explain everything," she repeated.

───────────

As they were wrapping up the interview, Kincaid said, "By the way,

Beth. We have several Jonathons on our list, which one are you referring to?"

Understanding broke, expanding across her features like a shock wave. "You didn't know about Jonathon."

Kincaid caught himself trying to distinguish Beth's disgust from her appreciation and hoped he was seeing more of the latter. He waited for her to go on.

Carlisle was unperturbed.

"Stein. Jonathon Stein."

"Thank you, Beth," said Carlisle.

"Yeah. Whatever. Fair enough. It was a good play." But she didn't look like that made it better.

Kincaid said, "Total improvisation. Right off the cuff." He shrugged. "It's part of the job."

Beth was still frowning. "Wait a minute, you thought there was a boyfriend. But not Jonathon." She shuddered. "Another one? God, that's awful."

"Anyone in particular?" asked Kincaid.

"*No.* I'm not falling for that again."

"Other than boyfriends and lovers? Does anything else come to mind, anything at all relevant?" asked Carlisle.

She looked at them absently. Thought about Missy Lombardi. The strange implied intimacy, the assumption that Beth and her son would embrace her now that Aurora was dead. The big fat check that hadn't come yet. She was probably being silly.

"No, nothing else."

———————◆▬▬▬◻▬◻⊦———————

Carlisle watched her partner watching their witness walk out of the bullpen. "It's okay, Jerry, you had her smiling again before she left."

"But things will never be the same."

Carlisle laughed. "I see it happening, Jerry. Mark my words. As soon as we've solved this case."

"Speaking of. Let's find Jonathon Stein."

She ran a DMV records search and found him pretty quickly. "This one's about the right age." They took a look at the face on her computer screen. "Damn. He *is* good looking. Caroline must only date Ken dolls."

"He's not *that* good looking," said Kincaid, sucking in his tummy.

"He is that good looking. But he's got nothing on you, Kincaid." Jonathon Stein had dark hair, dark eyes, olive skin and managed to look sultry in his DMV photo. "Let's go find this mother-fucker."

CHAPTER TWENTY-FIVE

IT WAS QUARTER PAST FIVE when they arrived at the Microsoft offices in South Lake Union. Carlisle had called ahead and Stein was going to meet them in the lobby in fifteen minutes, but he was already waiting. No problem recognizing him—he was even prettier than the pool boy.

"Mind if we walk?" he asked after they'd made introductions. They headed to a café a block away. "You realize I haven't seen the Stanhopes in years. I don't know how I can help you."

"It's actually years ago that we want to talk to you about," said Kincaid. "Around the time you broke up with Caroline."

He groaned. "I knew that would come back to me at some point. Man, that was a *bad* break-up." They had reached the café. "I wanna get a sandwich to bring back to the office. Working late tonight."

After they'd all gotten drinks and Stein had ordered a sandwich to go, they sat at a table by the window of the nearly empty café.

"They only stay open until seven, so when I work late I come by before they close and bring dinner back with me. Great sandwiches." He looked from Kincaid to Carlisle, saw that they didn't care. "Okay, okay." He took a deep breath. "Worst break-up ever."

Carlisle thought, *Nobody has had the worst break-up ever by twenty-five.* "What happened?"

"Look, I was a total asshole, I'll admit it. Caroline and I were together for almost a year and then I started fucking around on her. I mean, I should've just broken up with her when I started to, you know, wander, but I didn't. The whole thing was really bad. I really fucked up. I mean, it's my biggest regret ever."

Stein was circling the drain and Carlisle didn't have the patience for it. "Just tell us what you did, Jonathon." Smiling like she didn't mean it. "You'll feel better, I guarantee it."

He looked at her like a teenager caught in a stolen car. "I had sex with her mom. More than once." He gulped. "But Mrs. Stanhope was so flirty, I mean, she didn't care that I was dating her daughter. That last summer we were together, I spent a lot of time at the Stanhopes' pool and out on the lake and she was all over me. The minute Caroline turned around, she was there."

Kincaid wasn't going to interrupt the flow of information, but he wanted to tell this kid that after you've slept with a woman, it was time to start calling her by her first name.

"After a while I couldn't help it, she was *super* sexy and she obviously knew what she was doing, and it was so... *wrong*. Caroline was sweet, but totally immature and self-conscious." His eyes glazed over. "Mrs. Stanhope was so, like, knowledgeable."

Kincaid glanced at his partner and had to hide a smile behind his bottle of Coke.

"I didn't care that she was older, she really had it all. Know what I mean?" Stein raised his eyebrows, looked at the detectives, caught Carlisle's expression and had the good grace to look embarrassed.

"And that's why you broke it off with Caroline?" asked Kincaid.

"No, not exactly. I mean, yeah, but not just that. I knew we weren't going to be together forever. I mean, I had just turned twenty-one and Caroline was younger and just the fact that I could go to bars without her was stressing our relationship. We were way too young to get really serious. Plus, it's college. Time to play the field a little bit."

"And you chose Aurora Stanhope?" Kincaid said. Mocking.

"No, *no*. That's what I'm saying—*she* chose *me*. And I was already moving on from Caroline, emotionally, and she made it easy. So then I *really* had to get out of the whole situation because all of a sudden it was like an episode of *Pretty Little Liars* and I could practically see the headline: *Crime of Passion at the Stanhope Compound*. Freaked me out, man."

"It must've been scary," Carlisle said sympathetically.

"It *was* scary." Jonathon Stein shook his head of shiny black hair as if he still couldn't believe it had happened to him.

"Did Caroline find out?" she asked.

"Well, not at first." He sunk deeper into Carlisle's compassionate gaze and finally made the big confession. "I was being a real shit to her and I thought maybe she'd break up with me, but she just kept trying to work it out. Finally, I told her that I'd cheated on her and it was over and she started crying and then she slapped me and then she said that we could *still* work it out, that she could forgive me. But I knew we would never *ever* work that out and so after a few days of phone calls and screaming I couldn't take it anymore. Meanwhile, she's demanding to know who I'd slept with and I cracked. I mean, I'd really had it. I wanted her to leave me alone, so finally I told her. You know? I told her."

———————◆–■-◻-◻–◆———————

None of them spoke for a few seconds, the revelation sinking in. Carlisle clenched a fist under the table as a great wave of disgust passed through her. *He told her. Caroline knew.*

Head bowed, Stein added, "That did it. It was over. I thought she was going to hit me again but she just went all white and then red and started shaking."

"You were with her when you told her?" asked Kincaid. He'd pegged this kid for a cellphone dumper. Maybe even by text.

"She showed up at my place and one of my idiot roommates let her in. Meanwhile, I'm in my room, headphones up full blast and this cold little hand lands on my shoulder. I just about shit my pants; it was creepy, man. She kept saying that if I told her who it was, that she could forgive me. She *really* wanted to know who it was. I mean, at the time I thought she meant it about working things out, but later, I realized she just wanted to know who I'd fucked."

"Any reason to think she already knew? Or thought she did?" asked Carlisle.

Clearly, that had never occurred to Stein. "Already knew? How could she? I mean, if she already knew, she would've said something, right?"

Carlisle just stared at him.

He furrowed his brow. "When I told her, I'm pretty sure she was surprised. I guess it could've been something else." His eyes went wide. At last, the clouds parted and it all became clear. With a sick expression he said, "You don't think she killed her mom 'cause I slept with her?"

"We're just asking questions, Jonathon, nothing for you to worry about." Carlisle gave him a nod that was anything but reassuring.

As they gathered their trash and recyclables Kincaid asked, "What do you do at Microsoft, Jonathon?"

"Programming. My dad got me the job, but my band is my real gig."

They let him walk back to the office on his own and headed for their unmarked. "That's a huge load of resentment to dump on a freshman in college," said Carlisle.

"A freshman who already hated her mother."

"Fuck me. What the hell kind of a woman would do that to her own daughter?" Carlisle was offended at her core, as a woman, as a mother, as a human being. "Honestly, if she was still alive I might strangle her myself."

"Hard not to feel sorry for the kid."

"Yeah, well, sympathy is for her defense attorney to put in front of a jury. Our job is to put her in the courtroom." Carlisle's emotions sometimes walked the line between compassion and the law, but there was no doubt onto which side she would fall. If Caroline had killed her mother, no matter how awful the woman was, she had to go to trial for it—a jury could decide the punishment. But with Mrs. Chang's murder, as far as Carlisle was concerned, there were no mitigating circumstances. It was cold-blooded murder and whoever had killed her, no matter what the housekeeper had done for the twenty-five grand, had to go to prison.

"We gotta talk to Caroline, but no chance it'll be without Thorpe."

"If he lets us talk to her at all," said Carlisle.

"Think we've got enough circumstantial evidence to get a warrant for her phone records, bank stuff, anything?"

"Maybe, but I don't know how much good it would do us. We've got all the calls made to and from Aurora's phone and we've got Chang's records. Bank stuff? If she was at Gigi's on Friday, she might've paid with a card. Let's try it."

Kincaid started the car. "Speaking of phone calls. We still don't have an explanation for that second call from Steve Lombardi's phone on Friday night."

"It was him," said Carlisle. "Had to be." Still, she would feel better if he had just admitted it. Loose ends didn't make airtight cases.

———————————

Caroline had made up with her father. She'd told him how worried she'd been, that she'd only looked around his things because she had been scared. She'd let tears fill her eyes, brim over.

Her father had given her a tight hug and told her everything would be all right.

Now she was in the kitchen, iPad open to a recipe for lamb chops and risotto. She'd had the ingredients delivered that afternoon and now she pressed a finger hard into each temple, trying to stave off a headache; cooking held little joy for Caroline, and eating even less.

Which generally meant she didn't do much cooking unless it was for someone else. Learning to cook had been a part of her eating disorder therapy as a teenager, and she'd become quite adept, even shown some natural talent as a home chef. But she didn't like it. And she rarely ate what she cooked. Still, showing an interest in cooking had gotten her parents off her back, and that was reason enough to pursue it.

Pulling the big butcher's knife out of its walnut block, Caroline started cutting double chops and let her mind wander.

She wished Lucas would get off his high horse and play ball. She'd called him an hour ago and insisted he come to dinner, but she'd had to really press the poor-widowed-dad-doesn't-know-what-he's-doing card because Lucas was fed up with their father. First for not telling them why he'd been taken to the police station, and second for not telling them how he got out of it. Caroline had been able to fill in the details of the first, but she still didn't know for sure what their father had told the police to make them let him go. Though she suspected it had something to do with a woman. In any case, she was glad he hadn't actually been arrested. That would've been hard to live down.

———————◼◼◻————————

Kincaid hung up his desk phone. "No way on Caroline's bank, and no way on her phone records. After the Robert Stanhope debacle, they're gun-shy."

"Fucking district attorney," said Carlisle. "There's not a single spine in that office."

"*But*," said Kincaid, "Caroline's cell phone is on the Stanhope family plan, which we already got access to with the first search warrant. The on-call DA is going to pull the file and email it over."

"When?"

"After we have dinner."

They decided to get something to eat at a Caribbean place a few blocks away while they waited to hear from the DA's office. Carlisle called in a to-go order along the way because the restaurant closed at seven, not because they expected a response from the DA in the next half hour. Cuban dip sandwich and an empanada plate, extra chimichurri—her mouth was watering as she unpacked the food at their desks.

They ate in companionable silence until Kincaid's inbox dinged. He opened his eyes wide and swallowed. "Could it be?"

It was. Kincaid got a list of the phone numbers of all the players and they began comparing them to the list the DA had just sent over.

"There it is," said Carlisle, pointing at a number with her pen. "Caroline talked to Steve Lombardi for three and a half minutes on Friday night at nine-fifty-seven."

They both sat back in their chairs, dumbfounded.

"What do you think?" said Kincaid.

"I think she saw her mother having dinner with Steve at Gigi's and called him."

"To say what? Why didn't she call her mom?"

"I don't know." Carlisle thought about it for a few seconds. "Okay, she walks passed the restaurant—it's right by her condo—sees them getting cozy. She's seething, picks up her phone to call her mom, thinks better of it. Maybe she doesn't think Aurora will answer, or that she'll deny they're together, so she calls Steve instead."

"Why doesn't she just go in there and confront them both?"

"Maybe she doesn't want to cause a scene. Her mom had acceptable outfits delivered to Caroline for social events, I'm sure she drilled it into both of her kids that public outbursts were against the Stanhope rules of etiquette. Or maybe she calls Lombardi because she's already homicidal and doesn't want a record of a phone call to her mom." She caught the skepticism in her partner's eyes. "Come on, Kincaid, this is your theory, play along for a second."

"Okay, okay," said Kincaid. "She sees them in the restaurant together but doesn't want to rush over and start a fight. She takes out her cell and she's about to call her mom but thinks better of it—possibly because she doesn't want to leave a trail, but more likely, because she wants to take the two lovebirds by surprise. Steve picks up and she bitches him out, or Steve picks up and she asks to speak to her mom. Caught in the act, Aurora gets on the phone, and then what?"

"Then I call Lombardi and find out what the hell really happened." She started searching for her cell phone. "I swear if this guy doesn't 'fess up, I'll break his legs."

Kincaid held out a hand. "Let's track him down. Do this in person."

Half an hour later they were back on Lake Washington. "Up there on the left," said Carlisle.

An iron gate stood open and the house was lit up like Christmas. "Someone's home," said Kincaid. As they pulled into the drive next to a silver S-Class Mercedes, he let out a whistle. A sprawling three-story Federal Colonial stood in the center of a massive lot surrounded by Pacific dogwoods and big leaf maples. The brightly-lit windows glowed against the dark sky and when they got out of their unmarked, the sounds of water told them the lake was right on the other side of the house.

Carlisle counted five hundred-thousand-dollar cars in the drive. "Think they're having a little party?"

"Who do you think is responsible for turning all of those lights on and off every night?" asked Kincaid.

"The butler, of course." Shaking her head, she added, "Jesus, I thought the Stanhopes lived well."

"I'd like to think I could get used to living like this, but I don't know. Honestly, it's a whole different world."

They walked up the wide stone staircase, rang the bell and only waited a few seconds before the double doors opened and an older man in a tweed suit greeted them politely.

Carlisle told him they were there to talk to Mr. Lombardi and he led them to a sitting room and went off to fetch the man of the house. Kincaid sat on the edge of a stiff leather sofa while Carlisle made the rounds. "Was that *really* a butler?" Kincaid shrugged. She said, "I'll take the lead. He likes me better."

When Lombardi walked in, she was studying a seascape in a carved mahogany frame.

"Don't touch, Detective."

"Mr. Lombardi," she said, turning to face him and seeing two men standing in the doorway.

"To what do I owe the pleasure?" Sarcastic, but not angry. Ronny Buccio flanked his client as he entered the room.

Carlisle gave him a sultry smile. "Why Mr. Lombardi, is that a lawyer in your pocket, or are you just happy to see me?"

Lombardi was florid with scotch or bourbon or some other über-masculine booze, which made it somehow fitting when he said, "I have a poker game to get back to, Detective Carlisle."

"And I have a few questions, Mr. Lombardi."

He looked her up and down. "You forgot to bring your legs, Detective Carlisle. A skirt would've gone a long way convincing me to cooperate."

"It didn't do me any good yesterday."

"All right, all right, break it up you two," said Buccio. "Why are you here, Detectives?"

———————

Carlisle kept her eyes on Lombardi. "Caroline Stanhope called you at ten o'clock on Friday night. What did she want?"

He looked at his attorney, who nodded. Obviously, Buccio had already heard about the phone call. "She said she knew I was at Gigi's with her mother and she wanted to talk to her. I could tell by her voice that she was barely contained and I didn't want to deal with it so I handed over the phone." He shrugged. "Did not want to get in the middle of that."

He went quiet as if that was enough said. "And?" said Carlisle. "What happened next?"

"They talked. Aurora talked, anyway. Caroline sounded like a cat in heat from what I could hear across the table."

"Could you make out what she was saying?"

"Not at all. And Aurora didn't say a lot either because she couldn't get a word in edgewise. At first, she tried to calm Caroline down but then she gave up. Called her an asshole and said they could talk about it later if Caroline could compose herself."

"Is that a quote?" asked Carlisle.

"Paraphrase, but it's pretty close."

"She called her daughter an asshole?"

"That part *is* a quote."

"And she said they'd talk about it later?" He nodded. "Did she say when?"

"All she said was that they could talk about it when Caroline had settled down. Eventually she just hung up and handed my phone back."

"Did she say goodbye?"

"No. Caroline was still shrieking when she ended the call."

"Did Aurora say anything?"

"Just flashed me a smile and rolled her eyes. Aurora wasn't in the habit of explaining herself. Or her family."

Turning to Kincaid, she said, "Anything else?"

"Why does Caroline Stanhope have your number?"

"I don't know," said Lombardi. "I don't have hers, didn't recognize the call when it came in."

"But you weren't surprised she had it?"

"No. Honestly, it's easy to find. I *was* surprised she called."

"Why do you think she called you?" asked Kincaid.

He let out a little guffaw. "Because Aurora would've known it was Caroline calling and she wouldn't have answered. I mean, those two didn't get along on a good day, but a phone call after cocktail hour on a weekend night didn't bode well."

"Did you see Caroline in the restaurant?"

"I looked around when I realized she'd seen us there, but she must've left already. Or maybe she saw us from the street. We had a table by the window. I glanced at the bar—Aurora didn't seem to care, but I couldn't stand the thought of that weird little girl spying on us—but all I saw was a little commotion around the bartender."

Carlisle nodded at her partner. "The wedding ring."

"Wedding ring?" said Lombardi.

"An angry wife tipped the bartender with her wedding ring, came back for it a few days later."

Lombardi blinked at her, turned back to his attorney.

Carlisle looked closely at him.

"Anything else?" asked Buccio. He'd been silent throughout the conversation, but Carlisle and Kincaid had no doubt that he would've stopped it if he thought they were edging into the DMZ. That he'd let the questions stand without interrupting said a lot.

"Just one more thing," said Carlisle, now that they were on their way out. "Did you have sex with Aurora on the night of her murder?"

Lombardi flashed a sick smile. "In the backseat of my Mercedes."

———————■-■-■-□-■———————

"What a shithead," said Kincaid as he started the car.

"Total prick. But, he answered our questions. I even think he enjoyed answering our questions."

"Well, you were right on about that phone call."

"I was," said Carlisle. "That and a box of rocks will get us nowhere. We need hard evidence."

"We've got Caroline's hair in the car, and we've got her fingerprints all over her dad's stuff."

"So what? There's not a single article of clothing or square inch of my house that my children haven't tried on, pawed at, broken, bent, torn or stained. It's circumstantial at best."

"Okay, but put all of that together with the boyfriends and the phone call—which she lied about when she told us she'd last spoken to her mother on Thursday afternoon—and we've got a shot at a warrant of her bank accounts. Suppose she withdrew twenty-five grand in cash sometime in the recent past?"

Carlisle rolled her shoulders. "Always the voice of reason. I'll make the call." She talked to a DA, who reluctantly agreed to petition for a warrant for Caroline's finances. She hung up. "He said it's thin for the bank records, but he'll try. Head back to the station and wait?" Her partner grunted. She made another call. "Buccio drives the S-Class."

———————————

Kyle was still in the lab when they got back and she met them at their desks in the detectives' bullpen. "Anything new?" she asked, and Carlisle filled her in on the phone call to Steve Lombardi.

"I took another look at the blonde hairs I found in the Porsche," said Kyle. "There's Aurora's, Caroline's and one other."

"*Another* blonde was riding around in the car?" said Carlisle, exasperated.

"Well, another blonde *hair* was riding around in the car. The thing is, it's only one solitary strand. It could've been carried into the car on Aurora's coat or Robert's trousers or whatever."

Carlisle stared at her. "So, is it meaningful? In any way?"

Kyle frowned. "Well, I don't know. Maybe. But it's in the evidence file, so…"

"So," said Carlisle, "if we ever find another blonde and happen to subpoena a hair sample and send it off for DNA, we could test it against the errant strand you found in Aurora's Porsche?"

"Hey, I just collect it and report. You two have to figure out what to do with it."

Carlisle growled. "Shit. Do you have anything we can actually work with?"

"The reason I came up is that the technician who searched Aurora's suite found a few things of interest. I don't know what any of it means, but he found yet another pic of Aurora with the pool boy."

"Why didn't we hear about that last night?" asked Kincaid.

"I didn't know about it until this afternoon when I was sorting through some of the stuff we brought in."

"Well, you should've led with that instead of the case of the mysterious hair."

"Piss off," said Kyle amiably, "if I'd told you about the pic first, you wouldn't have paid attention to the hair."

"Because the hair is irrelevant," said Carlisle.

"Stop bickering, you two," said Kincaid. "Where?"

"He found it inside of Caroline's luggage which was in Aurora's room."

"In Caroline's luggage?" said Carlisle, flabbergasted. "And we're *just* hearing about it?"

"Look, if I had seen this stuff sooner, I would've told you about it. As it stands, I pulled it out, sorted through it, found out where it came from and told you two ingrates right away."

Kincaid frowned and turned to Carlisle. "She already knew about the pool boy, right? Does it make much difference?"

"It could help us get into Caroline's condo. I'm going to ask the DA."

Kyle said, "I didn't expect Caroline to have stuff in there so I didn't alert the troops to keep an eye out, but he should have let me know as soon as he realized it didn't belong to Aurora. It might not even fit within the scope of the warrant. I think it was an honest mistake on his part, but I'm not sure you can use it."

Carlisle nodded. "Don't worry about it. I'm gonna make that call anyway." She took her cell phone to the other end of the nearly empty squad room, came back a few minutes later. "Not a chance."

"Nothin'?" said Kincaid.

"He can't use the photo because Caroline's stuff wasn't included in the search warrant for her dad's house. And even if he could, he doesn't think it's enough. He said, quote, 'From what you've told me, those photos were ubiquitous. Everyone in that family probably had their own copy.' *Ubiquitous.* But," she raised a finger, "it might help us get a look at Caroline's bank accounts."

Kyle shrugged. "I'm going home. You two hardworking gumshoes can call me if you need anything else tonight. Otherwise, I'll be here bright and early."

She was walking away when Carlisle said, "You ever going to tell us why you and Lucas broke up?"

Kyle stopped in her tracks.

CHAPTER TWENTY-SIX

S HE TOLD THEM ABOUT THE weekend in San Diego.

"He was an asshole from the minute he picked me up at the airport. Interrupting me, staring openly at other women, talking exclusively about himself. He would shake his head when I told him about something new I'd learned or how amazing Quantico had been. Once he said, 'You really think all that shit's important, don't you?'

"I was furious and he apologized, but it was like he was placating an idiot, laughing, saying he'd been joking, don't take it all so seriously, and so on. We ended up having an okay night, but in my head, I was halfway out the door. I mean, I didn't have much invested in the relationship, except a little bit of my heart and nonrefundable round-trip ticket from Seattle. I thought I'd try to have a good time the rest of the weekend and then maybe I could just walk away.

"Saturday, I got up about nine and Lucas was gone. We had a nice suite. I ordered room service. Breakfast, coffee. Showered, got dressed and he came back about a minute after my breakfast arrived. 'Let's go,' he said. 'Right now. C'mon, you gotta see the waves, we have to get in the ocean.'

"It was April and the Pacific was ass-cold. But he was so excited—almost manic—that I went along, figured he'd stick his foot in and then change his mind. But he didn't—he tested the water, said 'Brrr,' and then ran headlong into the surf. He was out there for half an hour, splashing like a kid in a wading pool.

"Honestly, I didn't know what to make of it. He had always been so thoughtful and calm. I even asked him if he'd taken something. 'Like what?' he said. 'Like crystal meth,' I said. He laughed, told me he'd just tapped into his true energy, his Qi, something like that. I asked if he'd slept at all the night before. Maybe we should go back to the hotel and rest.

"'No time to rest,' he said. It was all very weird, and I was getting freaked out. It was like he was a completely different person."

She told them about the scene in the bar and finding him in the bathroom, absolutely terrified of something he'd seen in the mirror. "He'd urinated on himself. He started screaming and I called an ambulance.

"They kept him in the hospital overnight and I used Lucas's phone to call his parents. His dad said he would fly down right away. Could I pack up his things and leave them at the front desk. I was welcome to stay in the hotel room until my flight home."

She looked from Carlisle to Kincaid. "I never heard from him again."

———————— ✦ ————————

At the same time Carlisle and Kincaid were eating dinner at their desks, Caroline Stanhope was putting the browned double chops in the oven to finish cooking. The risotto was nearly done, the kitchen table set for three. She set a crystal dish of mint and pine nut chutney next to the salad bowl and went back to the kitchen island, where her brother was pouring her a glass of red wine.

"None for you?"

"I'll have some with dinner," said Lucas. "Thanks for cooking, by the way, it smells incredible." She enjoyed the compliment but couldn't tell if Lucas really meant it. The food was good, she could tell from the smell and the tiny bites she had masticated and then discreetly spit into her linen napkin. Since their mother had been found murdered, she'd begun restricting. Tonight, she had pushed the food around on her plate, lifting her fork to her mouth and then putting it down again before tasting it, wiping her lips to remove the occasional morsel from her tongue. She felt frail but knew she hadn't actually lost any weight yet. But that would come. It didn't take much for Caroline to go from thin to skeletal.

She figured she'd have some time before anyone noticed. First, her father and Lucas would have to pull their heads out of their asses. Then they might start to wonder, but she could layer her clothing, give herself another month, maybe six weeks before she would have to gain some back or face the loony bin.

Her mother would have noticed right away; her mother would have noticed before Caroline even started her fast. She could always tell, and she could always put a halt to it before anyone else could tell.

Now Caroline could do what she wanted, and she wanted to establish some control in the world around her. Most people thought that being hungry all of the time would be exhausting, restrictive, a constant battle of the wills, but there was an art to it.

You had to eat. Occasionally.

You had to consume enough energy to keep going. Just.

And after a little while, the weight of your body simply goes away. You are not hungry. Not tired. You are free. Light as a bird.

Light as a bird.

Until your body fights back. Then you go to war. Until now, Aurora had always decided the outcome of Caroline's battles, but now, Aurora was gone.

Gone except for the earworm named Kevin Stoddard that the detectives had insinuated into her life.

But Caroline was going to do something about that. She wouldn't just let it go.

CHAPTER TWENTY-SEVEN

A FTER KYLE LEFT, CARLISLE SAID, "Bipolar Disorder? Sounds like mania crossing over to psychosis."

"Could be schizophrenic."

"I don't think so. Not if he's able to function normally for long periods. But, hey, what do I know?" When she'd been in uniform, Carlisle had handled a number of calls about people in the clutches of mental illness. After the first few, she'd done some homework. Mental illness rarely translated into homicidal rage. "Probably doesn't have anything to do with our case."

"Volatile kid, crime of passion. We can't ignore it."

"No, we can't." They sat in silence for a while.

"Hey," said Kincaid, "have you heard back from Harry?"

"Not yet, but we were just there this afternoon. Why?"

"Let's go down there and show the photo around ourselves. Our case keeps doing circles around that dinner Friday night."

"I'm in," said Carlisle, noticing for the first time that she had been drumming her fingers on the desk.

She checked the time on her phone. "Almost eight o'clock. It'll be nice and crazy at Gigi's. Harry will appreciate the interruption."

They were waiting for the elevator when Kincaid's phone rang. "It's dispatch." He answered and gave Carlisle a look while he spoke.

Tucking his cell away, he said, "Change of plans. Patrol has been called to Kevin Stoddard's apartment; Caroline is over there threatening him. Dispatch, called us when he heard the name Stanhope. Thought it might be relevant," he said with a smile.

"You're kidding me," said Carlisle, immediately brightening. "Good news." They got in the elevator. "Well, maybe we won't need a warrant after all. We can haul Caroline down here for disorderly conduct and question her about our case."

In the car, she said, "She's a complete idiot for doing this."

Kincaid grumbled, "Let's hope."

"Maybe she just lost it." The issue that neither of them wanted to say out loud was that certainly Chang's murder, and at least some of the details of Aurora's murder, were pretty well thought-out. Not the actions of someone who would then run out and get arrested for attacking an ex-boyfriend. "Let's not get ahead of ourselves here."

They pulled up to Stoddard's apartment building and followed the sound of loud voices to his door on the third floor.

A uniformed policeman stood on the threshold and nodded at them. "He doesn't want to press charges, just wants her to go away, but she won't." A loud crash had Carlisle and Kincaid through the door in a second and they saw Caroline Stanhope standing in the tiny living room with the broken pieces of a flat screen television spread out around her feet.

"Caroline," said Kincaid, ignoring Kevin Stoddard, who stood, looking horrified, by the dining room table. When she fixed her glare on him, he said, "Caroline, you're going to have to come with us. Now, we can do this the easy way or the hard way."

"You gonna wrestle me to the ground?" she said, panting with adrenaline.

"Nope, not me. But she will," he said, pointing to the second uniformed officer, a tall dark-haired woman who stood mid-way between Stoddard and Caroline.

───────■─■─□─┤───────

Carlisle and Kincaid let the uniforms take Caroline back to the station in their patrol car. If they could convince Stoddard to press charges, she'd spend the night in jail no matter how fast her lawyer got there. Another call to the district attorney's office with updates about the most recent Stanhope event yielded a promise to get a warrant for Caroline's apartment.

They finished interviewing Kevin, who seemed utterly baffled by recent events but promised to follow through and press charges against Caroline, and were headed back to the unmarked when Kincaid's phone rang. Carlisle checked her messages while her partner finished the call. "Caroline's got her mother's temper. At least we know she'll be locked up for the night."

"Might not matter," said Kincaid. "That was Harry Cole again. He showed Caroline's photo around to the waitstaff." The engine growled to life.

"And?"

"And he said no one recognized Caroline, but the bartender saw a woman who could've been her mother."

"Caroline's mother *was* there. We know that. How is this helpful?"

"Not Aurora," said Kincaid, "they all know Aurora."

"Then who?"

"The woman who tipped the bartender with her wedding ring."

Carlisle was dumbstruck. "Who?" But then she knew. "Missy Lombardi. She looks like she could be Caroline's mother. Jesus, she was at the restaurant that night? No wonder Steve Lombardi got so squirmy when I mentioned the ring. He knew Missy hadn't been wearing her ring."

"Maybe she followed her husband. Saw him there with Aurora, freaked out. She gave her wedding ring away so she must've been furious. She doesn't want to cause a scene, leaves, goes home and comes up with a plan."

"And when Steve gets home that night, she uses his cell phone to call Aurora. Tells her she knows they had dinner. Convinces her to meet. Somehow, she knows that the Shermann home is empty for the winter. But how does she convince Aurora to meet her on a stranger's property?"

Kincaid shook his head. "I don't know, but we need to get a proper ID from that bartender before we run with this."

Carlisle made a call and when they pulled up behind headquarters on Cherry Street, she ran in and picked up a manila envelope containing a single sheet of paper with DMV photos of six similar-looking blondes, one of whom was Missy Lombardi, and six individual photos of each woman.

Twenty minutes later, Kincaid swung into a loading zone near Gigi's and they headed inside, straight for the bartender.

"That's her." He pointed at the photo of Missy.

"Are you sure?" asked Carlisle.

"It's not every day that a lady adds a five-pound diamond to my tip. Besides, I was here when she came back for it."

Harry Cole was coming out of the kitchen, and Kincaid gave him a thumbs-up, but didn't stop to talk. They needed to find Missy Lombardi, and they needed to talk to her husband again.

The drive back to Lake Washington seemed interminable. Carlisle used the time to put out an unofficial BOLO for Missy's car. "She was cool as a cucumber when we talked to her yesterday."

"Why retaliate now? Why take Aurora's shit for so long and now, suddenly, kill her?"

"It was a rage killing. Missy might've just wanted to scream and yell at her and before she knew it, she'd hit her with a rock and choked her to death."

"But if she knew beforehand that the Shermanns' house was empty, she must have been planning something."

"Missy might know the Shermanns. Or Chang told her their place was empty, maybe just in passing. Someone gave Chang twenty-five grand. If Missy was paying Chang for information about the Stanhopes, maybe paying her to plant evidence, her former employer could've come up in conversation."

Kincaid frowned. "Or Missy told Chang she was going to murder Aurora Stanhope and she needed a nice quiet place do it."

Carlisle said nothing. It was hard to believe Annie Chang would participate in murder for twenty-five grand from someone as rich as Missy Lombardi, but maybe another payoff was coming. Or maybe twenty-five grand was enough.

"And what about Caroline?" said Kincaid.

"One thing at a time."

It was almost ten when they pulled into the empty drive. "Looks like the party broke up."

This time Lombardi answered the door, holding it open for the detectives without a word. He stood awkwardly in the foyer, looking a little sick. "Uncanny," he said finally. "I was just considering what to do." His breath smelled of scotch, but his eyes were clear. "You'd better come with me."

"Where are your guests?" asked Carlisle, trying to get an idea of what they were walking into.

"I called an end to the game after you left the first time. After you told me about that wedding ring, I couldn't keep my mind on the cards."

They followed him down a stairwell and into the den. Open bottles of booze, the stench of cigar smoke, a felted table: the only thing missing from the cliché was a pack of dogs. Lombardi slumped onto one of a pair of leather sofas by the lacquered wet bar and pointed to a stack of photographs on a slab of marble and carved wood that filled the space between sofas.

Carlisle reached for the photos, flipped through the stack, passed them to Kincaid. All were dated almost twenty-five years ago, all featured Steve and Aurora, and two were of the unfaithful couple *in flagrante delicto*, Aurora astride him in the back seat of a car. The last pic featured a pregnant Aurora with her husband. Her bulging belly had been crossed out so hard with a ballpoint pen that it had torn through the photograph paper.

It wasn't lost on Carlisle that Caroline Stanhope was twenty-four years old. "Why didn't you and Missy ever have children?"

Lombardi smiled ruefully. "Missy couldn't. She had two miscarriages before we knew for sure. Didn't bother me much, but she was heartbroken."

"Do you think your affair with Aurora produced Caroline?"

"No," he said, nodding toward the photos Kincaid held, "but I'm starting to think my wife did."

"Did you tell your lawyer you had these photos?" asked Kincaid. "Ronny doesn't know anything. Conflict of interest. And I'm not really showing them to you; I'm letting you see them so you can do what needs to be done. Once you've arrested her, you'll get a search warrant for the house and find those in a locked drawer in her desk. She keeps the key in a glass with the paperclips."

Kincaid thought that Ronny Buccio had probably seen the pictures and advised his client that *if* he chose to talk to the detectives, he should not hand over any evidence and should deny ever speaking to them. As legal counsel for Missy and Steve, Buccio was bound by confidentiality and Steve's decision to hand over what he thought might be evidence was complicated by Missy's right not to have her husband testify against her. Deniability would protect them both.

This whole set-up reinforced Kincaid's belief that Steve Lombardi was a man of low moral character.

He said, "Trouble is that without the photos, we might not have enough to arrest her."

Lombardi was unperturbed. "You'll get something, detective. She's not done." He reached to a small table on his right and picked up another photo, handed it to Carlisle.

"Jesus Christ," she said, looking at a photograph of Beth Williams and Aurora Stanhope accepting some kind of award. Furious scribble lines marred both of them. Carlisle wanted to throttle the guy.

She asked, "What's her problem with Beth?"

He shrugged. "Dunno exactly, but she hates her. Maybe because she was like a daughter to Aurora? Another slap in my wife's face."

"Like a daughter until she fired her and stopped inviting her to Thanksgiving dinner."

"Don't feel too sorry for her, by the time that happened, Beth didn't need Aurora anymore. She was set, even if she didn't realize it."

"What do you know about Beth and Aurora?"

"I know that Aurora liked her more than either of her own kids. Not surprising—they're both fuck-ups in their own way. If you're asking whether there was any blood relation, that seems pretty far-fetched don't you think?" They all thought about that for a few seconds.

"Anyway. Missy would watch them together at the club or at a party and you could feel her get hot under the collar. She'd say, 'Aurora already has a daughter, why does she need Beth?' I just ignored her, but Missy hated Beth almost as much as she hated Aurora. I figured she was jealous. Missy couldn't have children, her archnemesis had two and then acquired another one when her own daughter disappointed her. Once she even went on a tear, positive that I was Henry's father. Don't know where that came from."

Kincaid went rigid. "Any truth to that?"

"Beth is lovely, but she's not my type."

"Because she's not filthy rich?" said Carlisle.

"Because he asked and she told him to fuck off," said Kincaid.

Steve looked pleased. "Do you have feelings for our Beth, Detective Kincaid?"

Carlisle broke it up. "Do you think your wife could have hurt Aurora?"

"Maybe. Missy could be nuts when it came to Aurora." He looked at them. "And it started long before I slept with her. They knew each other in college. Had a rivalry over Robert, probably a bunch of frat guys before that. Cat-fight stuff."

Carlisle smirked. "It was good of you to reinforce your wife's insecurity by having sex with her archnemesis."

Kincaid had gone back to staring at the photo of Beth and Aurora. "When did you find these?"

"After I sent everyone home, I started searching Missy's things. I don't know what I hoped to find. Certainly not these." He pointed. "You see, Detectives, Missy didn't wear her wedding ring all weekend. When I asked her why, she said she wanted to know what it would feel like if she divorced me." He smiled. "She can be a real bitch."

CHAPTER TWENTY-EIGHT

"**S**TILL NO ANSWER," SAID CARLISLE as Kincaid sped across town to Beth Williams's house in Bellevue. They'd already asked a patrol car to do a drive-by but hadn't heard back. The irony of living in a low-crime neighborhood was that there weren't patrol cars on every corner.

He hit the steering wheel hard with the palm of his hand. "Why the fuck didn't he give us that picture first?"

"It doesn't mean that Beth is in danger."

Kincaid didn't bother to respond. Carlisle called Beth's mobile again—no answer.

It was eleven o'clock on a school night; her ringer was probably off. But Carlisle could hear her partner's angry breathing, and the truth was, this didn't look good for Beth.

———————————

Beth Williams was flitting nervously around her kitchen, unloading the dishwasher, scrubbing a cast iron pan—fried potatoes and a cheese omelet for dinner—thinking about breaking out the Mint Milanos again.

Thinking about the phone call from Missy Lombardi.

Henry was tucked up in bed, sound asleep, but it had been a bear to get him there. *Just five more minutes, Mom.* Ten minutes to finish the last two drops of hot chocolate, ten more to brush his teeth. *Enough, Henry. No book tonight,* she'd said and he'd whined a little but finally curled up under the covers. It had been a long day and Beth needed some peace and quiet.

She made tea and got a cookie. Just one. Maybe two.

There was something odd about the call from Missy last week. Something odd about the invitation to lunch, out of nowhere. Right before Aurora was murdered. And then the generous offer and the intimate conversation right afterward.

It was silly—silly to worry like this, silly to be so suspicious, silly to speculate at all.

Still. Aurora had taught her to accept every donation, *and* to make sure she knew the motive behind it.

It was the phone call today that had really thrown her off. Awkward. There was no other word for it. But she couldn't shake the feeling Missy had wanted her to be uncomfortable.

Henry had come home from school and finished what passed as homework for eight-year-olds. Then Tonka trucks in the backyard. Beth had been leaning over the back railing, looking out at the water, when the sound of her phone made her flinch. She'd pulled it out of her pocket and read the caller ID. Missy Lombardi. She'd flinched again, certain this was the call that made the too-good-to-be-true offer go away. *So sorry, Beth, don't know what I was thinking.*

But apart from a quick reassurance in the beginning that she was still on board, Missy hadn't spoken at all about business matters. Which left Beth to wonder, why had she called?

Evidently, she had called to talk about Henry. Did he like his school, did Beth have any interest in sending him to private school, hadn't Aurora ever talked to Beth about the academy Lucas and Caroline had attended. Missy, had she been blessed with children, would never have sent them to public. Low expectations, inflated grades, bored teachers, violence.

Well-meant or judgment, Beth had wondered. Either way, inappropriate.

Then it got worse. Henry looks so much like you, Beth, dark hair, dark skin. She wondered, did he look anything like his father?

"Not much," Beth had said, wishing she could afford to tell Missy it was none of her business. Then, silence. For ten seconds. Twenty. Missy had said nothing and Beth hadn't known what to say.

Finally Beth had said, "I've got to get something together for dinner, Missy, can I touch base with you tomorrow?"

"I think it would be better if *I* call *you*, Beth."

Creepy. Truly though, everything felt creepy to her. And why not? Aurora had been murdered, her housekeeper had been murdered, the police had already questioned her three times. She'd been reliving all sorts of unpleasant memories. The cops weren't asking her about the good times. They were asking about the very worst times, about Aurora sleeping with her own daughter's boyfriends and antagonizing her friends. About Caroline's bad behavior and Robert's alleged affairs, about the animosity between Aurora and the Lombardis, between her and Aurora.

When Missy had ended the call, Beth had felt a little sick. Now, she felt a little afraid. Somehow, she was wrapped up in this mess and she had no idea what was going on.

Then the doorbell rang.

———————◼◼◻◻◼———————

Beth's stomach bottomed out.

She checked the time on the microwave. Just past ten. Who would be here this late?

She looked around for her phone, couldn't find it. The bell rang again; she took a deep breath. Maybe it was the detectives. Maybe something had happened. Maybe they came to warn her.

Beth Williams answered the door.

Threw it open without thinking. Cold, wet wind rushed across her face like a slap and broke the panic.

She looked at the tiny blonde woman standing on her doorstep, smiling, hands clasped behind her back and her mind went blank.

⸻

Lucas Stanhope was fuming.

He'd spent an hour at the police station waiting for Jim Thorpe to convince Kevin Stoddard to drop the charges against his sister, then he'd driven her back to Lake Washington, where their father had wrapped Caroline up in his arms and told her everything would be okay and wasn't the stress of it all just too much and wasn't she already getting a little thin, and he would be stronger for her from now on.

And actually, his father *had* looked stronger, looked like he would take care of Caroline and take care of the mess Aurora had left behind and take care of business in general. Before you knew it, Robert Stanhope would be richer than ever, dating again, have a new doubles partner, honeymooning on a sailboat in the Greek Isles. A man in full.

It takes a crisis to get over a crisis.

Disgusting. Lucas had stormed out, had slammed the front door on his manipulative sister and his stalwart father, had tried to rev the engine on his Prius—unsuccessful—and had finally driven home just as fast as his practical car would take him.

And now, now he was running—across Ward Street, south on Second Avenue to Mercer, right on Fifth. It was dark and cold and drizzling and the sidewalks were deserted but steady traffic made a constant slapping sound on the wet pavement. His face was wet, his hair, his neck. It felt wonderful—he'd been burning up since the call from his sister.

They'd had dinner. Lambchops. Caroline was a good cook. Of course, she hadn't eaten any of it. She thought no one noticed, but he did. She went through all of the motions of eating—cutting meat off the bone, dipping her fork in the potatoes, lifting it to her mouth, but somehow, nothing ever made it in. Pattering on the whole time about the new maid and taking time off of school and the social commitments she would have to take over since Aurora died. And their father had gone along with all of it. As if taking a semester off to attend charity luncheons made sense.

She'd been silent while they cleared the plates. Robert had gone off to find the scotch bottle, just the two of them in the kitchen, and then, all of a sudden, she had to go out for a while, could Lucas stay with Daddy until she came back, it wouldn't be long.

Et cetera.

And the next thing he knew, she was calling him from jail because she'd just shoved her way into her ex-fuckbuddy's apartment and was threatening him because he'd also slept with their mother. *This fucking family!* he thought, picking up the pace.

She would've spent the night in jail if Kevin hadn't dropped the charges. *Pussy.* Thorpe said the guy *felt bad.*

He should feel bad. He had slept with Lucas's mother and sister. Still, Caroline deserved a night in jail. *Fucking pussy.*

Aha. There it was. The Space Needle.

He ran down the path, circled the base. Nothing. Like nothing had ever happened there. Not even a scrap of crime scene tape. Annie Chang had just disappeared from their lives. Same thing at home. Her room was still intact, but no one ever went to that part of the house anyway. Lucas supposed Annie's family was feeling the pain, but as far as the Stanhopes were concerned, she might as well have quit her job, or been fired, or been killed in a car accident.

She just wasn't there anymore.

Tidy.

———————◆━■━■━◆———————

Beth took a surprised step back and Missy Lombardi swept into the foyer like she owned the place.

"This is beautiful, Beth." She marched into the kitchen,

surveyed the counters, appliances, cookie crumbs, kept going straight into the living room without breaking stride.

Beth trailed behind her, speechless. She watched her sit primly on the sofa, cross her legs, arrange her left hand on the arm of the couch, rest her right hand in her lap.

Holding a gun.

"Have a seat."

Beth sat opposite Missy, on the edge of an armchair. "What are you doing?"

Missy looked at her thoughtfully, smiled, and said, "I suppose I'm settling scores." She glanced at a mess of Legos on the rug. "Where's the boy?"

Beth couldn't speak. She couldn't talk about Henry with a gun involved in the conversation.

"Bed? Of course he is. It's after ten." She picked lint off of the arm of the sofa. "Let's you and I have a little chat before we wake him. Shall we?"

Beth began to shake.

"Why so quiet, dear?" Missy's open smile was so very close to actual bafflement that Beth almost relaxed.

But there was the gun. She couldn't move, couldn't breathe, couldn't speak.

"Fine. I'll start the conversation. I was never able to have children. Always wanted to, never could. Early on, Steve and I tried everything. Then we talked about adoption, but Steve was adamant about dealing with some stranger's DNA. Why would he want to raise someone else's child? he said, who knows what we'd get? he said."

Beth had no idea what this had to do with her, but she was beginning to think Missy Lombardi was a complete lunatic.

"It's such a blessing to have a child, Beth." Missy didn't make it sound like Beth was blessed. "You are so very lucky."

She didn't say anything more for a full minute while she looked wistfully at her left hand, at the huge diamond ring sparkling in the lamplight. Finally, she blinked.

"You're adopted, Beth, aren't you?"

She nodded, but had no idea why Missy wanted to talk about it. That gun was the only thing Beth wanted to talk about.

She tried to control her breathing, her shaking, to ignore the cold sweat prickling on her hairline, her neck, between her shoulder blades and breasts.

"Did you ever look for your birth parents?" Missy paused, thought about it. "No, you probably didn't. Weren't you curious?"

Beth's parents had loved her liked their own. Told her when she was young that she'd been adopted, but she was theirs, heart and soul if not biology. Told her, when she was older, that she might someday want to seek out her birth parents, and that was fine with them. Fine if she didn't. As long as she did what she needed to do.

She hadn't needed to.

But Beth didn't know why Missy would assume she hadn't looked for her birth parents, didn't know what any of this had to do with the gun casually pointing in her direction. But she knew it all had something to do with Aurora's murder. She finally tried to speak, stuttered a little, cleared her throat, then said, "No."

Missy waited a second, laughed. "A woman of few words. *Why* weren't you curious, Beth? I'd like to know."

"I guess I was just happy with the parents I had. I didn't need more." She felt oddly defensive.

"But you got more."

"I *got* more?"

Suddenly Missy was on her feet. Waving the gun around. "You had Aurora!"

———————

Carlisle got a call from dispatch. "Patrol got there, rang the bell, knocked. No answer, but he peeked through the windows, said everything looked in order."

Her partner was silent. They were still ten minutes out.

Finally, he said, "Tell him to go back. She would have answered the door."

———————

"What?" Beth started to cry.

Missy sat back down, sighed. Rolled her eyes. "Did you never wonder why Aurora took you under her wing, mentored you, invited you into her home, treated you as part of her family, and then *dumped* you?"

"Of course I wondered." Beth was getting sick of this. She wiped her eyes. "Who wouldn't wonder? But I wasn't going to fight it. If she wanted me gone, then I would go away."

"Bit passive." Missy frowned. "*I* would have demanded an answer, looked into it, done some research."

"I did look into it. Her nonprofit was going to get big bucks to move out of India. She knew I would never go for it. Therefore, *I* had to go. Simple as that."

"You must be an idiot, Beth, or obscenely naïve. If Aurora had wanted to keep you, she would have. She would've told whomever had made the offer to shove it up his ass."

Profanity did not become her. Missy's china doll mouth twisted and she looked like a different person. Beth recoiled. "What should I have done, Missy?"

"Figured it out!"

"I did figure it out! Aurora got a better deal. For a while I helped her nonprofit grow, after she accepted that donation, I would have hindered it. Aurora was ambitious. Case closed."

"Beth. You're so stupid." She sighed.

"Aurora was your mother."

CHAPTER TWENTY-NINE

CARLISLE'S CELL RANG. "POOL BOY dropped the charges," she said when she'd ended the call. "Caroline's been sprung."

"Christ. Where is she now?"

"Dunno. Lucas picked her up. Evidently, they never even booked her because Stoddard dropped the charges. Thorpe was up their asses the second he got the call so they couldn't even stall her release."

"When?"

"Nine-forty-five."

He checked the dash. Eleven-oh-seven. "Shit. Why are we just hearing about this?"

"Different precinct. They didn't know to tell us."

"So now we have another moving part out there." He drummed his fingers on the wheel. "But she didn't do it. Caroline didn't do it. Man. Call Beth again."

Carlisle called Beth's mobile. Voicemail. Again. Kincaid hit the dashboard with the palm of his hand. Technically, they weren't supposed to use the lights in a non-emergency situation, but traffic on Queen Anne Hill was inexplicably backed up and Carlisle finally slapped the cherry on top of their unmarked and turned on the siren.

They went faster.

"No she was not." Beth straightened. This was crazy. And crazy had a gun. And Henry was downstairs.

"She was, Beth. Didn't you ever wonder?" she asked again. Missy was *really* asking, *really* perplexed.

And so was Beth. "Did I ever wonder if Aurora Stanhope was my long-lost mother? No, I didn't." Was Missy threatening her because she thought Aurora was her birth mother? "Plus," she continued, trying to think through the logic, "if she took me on because she thought I was her child, why would she dump me?"

Missy laughed. Hard. Tears brimmed at the corners of her eyes. But she kept her hand tightly on the gun.

"It's so *sad*, Beth."

It didn't look like Missy thought it was sad. It looked like she thought it was funny.

The laughter stopped. Missy kept grinning but shook her head ruefully. "Aurora didn't take you under her wing because she found out you were her daughter. She *dumped* you because she found out you were her daughter."

"No."

"Yes." Missy reached into her shoulder bag, pulled out a sheaf of papers rolled up in a rubber band, and set the roll on the table between them. "See."

Beth hesitated.

"Read."

Beth read.

Indeed, they were adoption documents, indeed, they said Aurora was her birth mother. Beth felt a little sick, but she wasn't sure she bought it. "These could be fake," she said.

"Could be." Missy shrugged. "But let me tell you a little story."

"About two years ago I found a man who said he could get access to confidential adoption documents. Why was I looking? Because Aurora had pushed me too far. Getting herself on the board of one of my favorite charities. Telling me about yet another of Steve's affairs. Flaunting you and Henry. As if, even though she had two perfectly decent kids, she deserved another one who was even better. And don't deny that she preferred you to her own." Missy gave Beth a stern look.

"Anyway, I was fed up and I'd been thinking about the years between college and marriage. Aurora and I had always run in overlapping crowds, so even after we graduated, there was no being rid of her. Plus, the country club and the museum benefits and the restaurant openings and the charity galas—she was *always there*."

Beth was having a hard time understanding Missy's trauma. Feeling plagued by Aurora was one thing. But between the galas and the gun, she couldn't muster any sympathy.

"She was *always* there. Wherever I went. And she always got what she wanted. Always got what *I* wanted. The husband, the children, the attention. I was *nice* to people. But everyone loved *her* for being a bitch."

Nice is not how Beth would describe Missy Lombardi, sitting there with a gun, but she said, "Aurora could be awful."

"*Awful?*" Missy's eyes went wide. "Whatever. So, after college, Aurora took off for a year in Europe. Not so unusual. In those days, when a rich girl studied French literature for four years, her parents sent her off to speak the language. The thing is, she wasn't the only one, and none of our mutual acquaintances ever saw her there. I didn't know that at the time, because I never asked, but lately I've been asking a lot of questions.

"Another thing, there are no pictures of Aurora in France. None. It wasn't like now—snapshots posted all over the internet— but people took pictures, kept mementos."

For a second, Beth wondered how Missy would know there were no pictures, why she started asking questions only recently. But the thought was fleeting: bigger fish to fry.

"In those days, it wasn't unusual for a good family to send their pregnant but unwed daughter away to hide. The sexual revolution was more or less acceptable, but not an unwed pregnancy and Aurora's parents were pretty devout Christians. No abortion. And even more important than *that*, they were *prominent*. Status. And they wouldn't have given that up because their wild-child had gotten knocked up.

"And she did get knocked up. I became sure of it.

"So I checked around and I found this guy who, for a shocking sum of money, got me the documents, and two years ago, I had them delivered, anonymously, to Aurora. She took it hard. Chased her maid around the house and yanked a chunk of her hair right out of her head.

"And then, she fired you and threw you out of her life. I knew she would. She'd have to." Missy's eyes twinkled. "And I thought that was enough. Aurora didn't know it, but *I* had just taken away her most prized possessions. You and Henry.

"She changed after that. Shorter temper, even more volatile—I know because I watched. I think it actually hurt her to lose you. But she did it anyway, for her own good. Personally, I think something in your *skin*, something in the *smell* of you drew Aurora, and she had no idea what it was. She just liked you. Thought she deserved your loyalty, your hard work, your love.

"But once she found out you actually *were hers*, she cast you aside. The best part was she didn't know who sent the papers, never knew if it would come out. It ate at her.

"And it was good. It was enough." She shrugged. "Mostly, it was enough."

Lucas Stanhope circled the Space Needle three times, ran straight up Queen Anne Hill, and arrived home soaking wet and tingling with endorphins.

Water, shower, voicemail. In that order.

Caroline had called. Twice. No apology, no explanation, she

just told him their mother's funeral would be the following weekend and she needed his help planning it. What time would he be at the house tomorrow?

Another missed call. Another message.

Except, this one was important.

This one sent him running to the bathroom to throw up.

———————

"Missy," said Beth quietly. "Please tell me what you want from me."

Missy didn't say anything for a few seconds. Licked her lips. Beth noticed that they were chapped and cracked, that her nail polish was chipped, that she had mascara in the corners of her eyes.

Missy Lombardi was not herself. And Beth thought that might be very bad for her.

"A few weeks ago, maybe two weeks. I don't know. Aurora found out I was the one who'd sent her the adoption documents. She never told me how she knew and it probably didn't much matter.

"She came to my house." Missy's eyes focused. "You've never been, have you? It's just a few miles from Aurora's house, on Lake Washington. It's much bigger, much nicer, though that never bothered Aurora.

"Anyway, she showed up after breakfast with a huge bouquet of tiger lilies and snapdragons in a Baccarat vase. She was wearing jeans and a blue silk blouse, Jackie O sunglasses, huge smile. No jacket. The first thing she said was, 'Let me in, Missy. It's freezing out here.'

"I did. Of course I did. Fifty-seven years of good breeding does that to you. Makes it impossible to turn your worst enemy away when she comes bearing flowers.

"Anyway, she came in and we sat in the back library overlooking the lake. It was a weekday so Margaret was there to tidy up. I asked her to bring us coffee and she did. All the while, Aurora was prattling on about this and that as if we were old friends.

"Margaret brought the coffee. Aurora drank it black. When we were alone, she looked at me and said, 'A couple of years ago, someone gave me an envelope full of adoption documents, and a couple of days ago, I found out it was you.'

"I was terrified. Aurora could be a scary person." Missy spoke impassively, didn't seem scared at all. Not now anyway. "She could be like a rabid dog. Better to hit her from behind than shoot her in the face. And there she was, civilized, drinking coffee, sitting cross-legged on the chintz divan in my library and I knew she was about to spring."

Now Missy smiled, because, Beth supposed, no matter what Aurora had done that day, Missy had killed her. Game over. Missy won. Except that now, she was in Beth's living room, looking a little crazed, not at all like a woman who had triumphed.

"I don't understand what this has to do with me, Missy. Please."

"*What it has to do with you?*" she boomed. "That day, Aurora produced her own envelope of documents, but she didn't hand them over right away." Missy stood, paced back and forth a few times in front of the sofa. Kept a tight grip on the gun.

"You see, there was no father listed on the birth certificate, or on the adoption papers. I figured he was just one of a string of possibilities long forgotten."

Missy sat back down, looked pensively at Beth.

"She told me that she was impressed. It had been a bold move to hold those papers over her head. Though she said she thought I was a coward for doing it anonymously. Actually, what she said was, 'You almost grew a pair of balls, Missy. But in the end, you're still a fucking pussy.' She said, 'You're a tiny little ineffective Tinker Bell with no spine and no guts and no chance of ever coming out on top.'

"And then, she gave me the envelope. Her trump card. A couple of DNA tests and a summary of the results."

Beth had no idea what was coming, but Missy had begun to shake, and she knew it would be bad.

Missy was up again, pointing her gun at Beth, shouting.

"Aurora was your mother Beth. And my husband—*my husband is your father!*"

CHAPTER THIRTY

"**M**OM?" HENRY CALLED FROM THE base of the stairs
No! Beth kept her eyes on Missy Lombardi.

A roar started in her belly.

And there it was. Mama Bear.

"Go back to bed, Henry." A calm, cool directive. Usually did the trick with Henry.

"But Mom, I heard yelling."

She could hear his little footsteps on the Berber carpet. He was coming up the stairs. "Go back to bed, Henry."

Carlisle got off the phone. "Patrol got the address wrong the first time. They're on their way, but we're going to beat them."

"Goddammit," said Kincaid. "Call again."

She did. "No answer." They were two blocks away. One. Pulling into a spot in front of her house. Just Beth's car in the driveway.

Kincaid was out of the car in a second, Carlisle right behind him. They headed straight for the door, Kincaid balling his fist to knock when he stopped dead in his tracks.

Carlisle looked over his shoulder, could see straight through the kitchen to the top of the stairs where little Henry emerged, turned and stopped. The house was dark except for a glow coming from the living room.

"Something's wrong," said Kincaid.

"Yes, it is," said Carlisle and she pulled her gun out of its holster.

Henry kept coming up the stairs.

She turned to him, tried one more time. "Henry, go back to bed."

He didn't. His messy hair popped up first, then his monster truck pajamas, and then he stopped and peered through the bars of the steel railing, saw his mother, saw Missy. Took the last two steps. "Mom?"

Beth glanced at Missy. The gun had disappeared, but the look on her face was not comforting. She looked back at her son.

"Sweetheart, go back to bed. It's late. Please, Henry."

Missy said, "Why not let him stay up a while, Beth? This affects him too." Her voice was cold and clear.

Henry took a step forward, saw his mother shake her head no, saw the fear in her eyes.

"What's goin' on, Mom?" He just stood there holding the railing.

And then he started to cry.

Carlisle called dispatch and requested back-up, no lights, no sirens. They walked around the house to the back deck, testing the planks for sound, and when they got past the kitchen, had a clear view of Henry running for his mother.

And Missy Lombardi pulling a gun from the sofa cushions.

Kincaid didn't breathe until Henry made it into his mother's arms. "Fuck."

"Back-up?" said Carlisle. She knew he wouldn't wait.

"Fuck no," said Kincaid.

"Fine. I'll get in downstairs, come up. When you see me on the steps, get ready and we'll blow the fucking house down."

Easier said than done. Carlisle made it halfway down the steps to the garden before hitting the flashlight app on her phone, found the sliding doors to the lower level. Locked. Couldn't break the glass because it would make too much noise. She started looking for another way in.

———————

Henry ran for his mother and Beth stood.

Every muscle in her body was a high-tension wire. She could feel them humming.

Henry was cleaved to her side like he could disappear into her skin, his legs inching behind her, his head pressed between her arm and breast. He stared at Missy.

"Stay out here where I can see you, Henry," said Missy. "You've nothing to be afraid of, we're practically family. Right, Beth?"

But Missy Lombardi couldn't wipe the look of rage off of her face and Henry began to shake violently. Beth was perfectly still. Her vision sharp, her body coiled.

Like a cat watching a bird.

She knew what to do.

———————

Still on the deck, Kincaid was getting restless. Missy had rested her gun hand in her lap, was no longer pointing it at Beth and Henry, but she still had her finger on the trigger.

The trigger is the scary part.

He saw the pale blue of Henry's pajama bottoms darken with urine, saw him try to inch closer to his mom. Saw Missy say something that brought him to a halt.

———————

Carlisle slid a three-inch blade out of her inside coat pocket, opened it, cut a long hole in the screen of an open window and lifted the sash far enough to get herself through. She was in Beth's bedroom but didn't bother to look around, just went for the closed door and headed for the stairs.

Halfway up she stopped. Couldn't see her partner through the reflection in the glass, but she could see the top of Beth's head in the window, as clear as a mirror.

She crouched low and took two more stairs, saw Kincaid's fingers pressed to the base of the glass door. Five fingers, four, three, two...

———————

One.

Beth threw Henry to the ground, hard as she could, launching herself at Missy. Two shots rang out. A pane of glass exploded.

Kincaid flew through the splintered door, shards of glass chiming as they hit the floor, caught Carlisle vaulting the iron railing in his periphery, saw Beth leap the coffee table, saw her body stop in midair, saw her fall to the ground.

Then he put two bullets in Missy Lombardi's chest. One more just to be sure.

The room went dead silent.

———————

Over the ringing in his ears, Kincaid could hear the terrible keening sound coming from Henry as the child started crawling and then running for his mother. He swooped him up with one arm while Carlisle confirmed Missy was dead.

She was definitely dead. Carlisle stretched Beth out on the floor, dialing dispatch with one hand and prodding Beth's wound with the other.

Carlisle turned to Kincaid, saw Henry pressed to his shoulder, squirming to see his mother. She looked at him as she spoke into the phone.

"Adult female, bullet wound to the shoulder. Some blood loss, but she's gonna be okay."

CHAPTER THIRTY-ONE

"**A**RE YOU SURE YOU WANT to go?"

"Why would I want to stay?" said Beth Williams.

Carlisle looked around the hospital room, didn't have an answer. She said, "Crime scene is finished up at your place, Beth, but it's still a mess."

"They're going to the Marriott," said Kincaid, walking up behind his partner, slipping his phone back into his breast pocket. "Special discount courtesy of the SPD. All set up."

"Thank you, Jerome," said Beth, her good arm around Henry. "Parents are coming, brother and sister are coming, friends will come if I want them. When I want them. We'll be fine, but I want to get home sooner rather than later."

"I called a guy I know. He'll take a look at your door tonight, get it fixed tomorrow." Kincaid handed Beth a business card. "This is who you call for the clean-up." He glanced at Henry. "'They'll get everything out."

"I'm throwing that goddamn sofa away."

"They'll take care of that too, if you want."

"Tomorrow," said Carlisle, "nothing to worry about today."

They drove Beth and Henry to the hotel and got them checked in. Carlisle had gone back and packed some clothes while Beth had been in surgery. Kincaid had stayed with Henry, told him everything would be okay, let the kid pass out on his big chest.

"Call if you need anything. Anything," said Kincaid, giving Henry a bear hug and Beth a pat on her uninjured shoulder.

They drove back to the station, spent the rest of the day there.

Shooting your service gun during an incident required a lot of paperwork. Shooting your service gun at a person required a lot more paperwork.

Plus, there was the matter of understanding what had really happened. Because there were still some missing pieces. Important pieces.

———————

The next day, they were a little closer to understanding the narrative, but Carlisle and Kincaid still had some questions.

After a complete search of the Stanhopes' mansion, Kyle had determined that the big rock used to knock Aurora out had almost certainly come from the Stanhopes' own landscaping, where the flower beds at the front of the house were lined with big river rocks instead of mulch. They matched Missy's DNA to the hairs found in Aurora's car and in drops of saliva found on Aurora's chin and neck. The gun Missy had used on Beth was the same gun that had killed Annie Chang.

DNA plus motive, means and opportunity was enough to close the case on Aurora.

Carlisle had spent ten minutes on the phone with the Shermanns and learned that Edith Shermann was chairman of the board of the Seattle Orchid Society, of which Missy was a member. Everyone knew the Shermanns' winter schedule because the vice-chair took over the meetings during the winter months. Edith held annual tea parties for members in the gardens behind their house, which included a tour of the hothouse.

Kincaid summed up. "Missy Lombardi, having found out that her husband had fathered a child with Aurora Stanhope, calls her, goes to her house, snaps and hits her over the head with a rock, then drives her in her own car to the Shermanns' house because she knows no one would be home for a while. Strangles her to death, then dumps her body. Then, a day and a half later, she kills Chang because she knows too much. Gets rid of the Porsche when she dumps Chang by the Space Needle, plans to go back for Chang's car, but we find it first. Then she goes after Beth and Henry because they are the product of her husband's ultimate betrayal."

"I guess so," said Carlisle. "But there are still some question marks. For example, what did Chang actually know that got her killed? We assumed she was the one who told our killer about the Shermanns' empty house, but now we know otherwise."

"Maybe the bloody shirt? She found Missy stashing the shirt back inside the Stanhopes'. Missy would have had Aurora's house keys, could've gone back."

"But why? If the plan was to frame someone, I'd think it would be Missy's own husband, not Aurora's. And how did Missy get the shirt in the first place?" Carlisle shook her head. "Plus, Chang had that money stashed for a while. If she was blackmailing someone, it was long before Aurora was killed."

With Missy dead and plenty of evidence to prove she had killed Aurora, it would be easy enough to toss Chang's case in with Aurora's and call it solved even without motive. There was no reason to think Missy was working with someone—her call log had produced nothing out of the ordinary—and there was no reason to think anyone else had motive to kill Chang. Plus, there would never be a trial for either murder because Missy was dead.

Bottom line: the was solved.

But the inconsistencies didn't sit well.

———————

Beth and Henry Williams arrived home just before dusk. Beth's father gave the place a once-over, turning on every light in the house, inspecting the living room for signs of violence, checking the replaced door, then helped his daughter carry her bags in from the foyer.

Beth's mom followed behind with a bag of groceries and began putting them away.

Henry looked around suspiciously at first, but seemed okay after Beth said he could watch TV.

Beth's dad stood looking out the window at the clouds over the sound, his arm around his daughter's shoulders. "We never knew who your birth parents were. I promise you."

He didn't have to promise; she knew.

They wanted to stay with Beth and Henry. Beth said no, they were safe by themselves, needed to feel safe by themselves. Her parents went back to the Marriott to have dinner with Beth's brother and sister. They'd all be back at breakfast time.

━━━━━━╾■-■-□-╼━━━━━━

Kincaid and Stanley shared a bowl of granola with milk for dinner.

Beth had called. She and Henry were home, the house had been magically put back together, thank you for arranging it all.

"You okay there by yourself?"

"Honestly, I didn't want to let the ghosts fester. We're home, we're safe, better to get back to normal." Quiet for a few seconds. "I'm going to find us a counselor or something, just to be sure."

"The department can help with that. We've got all sorts of resources."

"I'm sure you do," said Beth.

Henry wanted to say hi before they got off the phone, wanted Kincaid to come over to play trucks sometime.

Kincaid wanted to come over and play trucks too, but he would wait until the invite came from Beth.

He refilled his cereal bowl, turned on Netflix. *Black Mirror.*

━━━━━━╾■-■-□-╼━━━━━━

Carlisle was trying to pay attention to what Janie was telling her but all she could think about was that bloody shirt. Something wasn't right.

"Mom! Can I stay over at Brooklyn's house this weekend or not?"

Carlisle turned. "That depends. Is Brooklyn a boy or a girl?"

"Mom!" Janie rolled her eyes, turned to her father.

Missy couldn't have gotten that shirt from Robert Stanhope's closet and put it back in the house without help. And why put it back at all? Annie Chang could have helped her. But why go to the trouble and why implicate herself to Chang? For a piece of evidence that might never have been found? Why not wear one of Steve's shirts. Why wear a man's shirt at all? Made no sense.

Unless the shirt hadn't been worn by Missy Lombardi at all.

Forgotten by someone who was used to throwing dirty clothes in the hamper, letting the maid take care of them.

Someone who lived in the Stanhope manse.

———————◼–◻———————

On the night Missy Lombardi died, Lucas had punched three holes in the wall in his bedroom waiting for her to return his calls.

Now, of course, he knew she was gone. He had heard the details on the news, read about it on the internet, even gotten a courtesy call from Detective Carlisle. *It looks like Missy Lombardi murdered your mother, but she's dead now.* Justice done.

"Why?" he had asked. But she hadn't told him. They were still sorting it out, she had said.

How much did they really know?

———————◼–◻———————

Phone to her ear, Carlisle was already heading for the unmarked in her driveway when Kincaid picked up.

"Either of those kids could have found out about the adoption and freaked out. Maybe Missy told them, maybe one of the kids told Missy." Beth had filled them in on Missy's version of events, but Carlisle didn't buy it. A sudden revelation after all these years that her archenemy might have gone away to hide an unwanted pregnancy, finding *a guy* who could get hold of the documents even though Missy wouldn't have known where or exactly when the adoption took place? Nah.

A little birdy had told her.

"We know it wasn't Stanhope, so it's one of the kids," she said.

"What's one of the kids?" said Kincaid, but he was already processing it. "The shirt," he said.

"The shirt," Carlisle said. The one piece of evidence that didn't fit. "I'm on my way."

———————————————

Waiting for Carlisle, Kincaid had called dispatch, gotten patrol cars to sit on the mansion, Caroline's condo and on Lucas's apartment. So far, no one had come or gone from the Stanhopes' and the lights were off at Caroline's and on at Lucas's, although, from the street it was impossible to tell if anyone was actually home.

He was standing on the sidewalk when she arrived at his house. He got in the car. "No movement at either place," said Kincaid.

Carlisle said, "Doesn't matter," and threw the car into drive.

"Which one?"

"On the way over I called in a favor from TSA."

"TSA?" said Kincaid.

———————————————

"It was Lucas," said Carlisle.

Carlisle was already speeding down the street. "He was never in the Honduran bloody rainforest. Why the fuck did we take his word for it?"

Kincaid's brain was turning. "We took his word for it because it didn't matter."

"It mattered," said Carlisle, "because the day he was supposed to have come home from his research expedition, Lucas Stanhope and Missy Lombardi were on the same plane flying from Maui to Seattle."

"Shit," said Kincaid. They hadn't thought to check Lucas's whereabouts *before* the murder. And Kincaid had just realized what Lucas was going to do next.

"He's going to finish it."

"What?"

But Kincaid was already ordering squad cars to Beth Williams's house.

"Why do you think he's going after Beth and Henry?"

"My gut," said Kincaid. And that was enough.

Carlisle hit the gas and Kincaid put the light on.

———————◆—■—▪—■—◆———————

Lucas Stanhope had never felt so utterly helpless and so wildly determined at the same time.

He had been watching the hospital, had seen Beth and Henry go to the Marriott. Had called the next day and found out they had checked out that morning.

He had waited till dark, parked down the street from Beth's house. Circled the block on foot, once, twice. The thing about living in a safe neighborhood was that nobody paid attention to a well-dressed stranger going for a post-prandial walk. Nikes. Ear buds. Thousand-dollar phone. No cause for alarm.

He walked up the drive, around to the back deck, checked the five-inch hunting knife he had sheathed under his windbreaker and made himself comfortable on the wooden planks while he watched his half-sister and his half-nephew cuddled together in front of the TV. Eating popcorn.

That was nice.

He couldn't recall ever eating popcorn with Aurora.

But he vividly recalled the moment he had smashed her head with a rock.

———————

Beth sat in a big armchair—the sofa was gone—Henry cuddled up against her, blanket, popcorn with real butter. They were watching *The Incredibles*. The first one. She was happy to be home. A little jumpy, perhaps, but she was glad they were home.

She looked at the panels of glass, saw only her own reflection.

Missy was dead, the dragon slain. Nothing to worry about.

———————

She was looking straight at him.

Lucas felt panic rise. Should he do it right now? Should he kill them right now?

Then Beth turned her head back to the television. She hadn't seen him. Couldn't see him out here in the dark.

Beth and Henry made a good pair, he thought. He had always thought so. Had always liked them both very much.

Why had Missy wanted them dead? Looking at the two of them now, snuggled up together, he had a hard time understanding why Missy had hated them so much. Steve, Aurora, he understood that, but Beth and Henry didn't seem so bad.

But Missy was always right. He didn't need to understand. And this was the last thing she had ever wanted. She had told him so in a voicemail. And then she had been killed.

And Lucas would do it. He would do it for Missy because he loved her more than anything.

Beth and Henry had to go.

———————

Kincaid turned the lights and sirens off. They were close to Beth's house and didn't want to spook her if nothing was wrong.

He had called her cell phone a few times, but it went straight to voicemail. Off wasn't good, but it didn't mean Lucas Stanhope was holding them hostage.

They turned onto West Bertona and Carlisle hit the brakes. "What?"

She pointed. Lucas's car was parked half a block down from Beth's house. She pulled over behind it.

Pulled her gun out of its holster.

She and Kincaid crouched low and approached the Prius. Popped up, guns pointed. No one home.

"He's already in there," said Kincaid.

They ran, guns to the ground. No time to wait for the squads to get here, no time for recon. They ran straight for Beth's house, straight up to the front door.

Saw the flashes of a television screen in the glass walls at the back of the house, saw the popcorn maker on the kitchen counter.

Saw Lucas Stanhope rise up from the back deck, saw him raise a crowbar to the glass.

Kincaid was around the corner in a second, howling like a bear.

Carlisle turned the corner just in time to see her partner tackle Lucas, throw him to the ground so hard she heard the air forced out of his chest.

She heard the muffled screams of Beth and Henry Williams through the glass, heard the crunch of Lucas's nose breaking against the cedar decking, heard sirens wailing in the distance.

And then she was on Kincaid, pulling him away, cuffing Lucas, taking the knife he had clipped to his belt.

She turned to her partner, panting, saw him leaning against the railing, unhurt. Turned again, saw Beth Williams standing in the open door.

It had begun to rain again. A cold drizzle. Felt good on her face.

A minute later the cavalry arrived with lights, and sirens, and pounding footsteps.

CHAPTER THIRTY-TWO

"'Schizoaffective disorder,'" Carlisle read from a summary the department shrink had prepared after studying Lucas Stanhope's psychiatric records. "'Diagnosed schizophrenic during his first psychotic episode, age fifteen. Amended to Bipolar Disorder I after months of relatively normal behavior. Amended once again to schizoaffective disorder, when, after a period of mania which ultimately led to a psychotic break'— this is the weekend Lucas and Kyle spent together in San Diego—'he was hospitalized for seven months during which he suffered auditory hallucinations, illusions, mania and recurring periods of profound depression. Eventually stabilized, the diagnosis was amended again to Bipolar I. He returned to his home for several months during which time he was closely monitored by a psychiatrist and treated with medication.'

"When Lucas claimed to be in Honduras, he had actually been hospitalized again. In a psychiatric rehab facility in Hawaii. Missy had gone to meet him after he was released."

"History of violence?" Kincaid asked.

"He went after Aurora during his first episode, Robert stopped him. And, obviously, when he bashed her head with a rock just recently."

"Bipolar and schizophrenia don't usually cause violence," said Kincaid. "Unless maybe drugs are involved."

"Sometimes mania plus stress..."

"Plus, an earworm named Missy telling him to kill."

It had been two weeks since Carlisle and Kincaid had arrested Lucas Stanhope, and the two murders that had begun this whole mess had finally started to make sense.

As much sense as murder ever made.

Lucas was currently under medical supervision in a secure hospital. Since Kincaid had wrestled him to the ground on Beth's deck, he had been weaving in and out of psychosis, but a search of his house, text messages they found on the pay-as-you-go phone he had been using to communicate with Missy during the last few weeks, lab comparisons—soon to be DNA comparisons now that they knew who they were looking for—had all corroborated the bits and pieces Lucas was giving them during his more lucid moments.

They had pieced the story together pretty well over the last few days. Though there were some parts of Lucas's past they would never be able to prove, everything he had told them about Missy's involvement in Aurora's and Annie Chang's murders checked out.

They had found matching burners in both Lucas's and Missy's possessions. Years of cellular call logs showed a long history of communication between Missy Lombardi and Lucas Stanhope.

Lucas had called Missy on the night of the murder. According to him, Missy had told him about the stunt Aurora had pulled at her house. About the DNA tests. About Steve Lombardi fathering a child with his mother. He had gone to the house to speak to his mother knowing that his father was away on business and Caroline didn't spend any time there when Aurora was around. He would have her to himself.

He had wandered through the empty mansion for hours, furious that Steve Lombardi was the father of his mother's illegitimate child. Even more furious that his mother had told Missy Lombardi. Aurora knew what that would do to her. She was so spiteful.

Pacing, stomping, twiddling his thumbs, Lucas had worked himself into a frenzy. He needed to calm down before his mother got home. If she saw him in this state, she would blow him off. She needed to *listen*.

He'd needed to relax. He'd gone to the bar. Whiskey. Good whiskey. Lots of it.

Spilled some on his shirt. That wouldn't do. She'd know he'd been drinking. Smell it. See it.

He'd washed his face. Brushed his teeth. Taken a clean shirt from his father's closet.

Better.

When she'd come home from dinner, he'd been waiting just inside the front door. Heard her car, had gone outside.

He had told her she had to fix the situation. She had to make it all right. She had to undo what she had done to Missy, the only person who had ever really cared for him. She needed to *undo* it.

But she'd kept telling him he was sick again. Acting crazy, not making sense.

He had to shut her up so that she could *hear* him. *Understand what he was saying.*

Finally, he'd hit her. He had picked up a rock and hit her with it just to shut her up.

And it had worked. But there was blood. Lots of it. Everywhere.

He had called Missy. She would know what to do. She'd told him to put Aurora in the Porsche and drive to the Shermanns' house. No one was home. It would be safe.

<hr>

"She came. Told me to bring my mother into the greenhouse. Told me she would take care of everything. Told me to walk back, get my car, go home.

"And I did. But there was blood on the shirt. All over it. I took it off, threw it in the laundry basket. Went home."

Lucas had claimed he didn't know what Missy would do to

Aurora. Hadn't known until his father had called him with the news on Saturday morning.

"Possible he didn't know," said Carlisle. "Also possible he did know and can't handle it. Convinced himself he didn't have anything to do with that part of it."

What they did know for sure was that Missy Lombardi had done the strangling. The bruises on Aurora's neck were a perfect match to Missy's little hands.

They also knew that Missy had shot Annie Chang. A single strand of fine blonde hair found on Chang matched Missy's hair. Her prints and only her prints were found on the gun.

They had also found a bank record of a one-time withdrawal of twenty-five grand from Lucas's account, dated a year ago. According to Lucas, Annie Chang had found the adoption documents in his room.

Lucas had found the papers in an old file cabinet in his grandparents' home. "Spent a week with them on Bainbridge a couple of years ago. Missy told me to look around." He had made copies of the documents, brought them back to her, kept his own set under the bed.

"She was so happy when I gave them to her. So happy." Lucas had drifted off for a while at that point, remembering how happy he had made Missy.

"Last year, Aurora bought a new bed for my room. New bed did me in." Lucas had told them Annie had supervised the delivery and found the documents when they fell from under his old mattress.

"She only asked once, though. Said she'd never tell if I gave her the money. Would never ask again. And she didn't."

That is, until after Aurora's murder. She had called Lucas. Wanted more, a lot more. "Missy made that go away too." She had used Aurora's phone to contact Chang, told her where to go, shot her in the head. Lucas had been there. Seen the whole thing.

"She said I had to help her now. I had to get rid of the body, get rid of the car. Hide them where they wouldn't be found."

But the task had been too much for Lucas. He had panicked. Thrown Chang under the Space Needle—"Then I could keep an eye on her from my apartment"—had dumped the Porsche and forgotten about Annie's old car, had run all the way home in the rain and hadn't slept since.

Chang's car had been found before he could move it.

"I screwed up and Missy said she was probably going to get caught, but that it was okay. She left me a message. Said it was okay, but now she was going to finish it. Was going to Beth's house.

"She *hated* Beth."

It had taken a swift deal with the DA not to prosecute Lucas Stanhope for murder, and then several supervised interviews over several days to get the salient bits out of him, but Carlisle and Kincaid where pretty sure they had it straight.

Missy had begun her relationship with Lucas sometime in his adolescence—they would never know exactly when—but it had been before Lucas's first psychotic break. It had begun with friendship and compassion, quickly become sexual, and by the time he was a young adult, Lucas Stanhope had been completely emotionally dependent on Missy.

In hindsight, Lucas's state-appointed psychiatrist said that his relationship with Missy could have exacerbated or even caused his initial break from reality. According to him, she had been openly and justifiably hostile about his mother, encouraging him to dismiss anything Aurora told him as a deliberate attempt to misguide her only son.

She had mentored him. As a mother, as a lover, as a friend. She had encouraged his interest in environmental biology, had guided him through his first sexual experiences with her, and even advised him on his relationships with other girls.

After his psychotic break, she had spent years conditioning him to mistrust Aurora. Had convinced him that Aurora wanted him locked up where he couldn't burden her anymore. Convinced him that he wasn't really mentally ill but was being manipulated by his own mother so that she could be rid of him.

Missy Lombardi had fed every paranoid thought, every uncertainty, every delusion Lucas had ever had.

"Here's what I want to know," said Carlisle, "of all the people in this bizarre love story, why didn't she kill Steve?"

------◆━■━■━◆------

When it was all said and done and the legal negotiations were settled, Kyle stopped by Carlisle's and Kincaid's desks.

"So, he's not going to go to jail. Right?"

"Right," said Carlisle.

"Hmm."

"How do you feel about that?"

Kyle didn't say anything for a few seconds. Then, "I think that's the right call."

Kincaid said, "Right or wrong, it's what Stanhope's lawyers and our DA agreed to. He'll spend some time in a locked ward, but then, he'll probably be out." He sighed thoughtfully. "Under a doctor's care, Lucas is probably not a danger to anyone. *But*, we know that under certain circumstances he can be persuaded to violence."

"The court will have to be vigilant. And so will the Stanhopes," said Carlisle. "Robert had no idea that Missy Lombardi was grooming his son for all those years."

"He knew Lucas was sick," said Kincaid.

"With an illness that rarely causes violence, and even then, it's usually self-inflicted. Besides, how much control did he and Aurora actually have? A grown man, a successful scientist, handsome, charming."

"Clever enough to hide his anger."

Kyle said, "Or Missy was clever enough to *control* his anger."

"Either way," said Carlisle, "the deal is done. He'll be in a hospital for a while and on probation for a long time after that." She looked at Kincaid. "How does Beth feel about it?"

"She's having motion detectors installed around her house. A pretty sophisticated alarm system. But she doesn't want to move to a house with no windows. Actually, of the two of them, Beth thinks Missy was the boogeyman and Lucas was just under her influence. So she's mostly okay with it. Taking the kid to therapy, keeping things as normal as possible. Henry ends up in bed with her a few nights a week, but that's about the worst of it as far as she can tell."

"Keeping in touch with Miss Williams?" Carlisle winked at him.

"All right, you two," said Kyle. "I gotta go home and change." She grinned. "Hot date."

Carlisle watched her go. Said, "Come to dinner. Tom's making something French."

"Can't," said Kincaid. He grinned. "Hot date."

ABOUT THE AUTHOR

Ava Parker is an author and traveler, a freelance researcher and writer.

Email: avaparkerauthor@gmail.com
Facebook: www.facebook.com/avaparkerauthor
Twitter: www.twitter.com/avaparkerauthor
Instagram: www.instagram.com/avaparkerauthor
Website: www.avaparkerauthor.com

Made in the USA
San Bernardino, CA
30 March 2019